A Time to Gather Stones

A TIME TO GATHER STONES

ANNABEL JOHNSON

THORNDIKE
CHIVERS

This Large Print edition is published by Thorndike Press, Waterville, Maine, USA and by BBC Audiobooks Ltd, Bath, England.

Thorndike Press, a part of Gale, Cengage Learning.

The text of this Large Print edition is unabridged.
Other aspects of the book may vary from the original edition.
Set in 16 pt. Plantin.
Printed on permanent paper.

LIBRARY OF CONGRESS CATALOGING-IN-PUBLICATION DATA

Johnson, Annabel, 1921–
   A time to gather stones / by Annabel Johnson.
      p. cm. — (Thorndike Press large print clean reads)
   ISBN-13: 978-1-4104-2300-9 (alk. paper)
   ISBN-10: 1-4104-2300-X (alk. paper)
   1. Women—United States—History—20th century—Fiction. 2. Self-actualization (Psychology) in women—Fiction. 3. Large type books. I. Title.
PS3560.O37134T56 2010
813'.54—dc22   2009039724

BRITISH LIBRARY CATALOGUING-IN-PUBLICATION DATA AVAILABLE

Published in 2010 in the U.S. by arrangement with Annabel Johnson.
Published in 2010 in the U.K. by arrangement with the author.

U.K. Hardcover: 978 1 408 47790 8 (Chivers Large Print)
U.K. Softcover: 978 1 408 47791 5 (Camden Large Print)

Printed in the United States of America
1 2 3 4 5 6 7 14 13 12 11 10

To

The strongest woman I ever knew
The wisest woman I ever knew
The best friend I ever had

My mother

PROLOGUE

1919

The great touring car moved across the Kansas plains like a powder-blue yacht breasting an ocean of green. Last week's punch-and-run snow storm had brought the young wheat to riotous color. It had also left a tang of chill on the air that breezed through the vehicle in spite of the side curtains.

In a corner of the back seat Lindy Forrest bunched down into the folds of the sealskin coat, privately withdrawing from the others, those nouveau aristocrats with their golden hair and implacable self-assurance: The DeMilles of Independence, Missouri (and Texas, they would always remind you.) Oil-well rich, and never mind the days when the grandfather punched cattle. She marveled at the inexhaustible store of banalities which they managed to invest with an air of utmost importance.

"We should have bought a Cadillac. Their

new V-8 engine is a honey. All the Army staff cars are Caddies," Austin was saying, leaning forward to speak over the seat to his father who was driving. A bit of a dandy, in tweed jacket, tailored pants and a suede vest, his air of authority on practically all subjects was impeccable. But no match for his dad.

"The Pierce-Arrow is the finest driving machine ever built." Mr. DeMille smacked the steering wheel with a finality that brooked no argument. "The dual-valve six-cylinder is an engineering masterpiece."

Arguing about horsepower in bluff masculine tones, as if that bully-voice impresses people. Lindy had been in a rebellious mood lately — in fact for most of the last year, as the War brought home a lot of sobering truths. You can't work week-after-month as a Red Cross volunteer greeting the trains, helping the wounded, down at Union Station, without taking on a whole new outlook. She was vested with such strong opinions that her own mother had advised her to curb her remarks, especially around men. But she was finding it harder these days to suppress a growing impatience with triviality.

"Go on, Dad, pass him!" Austin was hunched forward, flushed with excitement as the Pierce-Arrow picked up speed, gravel pinging the bottom. When they overtook the Stanley Steamer in a rush, lavishing dust over the occupants of the ancient car, they had achieved some kind of glory in Austin's mind. "Forty-seven miles an hour! Keep going, Dad. Don't slow down. Let's get there!"

At least that was a sentiment with which Lindy could agree. They had been on the road for over two hours.

"It's absolutely ridiculous," Mrs. DeMille was stating in her rather silly high-pitched voice. "Why couldn't they let the boys off in Kansas City? Why bring them clear out here in the sticks to dismiss them from the service? Haven't they given up enough?"

"The term is 'muster out.' The Army works by its own rules and in its own way," Austin informed her pompously. "In a war you learn not to question orders. It's only fitting that our troops be discharged in proper military style."

Lindy bit down on a comment. Austin DeMille hadn't seen any more of the war than could be glimpsed from the back room of the Recruiter's Office, which he had presided over without ever leaving Kansas City, a safe plushy job that his father had arranged. You'd think to hear him talk that he had personally brought about the Armi-

9

stice. It was going to be interesting to see whether he could still lord it over Cocky, his younger brother, object of this lengthy journey.

Crockett DeMille had refused to be routed off to a fashionable prep school. He had insisted on enlisting and shipped out for France with the rest of the doughboys. Lindy had written him regularly during the war and sensed, from his letters, that he was growing up rapidly. In high school he had been a devilish little tease, but the Field Artillery was an education all in itself, he had assured her. He was in the 60th Brigade, had been through the same battles, but in a different Company from Bernie's. Just chance that they'd be arriving home on the same train.

A shiver of emotion rippled her spine as she realized again: the waiting was over. All through the long year she and Bernie Jones had exchanged letters, heartfelt, but with much that remained unspoken. In the early days his had been full of excitement, wonder, humor — he drew marvelous cartoons of Army life and sketches of each new billet. In fact, his talent with a pencil and paper had got him the job of map-maker for the General. Then during the Argonne the lines of communication went dead. Even after the battle was over he only scribbled a line or two. His best friend had succumbed to the flu the same week as the Armistice, and from then on he seemed to have withdrawn to some place she couldn't imagine.

In the front seat of the car Mrs. DeMille's broad-brimmed hat, piled with yellow chiffon roses, swiveled as she craned to look over her shoulder. "Uh, Lindy, dear, just who is this young man you're meeting?"

"His name is Bernard Jones," Lindy said, on the verge of being curt. She was expecting that lifted-brow. *Jones? Oh my!* She had seen it on more than one face among her mother's blue-blooded friends. She called it their "Ellis Island look." Defiantly she went on, "He's a Lieutenant, on General Berry's staff. He was one of the General's liaison officers during the Battle of the Argonne. Afterward he was in charge of Intelligence, prisoner interrogation. He speaks German fluently. His mother is of German extraction. His father is Welsh." She said it deliberately, aware that they probably already knew. Mrs. DeMille and Merle Forrest were friends. These pillars of Kansas City society gave off such irritating echoes of *noblesse oblige:* My dear, it's all very well to keep up the spirits of our soldiers, but the war is over. One must remember to be true to

11

one's own class. And so forth. *Don't say it, don't say it!*

Her ladyship must have caught the glint of warning. "Well, I'm sure he's a fine boy," she commented bleakly, and turned back to stare out the front window.

Austin seemed about to say something, but he too sensed a fortified barrier and shut his thin lips in a tight line. He had treated Lindy like some irksome little sister ever since the Debutante Ball a couple of years ago, where he had been her escort at her coming-out. That had been arranged between mothers, with an eye toward aesthetics. Everyone said they made a handsome couple. The implications of that comment had sent Austin feverishly back-pedaling as if worried that Lindy might expect him to follow up with further attentions.

She wasn't his type, with her snappy tongue and her strong face, too clever for a girl. Too unconcerned with the fashion of the day, cutting her hair, letting it flourish in ruddy curls, instead of sweeping it up into a coil. He had once called her "Squirrel-head," and pointed out that, like a small beast, her movements were too quick to be graceful. His taste in women was a good deal more sophisticated. Thank heaven, Lindy thought with amusement. He was the dullest date she ever suffered through. A stiff and ungifted dancer, he didn't mind showing with a yawn how bored he was with the entire concept of coming-out balls. He hardly tried to make conversation unless in company with other golden young men who were interested in stocks and bonds and race cars.

"Shouldn't we be there by now?" He dug a large watch from his vest pocket. "Been on the road since ten o'clock and it's after noon. The train's probably already arrived."

"I had Clarissa pack us some sandwiches," his mother said. "They're in the hamper back there."

"Just hold off a bit," Mr. DeMille muttered. "I see buildings."

Ahead was a whole compound of barracks beyond a spread of rail yards. As the car topped a rise in the rolling prairie they could see a train moving slowly, heading for the loading docks. The open area beyond was already full of parked vehicles, people milling about, watching the approach of the tall black engine which shot out eruptions of steam as it crawled forward.

Something began to simmer inside Lindy, fear or dread or wishfulness, though she didn't know exactly what she wished. *Let*

13

me call you 'Sweetheart' . . . If she could just waltz around the dance floor in his arms once more, she thought, everything would settle back into place. They could reclaim the days when they were both so innocent. But that time was shattered forever, everyone a casualty, and some wounds not accessible to a healing touch.

As soon as the car had settled into a parking spot, she was out the door — almost stumbled. The skirt of the new traveling dress was too tight around the ankles, she couldn't take a proper stride. A beautiful creation, her mother's seamstress had made it for her of dark blue silk with touches of velvet, elegant. But Lindy was used to the full skirt of her Red Cross uniform, the toughness of the flat shoes. These high-heeled pumps had paper-thin soles; she could feel every piece of gravel as she trotted across the rail yard with small fast steps, trying to keep pace with the train.

Behind the engine were two long luggage cars, trailed by a line of Pullman coaches. And on the top step of the first a familiar figure — Army cap shoved back on his head, brown cowlick sprouting forward. With heart pumping, she waved both arms. *Over here.*

Bernie saw her and his face lit up with a

broad grin. The world steadied. That one swift smile brought back everything, the time they met over the punch bowl at the War Bond party, dancing at the Muehlebach Hotel, clasping hands in the movie house where they had watched *The Birth of a Nation* in electrified horror. The goodbye moment when they had almost kissed, and all the letters that followed. She had signed them "Your friend," hoping the unspoken depth of the word had reached him across the thousands of miles.

When her mother had asked what there was about Bernie that was so special Lindy could hardly put it in words. He certainly wasn't handsome, no classic sculptured face. His warmth was of the earth, the keen brown eyes full of the joy of living. As he jumped down from the train and came toward her in a rush he moved with an open zest, so different from the posing of the other men she knew. Haughty young sophisticates, they held themselves aloof, as if it were beneath them to have fun.

They would never envelop her in a hard hug and dare to plant a quick kiss on her lips. It caught Lindy by surprise. As she scrambled to grab her hat, a small twist of the same silk as her suit, she was laughing. And then, still in his arms, she looked up and, inside her, something went very still. She had just been bussed by a stranger.

His whole face was shaped in harder planes. The brown eyes, even while bright with delight at seeing her, were shadowed with an inner darkness. It was a look she recognized. She had seen plenty of it in the battle-worn men she had tried to help, down at the station where just a cup of coffee and a doughnut were a treasure, a brisk hopeful word made them hang onto her arm. Like prisoners who had crawled out of a hole into bright light they were disoriented. It was the inheritance of The Front. And it would pass! Lindy determined she would not let it stunt the happiness on this day.

"So good, so wonderful to see you," she told him fervently. "I can't tell you how glad I am that you're home."

"What are you doing all this way out in the boondocks?" he marveled. "How'd you get here?"

"Oh, I caught a ride with the DeMilles. Do you know Cocky, their son? He's on this train too."

Bernie glanced at the hundreds of men pouring off the cars and gave a little chuckle. "Don't know any of 'em. Most of my oufit came home ahead of us. I heard they had a big parade."

"Oh yes, it was grand. I'm sorry you missed it."

"I'm not. Last thing I need is a brass band. Only parade that counted I watched over in Saint-Mihiel, the day the Armistice was signed. Just three old people, one of them carrying a French flag — they were all that was left of the town." His mouth took on a twist of bitterness, but he let it go and smiled at her. "This right here" — he took her shoulders and gave them a little shake — "is all the home-coming I need. It was swell of you to come. Hold on, I want you to meet somebody."

The little group advancing toward them had to be the Jones family. It was led by a sturdy man, his square face studded by the bluest eyes she had ever seen. Bernie left her, to envelop his father in a bear-hug. Shades of the little boy in that. His kiss on his mother's cheek was more reserved; she embraced him, looking embarrassed as if it were a breach of etiquette. Beyond them skulked a bony tall girl whom she knew to be his sister, Dolly, the family crank. Bernie planted an unwanted smack on her cheek and seized the gnarly little old peasant woman who tagged along behind. Wrinkled beyond belief, she was grinning toothlessly as he lifted her off her feet in a clasp of sheer joy. That had to be his grandmother, Lindy thought, the one he called "Grossmutter."

"And you must be Lindy," Mr. Jones was shaking her hand in a powerful, but respectful grip. "Heard a lot about you, young lady. This is my wife, Bernie's mom."

"Yes, we've met," Mrs. Jones said beaming. "At several of the charity affairs." A tall woman she was overdressed in a handsome gown of ultramarine silk with red sequins patterned on it, her sweeping hat topped by a small stuffed bird.

"You're President of the Delphian Society," Lindy nodded, knowing instinctively what would matter. Bernie's mother also lived in a world of caste, always trying to reach those upper regions of the socially elite. She practically bowed to the Forrest name.

"How good of you to come all this way to meet our boy," Mr. Jones was saying. "He thinks the world of you."

Bernie now was urging the elderly woman forward, and for an instant Lindy's eyes were engaged by a hard black stare from the wrinkled old face. A work-worn hand gave her slender one a grip that tested her, and found her satisfactory. In German she said to her grandson, *"You picked a pretty one."*

To which Lindy answered, with a grin. "Danke!"

It seemed to have been the right thing, the ice broken gracefully and the family automatically broadening itself to include her. Everybody seemed to be talking at once. The mother saying something about a "Welcome Home" party and his father was talking about real estate.

"Bernie's going to be a good salesman," he told Lindy. "I'm going to take him into the business, make him a partner. Big boom right now. I can afford to expand."

And Grossmutter rattling on in her own language so rapidly Lindy couldn't follow.

His sister had wandered off to look at the steam engine judiciously, as if she just might purchase one.

". . . appreciate the thought," Bernie was telling his dad earnestly, "but the fact is, I'm going on to college."

That brought them all to a halt.

"I decided I need more education to work on a newspaper," he went on. "I think I could draw editorial cartoons. But I need to know more about history and politics and all that. So I'm going to M.U.; they've got a great School of Journalism."

The others were speechless. Then Lindy burst out, "Bernie, that's a wonderful idea!

You could do better than those sketch artists they have now. You'll be great."

As the Jones family began to adjust to the idea, their words fumbled with false enthusiasm, but their eyes were troubled. His father said, "Politics is a pretty dirty business, son. You want to think before you start messing with that."

"I'm sure M.U. is a fine school," his mother kept saying, "a fine school. But you'll come home weekends, won't you?"

Lindy was thinking — another year of letters. Maybe longer than a year, if he goes the whole way and gets a degree. She was fixed on his face, trying to read between the lines. There was an underlying grimness about his determination, as if he'd been ordered to do a thing he secretly hated.

"Sure, I'll be home a lot. Don't worry."

"We can talk about it on the ride back," Mr. Jones said. And turning to Lindy, "I'd ask you to come with us, but the old Dodge is going to be pretty crowded. I'm afraid you wouldn't be comfortable."

"Oh that's all right," she hurried to assure him. "The DeMilles are expecting me."

"In fact, I don't want any of you to wait around for me," Bernie told them. "I have to supervise the unloading of those baggage cars, and I'd better get about it. I have to inventory every darned item on a long list. And the fellows are waiting to get their gear." A crowd of servicemen had formed toward the front of the train. "I'll call you when I get home," he added to Lindy in a low voice. "Sorry we don't have more time to talk."

She left them, the family still dithering about whether to go or wait. She eased away toward the spot where she saw Cocky, surrounded by his family. He had put on muscle, stood straighter. Still the impish manner, but there was a hint of his namesake about him now — he'd been christened David Crockett DeMille.

When he turned to greet her his hazel eyes took on a beam of discovery. Sweeping off his service cap he bowed, the short-cut hair bright as a brass brush under the sun.

"Well," he said, "the war has failed to ruin civilized society completely. You look good enough to eat, girl!"

"Crockett!" his mother protested mildly. "Don't be vulgar."

But his dad thought it was funny. With a tolerant chuckle he said, "Speaking of lunch . . ."

■ ■ ■ ■

1921

■ ■ ■ ■

ONE

"My dear Belinda, you look pale as a feather." After half an hour of boring small talk, she had finally worked up to it. "Surely it was more than just a fever?" Eunice Williston, paying a call on an invalid friend. Not lacking in color herself, round cheeks too red, curly yellow bangs, topped by a fat little straw hat sprouting a feather, she looked almost muscular in her leg-o-mutton pink sleeves.

Feeling uncomfortably thin, Lindy summoned her manners.

"I'm quite fine now, Eunice, but thank you for your concern." They were ensconced on a loveseat in the small sitting room in the upper story of the Forrest mansion, a close little chamber with the brocaded draperies shut against the drafts of a rainy spring day outside.

"Well, you obviously need nourishment. Can't I help you to some more of this marvelous — whatever it is?"

"Marzipan, and it's too sweet for my taste. I'd rather have a good beef steak." Bravado talking. Lindy had hardly been able to look at food for months.

"You're . . . you're joking." Eunice tittered. "Well, I know what will promote a rosy cheek. I've brought you a present." Lowering her voice, she went on, "You mustn't tell your mother." And from her reticule she produced a book. "It's really quite naughty. But lots of fun!"

Lindy took it, didn't have to look. The tatty red cover was familiar. "The Sheik." The novel had been causing whispers all over the social scene for months now.

"You will positively *expire* when you get to Page 58 where he forces her —"

All at once Lindy had reached her limit, social graces be damned. "Eunice, I've read the thing. All of it. My mother has, too, and advised me not to waste my time. But I wanted to see whether the book had any redeeming value. It doesn't. In fact it's an insult to women, with its ridiculous message that we need to be brutalized by some strutting bully in order to find love. The whole idea, that a girl could enjoy being enslaved and adore the man who ravaged her, is so demeaning I strongly advise you to toss this in the fire and turn to better reading matter." She handed the book back and stood up, a signal in anyone's etiquette that it was time for the visitor to leave.

When the girl had gone pouting off with a twitch of taffeta skirts, Lindy felt a touch of remorse. Nine-tenths of the ladies at the meeting of Colonial Dames the other day had been talking about the novel, pleasantly scandalized. One had said, "Well, it isn't that far from the Brontes, you know. Just a trifle more explicit."

Good literature is defined by trifles, Lindy thought irritably, as she cleaned up, placed the teacups and the napkins back on the tray with the unfinished marzipan. What a waste of time. Surely, in a new world where nations congregated at broad tables and disputed to define international values, the custom of the social call should be declared obsolete. There were so many more important things.

These days a restlessness had come over Lindy, the sense of history coming on like a high tide, a surge following the deep receding waters of the war. One of the few benefits that had come to pass during that terrible conflict was the realization that a wealthy woman need not be consigned to some gilded salon.

All those months with the Red Cross at Union Station she had immersed herself in hard un-ladylike work, nothing she relished, but it did bring a feeling of satisfaction. It had given her a sense of her own capabilities. Now, in the aftermath, she was adrift again on the endless cycle of empty days, no sense of fulfillment. Nothing to look forward to.

Of course, when she had expected to be married the future was taken for granted. Taking care of a family was challenge enough for any woman. If she and Bernie had gone straight to a preacher her life would have been blueprinted. She had been a little disappointed when he had chosen to go back to school instead.

Now, it seemed providential. *He's more mature than I am.*

He knew it was too soon after all the confusions of war to make permanent commitments. An honorable man, he was determined to lay foundations for his new life and any woman who shared it. Which was all right, she admired him for it.

Only now, it's too late. The sudden welling of tears was something she wasn't used to. It had only begun recently, this tendency to weep.

"Oh, my darling girl!" Merle Forrest had

come in quietly and moved to hold her daughter in protective embrace. "I saw Eunice leaving. What did she say? The stupid little twit! Just like her mother — they're both social climbers of the worst sort."

"It's not her fault," Lindy sniffled into the folds of a handkerchief. "In fact I'm afraid I wasn't very polite. She wanted to have a girlish giggle with me over 'The Sheik' and I treated it seriously. Began lecturing her about men. And women. What a laugh. What do I know about relationships, for heavens' sake? I don't even know how to tell Bernie that I can't marry him."

"Rainy days bring on the blues." Merle moved over to the hearth and poked the dwindling fire. A tall elegant figure in ivory silk, pale patrician face delicately touched by cosmetics, she was beautiful as a porcelain figurine. "You'll get through this, as soon as you're fully recovered from the operation. Don't make any hasty decisions. Then, if you do conclude it's necessary, perhaps you could write him a letter. That way you can revise and rework it until you have put things as well as possible."

Lindy was shaking her head, more tears leaking into the handkerchief now. "I am going to tell him in person. Face to face, as soon as he comes home. I'm going to tell him the truth: that I am no longer a whole woman, I am unfit to be anyone's wife, and no man in his right mind would want a girl who couldn't bear children." The sobs took over now.

Her mother held her wordlessly. It came to Lindy, the realization that this wonderful woman, whose love had never failed her, couldn't help this time. Merle Forrest was of a generation where wives were mere ornaments to a man's world. All that urgent fund-raising was nothing more than an instinct to fulfill the tremendous potential that was usually wasted in the life of a society matron. She would never understand the deeper unrest that Lindy felt, at the boundaries she perceived to be closing in on her.

And yet there had been a time, Lindy remembered suddenly, when Merle had written poetry. Lovely little sonnets. Abruptly she demanded, "What ever happened to that book of verses you wrote?"

The question should have seemed incongruous, but Merle nodded. "Just a fond memory. Pursuing a foolish course can ruin your whole life, unless you are incredibly gifted. To be a serious poet, or writer or musician, is to put your creative self ahead of everything, including your marriage. It may be fulfilling, but I doubt that Emily Dickinson was very happy. That's what growing up is all about — we make mature decisions. Just remember what you do now you'll have to live with for a long time, so think carefully, my dearest girl."

"But I don't have a choice. Where's the 'decision' in this?"

Merle hesitated. "You surely don't think your life is over, Belinda, you're too intelligent to settle for failure at such a young age. Oh dear, I think Clemma's calling me. I promised to go over the menu for the luncheon on Saturday . . ."

With a tormented mind and a body in which the surgery had left a chasm, Lindy gravitated back to her bedroom. A girlish chamber of pink ruffles and flourishes, Victorian scenes depicted on the wallpaper, a Queen Anne bed with sheets helter-skelter, yet there was an ambiguity about the spacious chamber. A typewriting machine sat on the mahogany desk in the corner, and next to it a heavy unabridged dictionary, newspapers in the magazine rack. A copy of Harpers on the floor and drafts of a letter-to-the-editor that she had never been satisfied with — it was too busy a room to be totally feminine.

31

As spring rain pelted the windows and a young wind flung the branches about on the old oaks outside she stared at herself in the full-length mirror of the elegant vanity dresser. The flowing blue chiffon morning gown was princess-cut, but the square stance, hands on hips, was hardly that of pampered royalty. And those unseductive short red curls were an instant giveaway that she was no fashion slave.

(*But Bernie said he loved them.*)

The ache that came with that thought made her anxious; she ran a few inward investigations, but the pain didn't come from the belly, it was of the heart. That kind of hemorrhaging couldn't be cured by the knife. Maybe by the flames?

Her glance tilted toward the bottom drawer of the dressing table. Against her will she went over and took out the satin box full of letters. It was a first step. Taking them back to the sitting room, where the fire had burned to embers, she settled down cross-legged, thankful of the lingering warmth that made a haven against the clammy chill of the day.

The packet was tied with a blue ribbon. The older ones were hard-worn, the edges dog-eared from many readings. But there were newer ones, those that had arrived faithfully each Monday this past year, while Bernie slaved away up at the University.

To make his expenses he'd had to take a weekend job with the local newspaper, so she hadn't seen him in months, but the letters were vivid. He wrote as if they were having a conversation and illustrated them with drawings. She realized, in a newfound detachment, that the tone was different lately. His humor was still boyish, but touched by ironic wit, and his cartoons were rendered with a new boldness that had begun to look like the work of a professional artist.

The first was dated in September, last year, only a few weeks after he had got out of the Army. Barely settled in up at Columbia, he had drawn a sketch that brought a tremulous smile, of a spindly figure confronting a group of football players in letter sweaters.

"I had hardly arrived when a committee of upper-classmen cornered me and informed me that, as a freshman, I was required to wear a beanie. This is an obnoxious skull cap in the colors of our Alma Mater. I wouldn't have worn the silly thing in high school. Which I told them, adding that they should feel welcome to try to make me, but it would not be without some pain and suffering on their part, and still wouldn't accomplish their objective. I also mentioned that the next doughboy they tried to lord it over, they had better come in numbers exceeding five-to-one. Some of the guys returning from the trenches are not all that polite. By then, the youngsters had prudently decided to reconsider the matter."

Lindy could picture that confrontation. Bernie didn't present an impressive physique, but there was an innate toughness that he had earned in childhood days running with a gang over on the west side, where Kansas City verged on prairies only a few years removed from pioneer times. The war had given a new edge to that basic metal, a grimness that she thought of as his "battle-field look."

But there was vulnerability too. She opened the letter he had sent last Christmas: not going to make it home. He had found a holiday job there in Columbia, helping a local printer turn out greeting cards. The pay wasn't much but he would learn a lot about plates and printing which he needed. This time his drawing showed a forlorn Bernie sitting before a press which was somehow endowed with touches of femininity. Above it a sprig of mistletoe. His caption was: "Sorry, but your type is not my type."

A knock at the door roused her. Merle, with a tray of food — she took in the scene at a glance, letters, fire. "Clemma made you some lunch, dear. I have to go out — the D.A.R. is choosing its officers today, and I'm up for Treasurer."

Lindy scrambled to her feet, discomfited to be found sprawled on the floor like a love-sick adolescent, maundering over a boy's letters. She took the tray. "That looks wonderful." It didn't. Last night's squab that she hadn't had the stomach for, warmed over now, along with biscuits and gravy, and *blancmange* for dessert. "Thank you, Mother."

Merle hesitated, then spoke out bluntly. "Lin, darling, if you don't mind a bit of advice: don't be in a hurry. Right now you are in a very human state of disarray. Your emotions are in chaos. Give yourself some time to adjust."

A wave of love swirled around them as Lindy hugged her. "Don't worry about me, I'm fine. Really."

"Of course you aren't," Merle's arms tightened briefly. "Let me just say, when I was your age I didn't have a grain of com-

35

mon sense. Today everything seems easier, but I do think I've learned a bit. So I advise you to wait and see what happens before you — er — burn your bridges."

It surprised Lindy, the urgency of the words. "That's odd. I thought you weren't very keen on Bernie."

Her mother gave a helpless shrug. "Maybe I wasn't. But one has to face the fact that it was a very narrow-minded time when I was young. To marry within one's class was *de rigueur.* I can't say it was wrong, but it limited a woman greatly. Today you have wider opportunities. I just want you to be happy." Then, with a quirk of a smile, she reached in her pocket. "I have today's mail, if you want it."

Lindy couldn't hide the leap of pleasure inside when she took the letter with the familiar handwriting, strong, masculine, but with an artistic flourish. When her mother was gone, she sank onto the unmade bed and tore the flap, not bothering to look for the letter opener.

"Lindy, my love.
I have great news. I won't go into it until I see you, but it won't be long now. First of June I'll be done with this place for good. I've run into a piece of luck that's going to

36

change our lives. I can't wait to tell you all about it. Meanwhile, though, I need a favor. Enclosed is a check . . ."

She realized a slip of paper had fallen to the floor and picked it up. A check, made out to her for a hundred dollars.

. . . My sister Dolly is getting married in a couple of weeks, and I need to buy her a wedding present, but there's no place in this little burg to find anything that fancy. Plus the fact that I don't know anything about bridal gifts and so forth. I don't even know my sister all that well, truth to tell. She and I never got along. She's three years older than me. I didn't even know she was engaged.

The groom is a parson of sorts (I don't know exactly what sorts.) He runs a settlement house over in The Bottoms. She's been working there as a volunteer, and they'll be living there after the wedding, so I doubt if silver punch bowls are in order.

I hate to wish this onto you, but I am truly stumped and studying hard for exams. I have to turn in a major project to pass Journalism. I'm hoping they'll accept a series of political cartoons. Of course, if you'd rather not tackle this, I'll understand. But if you can do it I will be most grateful."

It was signed by a sketch of a scrawny figure stretched out asleep over a drawing board.

Staring at the letter in dismay, Lindy felt disoriented. She had been peddling so hard on her own course, head-down and hell-bent, it was like coming up against a stone wall. But one with that tantalizing rose blooming high up and out of reach.

Change our lives.

Bernie had never asked her to marry him. Now she knew he was already ten steps ahead.

Two

An aroma . . . Lindy wasn't sure what it was, an emanation of law books, shelves of which lined the office, or a faint aura of soap that hung over the young man at the desk, her father's clerk. Albert, his name was, very tightly packaged in a stiff white collar and neatly buttoned coat, plastered down hair, meticulous wire-rim glasses. He felt her scrutiny and glanced up. Nervous smile.

"I'm sure the Judge won't be much longer. He gives these instructions to the jury, marvelous explanations of the law." The awe was apparent. "He's — well, here he is."

Whittaker Forrest looked every inch a judge. Six feet six inches tall, a lanky hundred and ninety pounds, square shoulders as if built for the burdens of decision-making, he never quite discarded the robes. Even at home in dressing gown and slippers he exuded power. The poker face was well cultivated, but it broke open in a grin when he saw his daughter.

"Lindy! What a nice surprise. Come join me at lunch — at least I think we have some lunch inside?" He glanced at his clerk who blushed like a girl.

"Oh dear. It's only a sandwich." Albert was headed for the door. "I'll run down and get something, whatever you'd care for, Miss Lindy."

"I've already eaten," she intercepted him gently. "Thank you anyway. I'll just have a word with my dad while he eats his."

"Have to stick around," he told her. "I know this jury. They will want to ask questions. Come in." Ushering her into his chambers, he closed the door and set two chairs in front of the desk. "Mm. Let's see . . . corned beef on rye. Good man. What would I do without Albert? He'll make a fine lawyer some day. Not a litigator, though, he doesn't have the panache. Now your boy, Bernie, he's got plenty of that."

Seated almost knee-to-knee, Lindy felt unnaturally shy. She seldom talked to her father about matters of the heart, and never about ailments of the body. "He's the reason I came today," she said. "I believe he's going to ask me to marry him."

"I should hope so. It's been taking him

40

long enough. Must be eight, nine months since he asked for my approval."

"He did *what?*"

"Right before he went off to college, and incidentally that was a very mature thing for him to do, go back to school. Came to me and announced his intentions, like the good man he is. Said he wanted everything to be on the up and up. Asked me not to mention it to you, though, as he wasn't going to make his proposal until he had something to offer you, some specific plan for the future. I admire that."

"And you gave him the — your —"

"I believe the word is 'blessing,' " the Judge chuckled. "This is a good sandwich. Sure you won't have the other half?"

Lindy shook her head. "So what did you say?"

"Told him he'd be taking my most prized possession and he'd better darned well be careful of it. Oh, shoot, Lin, this is a new world we're in. Used to be society families inbred so diligently their bloodlines got thin. It's good, that a solid young fellow made of different raw materials should bring new muscle into the mix. A whole new generation —"

Abruptly he fell silent, trying to swallow the last bite of sandwich. His lean face took on a pink tinge, and he was in such obvious distress Lindy had to rescue him.

"It's okay, Dad. I know what you mean. Of course, for me there won't be any further additions to the Forrest family tree, but if there were I'd be proud if Bernie had contributed. I wanted to ask you, not as a father but as a very wise man: Do you think it would be quite honorable of me to marry — anyone?"

The Judge looked as flustered as she had ever seen him. "Dear child, there's only one way it could be considered unjust, and that's if you neglected to tell him of your problem."

"And supposing he wants to marry me anyway, at least for now. Couldn't this lead eventually to a resentment on his part?"

Her father stood and went to the sideboard where he poured two glasses of water from a decanter, brought one to her. "You're putting my wisdom to a pretty stiff test," he said. "I will only tell you that none of us can imagine what the future may hold. It's a mistake to base our lives on suppositions and possibilities. We just plug along doing our best, and take each new day as it comes."

Lindy had pretty much expected that. With a rueful smile she said, "I guess I should stick to my current problem. Bernie wants me to buy a wedding present for his sister. And I don't even know her. Dolly isn't very approachable. And she's marrying a man of the church, runs that Settlement House over in The Bottoms. In fact they plan to live there. So Wedgwood and Sterling seem a bit inappropriate."

The Judge cocked his head, a familiar stance, lower lip jutting. "I have a suggestion. It may not be fashionable, and yet I have an idea it might be welcome in this case. What about Liberty Bonds? Treasury notes? Nothing crass like common stock, but gilt-edged certificates that could be cashed in or set aside for the future? The way our economy is booming their value would increase by leaps and bounds over the next few years."

Marveling, Lindy stared in awe. "Dad! You've hit it on the head. This is exactly the gift for a pair of earnest good Samaritans."

"Tell you what, why don't you go over and see Cocky DeMille. He's a bright young whippersnapper. Handles my own portfolio, keeps me up-to-date on the newest stock offerings. I'll wager he could fix you up with bells and whistles."

She was on the move. Wrapping her arms around him in a hard hug, she gave a kiss on the cheek. "I do love you, Dad!" And left a very happy middle-aging man behind, watching her go, fondly.

At four in the afternoon the tea room of the Muehlebach Hotel was a bevy of colors. Since the war the young matrons of Kansas City had blossomed into a whole new garden of finery. Discovering the scissors they had cropped their long locks and taken to marcelling their hair. It tickled Lindy a bit — these girls who had snickered at her when she cut hers during the War. Now wearing spit-curls and bright bands around their heads, they affected long strings of beads, those silly galoshes that flapped when they walked. She felt practically conservative in her green wool tunic and pumps, though it was a trifle daring to wear a hemline almost up to her knee.

Cocky was eying her with open appreciation. A natty dresser himself, sharply defined in a well-tailored suit of gray tweed, his blue four-in-hand perfectly knotted, wavy blond hair, he looked quite the sophisticate. But there was still a glint of boyish delight in his eyes.

"My dear lady, as always, you look delectable. But you're aware that you could find yourself in a Utah jail?" The headlines this morning had included an item about that state and its new decree against short skirts. "I understand that Pennsylvania has also passed a statute. In the City of Brotherly Love, modesty begins at four inches below the knee."

"The day the State of Missouri dictates how I dress is when I sic my dad onto the legislature. He'll take it to the Supreme Court."

"Your father is a formidable man. It was kind of him to steer you my way, with your investment problems. How can I help you?"

Lindy sipped her tea, excellent green Pekoe straight from the hillsides of Ceylon, according to the menu. "I have a bit of a dilemma." She lowered her voice, though the ambient sounds of the tearoom were muted by the wealth of potted palms, the softening influence of the rich carpeting. "I've been asked to buy a wedding present . . ."

It was easy to see why Cocky DeMille was successful in his chosen arena. His answers were quick and understandable, he knew his subject. "Your father's suggestion was inspired. You may not think of a Treasury Note as a fancy nuptial offering, but we can fix that. Concoct an accompanying certificate with red ribbons and a large gob of useless but decorative sealing wax. I keep a signet ring in my office, just to put the official stamp on such things. Makes a very spiffy gift. And more to the point, one that is bound to increase in value by leaps and bounds. Optimism is the byword of the day, in spite of Mr. Volstead and his dry friends. Actually, in a curious way, Prohibition has intoxicated us all with the spirit of rebellion. Speaking of which, can I refresh your tea, dear girl?" He opened his suit coat to reveal a flask in an inner pocket. "Brandy is more appropriate to celebrate a reunion of old friends."

Lindy started to refuse, and then some contrariness made her change her mind. "Why not? I've been having trouble with my appetite lately."

"I noticed you seem remarkably delicate." He quickly poured and the flask disappeared back into his coat. "How are you doing these days? What are you doing?"

"That's just it. I'm not. Since my Red Cross work is over I have been at loose ends. I envy you, Cocky, with a vocation that obviously suits you."

"But there must be avenues for you to pursue. Women have the vote now. You could even run for office. Belinda Forrest for President!"

"How I would love to get my hands on the government for just a few days and make some changes," she agreed, laughing. "I would set up a bureau to take care of all those returned veterans who are adrift in our streets. I would legislate against foreclosures on farms . . ."

"Hear, hear! We can't afford to lose our rural constituents. The trouble with that is, you'd also have to rescue the banks who loaned the poor devils money that they can't pay back. How do you make laws against a drought?"

"I would appoint rainmakers to go forth and solicit the heavens," she said soberly. The brandy was having a pleasant effect upon her.

"Grand. I will be your campaign manager. At least you won't bloviate endlessly like our present leader." It was a word that President Harding himself had invented without apology.

"And I would never return the country to 'normalcy.' " She shuddered over another of the President's concoctions.

"I should hope not! We deserve greatness in our future, no less. Shall I call for another pot of tea?"

"No, thank you, I have to go home. Mother's having a big dinner for one of Dad's colleagues who's resigning. My presence is requested."

"I know how that is." He helped her on with the feathery wrap. "Fortunately Austin handles the formalities in our house. Favorite son, he loves it. All spit and polish and small talk. Like a wind-up tin soldier, he's bright as new paint and rather hollow inside. An elegant degree in law and the poor chap doesn't know beans about handling money. When he inherits our father's estate I'm going to have to step lively to teach him how to manage it. You need to set goals."

"And I'll bet you're good at that." She took his arm as they walked out through the sumptuous lobby. "Tell me, Cocky, what's your secret ambition?"

"To make a million bucks, and there's nothing secret about it. Mainly, I enjoy the game. That's what it is, you know, a great game to play the market, guess which stock has promise, watch it go up and up and up. I bought RCA when it was almost unknown, and now — well, you've seen the new crystal sets haven't you?"

"Yes. I have." She smiled at the recollection. "At a party the other night one of the fellows had one. We sent a boy up onto the roof with the — what is it, aerial? And all of us got in a huddle with a cloth draped over, crouched around this little box and its knobs. It did a lot of squeaking and wheezing and then, like a miracle, the tiny voice said, 'We are coming to you from the ballroom of the Muehlebach Hotel.' And we were miles away in the Country Club. How do they do that?"

"I'm no engineer. But they say that in a few years those boxes will have amplifiers and we can set one up in our living room and hear people talk as far away as St. Louis. I'd advise you to invest in their stock. One of these days it will skyrocket."

He had led her along Twelfth and around the corner to a side street where his Daimler was parked. Patting a long blue shining fender, he said, "Here's another good investment. Car most likely to prevail for the next fifty years. Hi, there, Jip. Good boy, not a finger-mark on her." He flipped a coin at a street urchin who caught it in midair with a grubby hand. "He's my man. Every time I park anywhere near Twelfth I use him to stand watch over the property. I told him, as soon as he makes his first fifty bucks I'll invest it for him."

"And I'm sure no one could do it better. I am beholden to you for your help."

"My pleasure. Come by my office next

week and I'll have the precious paper done up in such style you'll want to hang it on the wall." He started the engine and listened to its quiet hum. "Lindy, we live in great times where the future is limitless. No reason why a woman shouldn't ride the gravy train too. Just don't wait too long to get on board."

THREE

Driving slowly through the middle-class neighborhood with its rows of sturdy brick houses, front porches, dormer windows, Lindy sensed that behind those lace curtains there were watchers, curious about the stranger in their streets. The red Franklin roadster with its rakish canvas top was as sassy as a race horse in a field of plugs. One of her few self-indulgences, she had picked the car out and paid for it with her saved allowance. She never asked her father for money to spend on frivolities. In fact it gave her a special elation to have bought it herself, and she usually enjoyed the envious stares. Not today.

Parking midway down the street in front of an undistinguished home, similar to all its neighbors, apple tree in the yard, porch draped in honeysuckle, she went slowly up the front walk between a color guard of tulips. Perky flowers, they were the same blithe pink as her linen suit. It was a modest style, old-fashioned in its length down to her shins. She had dressed carefully not to look like one of the elite. She had seldom felt such uncertainty about a visit to another woman.

When she had called to make the appointment Dolly sounded strange. "Okay. Yes, of course you can come over if you want." Less than enthusiastic. *Probably doesn't like me. I hope I don't come across as some kind of snob. Never mind, I have handled difficult people before. We can talk about the wedding, I will jolly her along . . . just doing a favor for Bernie . . . hope she'll be pleased with his gift . . .*

The Treasury Certificate had been done up by Cocky DeMille's secretary in style, with festive ribbons and sealing wax, then placed in a white stationery box topped by a large white satin bow. That part was well done. What was slightly embarrassing was that she hadn't been invited to the wedding.

"It just isn't polite," her mother had fretted. "I do think Bernie should have a word with her about including you in the list of guests. When is the ceremony to be?"

"In a week or so."

"I wonder why they didn't wait until he came home from school? He's due back

52

soon, isn't he?"

"Classes are over the first of June, but he may still have business up there in Columbia, some scheme that he hasn't explained. He won't set a time yet for his return here."

"Well, I think it's asking a lot of you to do his family chores, especially when the Joneses haven't exactly been eager to mix with us socially."

"I don't think they know how. They're not in a set that pays calls or sends around cards. And after all, Bernie and I are officially just friends. Don't blame them too much, they mean well." The few times she had been with his folks they had been warm and extravagantly solicitous. As she mounted the steps to the porch a calico cat lying in a patch of sun gave her an indolent flick of the tail. *Now there's a true snob.*

"Hello, Puss. Are your folks at home?" She pulled the chain and a bell rang distantly inside.

A long wait, someone moved behind the curtained window in the front door. Then, slowly, it opened. The girl who stood there looked tense, defiant, hugely embarrassed. The reason was obvious. A cumbersome bulge boosted the front of the shapeless brown smock she wore. On that tall, bony body, pregnancy was as awkward as a bowling ball stuck in a croquette wicket. Lindy had to summon every inner resource not to twitch a hair of her eyebrow as she smiled.

"Hello. How are you Dolly? Thank you for taking time to see me. I have a . . ." the word "wedding" stuck . . . "something from Bernie to give you."

"Come in." There had always been a kind of darkness about the girl, a shadowy strangeness which now had become painful. Brown hair swept back in a bun, angular face stiff with distress, she had trouble rallying some crumbs of dignity to say, "Won't you have a seat?"

"Thank you."

"My mother's not home. Nobody's home." She sounded resentful and frightened.

"Well, actually it's you I wanted to see. Bernie tells me you're going to be married soon . . ."

"A week from Saturday."

"And he asked me to bring over his present, which is accompanied by his love and best wishes. He's sorry he couldn't be here, he's getting ready for exams. So he asked me to do the honors." Lindy handed across the package, thankful that it didn't contain anything frilly.

"Bernie did that?" She took the box

absently and set it aside. "Well, I'll have to write and thank him. I mean, thank you, Lindy, for bringing it. Uh . . . would you like a cup of tea?"

"If you'll let me go get it. Why don't you just rest here on the sofa." It was obvious that she had just gotten up. Pillows were piled at one end and a crocheted afghan was in disarray. "That's a lovely piece. Did you make it?"

"No, Grossmutter did. I never was good at handiwork." Dolly sank down and drew the woolen coverlet around her. "I can't seem to get warm these days."

"I sympathize. I'm just recovering from surgery myself, and it seems to take a long time for the circulation to come back. Maybe a cup of warm milk would be better for you than tea?"

"I think there's some soup in the icebox," the girl said vaguely.

Lindy left her, thankfully, struggling to get reoriented on the situation. *No wonder she didn't want anybody to come. But I'm here now, so . . .* Going through the dining room, she was aware of a tall grandfather's clock on one wall, a handsome piece with a hollow tick-tock that gave presence to the room, with its humble oaken furniture, the big round table, chairs. One wall contained a sideboard full of dinner china, the cobalt-blue ware that was popular before the War. On a window seat a row of budding geranium plants was dominated by a large aspidistra.

In the kitchen she found the icebox almost empty except for a jar of chicken soup. Locating a saucepan in one of the lower cabinets she put it on the stove. Gas stove, modern enough, but the rest of the room harked back to the turn of the Century: worn linoleum on the floor, a wooden counter by the stained porcelain sink. Through a window that overlooked the back yard Lindy could see a crabapple in bloom. She could picture Bernie as a kid climbing that tree. It brought a welling of tears, for some reason. She had never missed him so acutely as here in his boyhood home. *Does he know about Dolly's condition? Probably not. Awkward thing to write about.*

A jug of orange juice was cooling under a wet dish towel. She poured a glass full, and got out a soup bowl. Bread in the pantry, fresh from the baker's truck, and in a covered dish she came upon some tapioca pudding. Taking it all over to the kitchen table she set a place on the checkered red oilcloth.

Going back to Dolly, she said, "Come

have some lunch. I think you'll feel better when you've eaten."

"I know. They keep after me to eat, eat, eat. For the baby's sake. I'm really not hungry." But she tagged along back to the kitchen. "Truth is, I wish I — I wish it — I don't really — oh, tarnation!" She slumped down at the table and buried her head in her hands.

So obviously this was not a little bundle of joy. Lindy pulled up a chair close beside her. "Don't cry, my dear. They say that even before birth, children are susceptible to moods. Surely things will look better after you and its — the father — are married."

With a hiccup, Dolly rallied and swallowed hard. "Oh, Hereford's not the father. He's just a very responsible man. He feels to blame, I guess. Not his fault, but he does run the Settlement House, and that's where this happened." She began to dip into the soup, listlessly.

What did happen? But Lindy hesitated to ask. She felt woefully naïve. "You worked there too?"

"Volunteered. I mean, those poor men, all of them needy and damaged by the war, and homeless. I can't imagine what it would be like to wander the streets, no place to sleep at night. It's tragic."

57

"I understand how you feel," Lindy said. "I worked with the Red Cross down at Union Station all through the war."

Dolly slanted a glance at her. "Yes, Bernie mentioned that. You gave them coffee and doughnuts?"

"And a lot more. As the wounded started to come home we fed them and comforted them and helped them make connections to the right trains. I wrote letters to their families. We washed their faces and got them clean clothes, and put on fresh bandages. After a long day we workers would sweep up all the trash, the messes that were left. It wasn't pretty work, but it made us feel useful."

Silently Dolly finished the soup. "I didn't know you really did all that. I guess you do understand. I mean you can see why I would go down there and volunteer."

"Yes, I do. I'm not sure I'd have the nerve myself to go into those dangerous streets in the West Bottoms."

"Oh, they're not so bad. The Boss keeps order — Tom Pendergast, he lives down there. He runs the Ward from a little office over a saloon. Or at least, since Prohibition they pretend it's not a saloon, but the laws don't matter a lot. Tom makes his own."

About that Lindy didn't know. She had

only heard that it was a slum district, rank with poverty and crime. "Poor people crammed into tight quarters, must give rise to a lot of desperation."

"Oh, it wasn't them that did this. It was one of our own boys." She was tackling the tapioca with more appetite. "We take in veterans. After all, they served their country well, put their lives on the line, and then they come home shell-shocked and gassed and scarred, their minds all twisted. Can't hold a job, can't pay for a room. All they can do is panhandle and use the money for whiskey. So somebody sells them some bath-tub gin . . . attack a woman . . . right there in the kitchen of Settlement House. It was last summer. The kids set off some fireworks outside and this fellow just went crazy." She pushed the dessert aside and got up heavily.

"What happened to him, the man who did this?"

"Oh, they sent him to jail. But what good does that do me now?"

"When are you due?" Lindy asked, walking with her back to the front of the house, ready to support her if she wavered. Her balance seemed unsteady.

"In about a month. I know I should have done something to — fix it — right away when it happened, but I couldn't bring myself to tell anybody until it began to — well, it became obvious. That's when Hereford stepped in with his proposal. He keeps saying he feels responsible. It won't be much of a wedding, but then I'm not much of a bride." Her chin puckered.

In a wave of pity, Lindy hugged her. "Of course you are! You've done nothing to be ashamed of. You'll be beautiful, and you'll make that man a wonderful wife."

Brushing her tears away, Dolly turned with watery wonder. "You mean that? Would you stand up with me? I don't know anyone else who would."

"I'd be honored." A hundred rampant thoughts gusted across Lindy's mind, reasons she shouldn't do this. "In fact, we've got to make some preparations. You'll need a suitable dress in a hurry. I have a clever seamstress who can whip up a gown in a matter of hours. Oh, yes, we're going to deck you out in ribbons and flowers. This is one day you must enjoy remembering. It will be my wedding present to you."

Dolly blinked in awe, a barely dawning shadow of enthusiasm. "Why? Why would you do that for me?"

Lindy plunged rapidly over the barricades. "Because I feel like you're practically my sister. That means a lot to me. I always wanted a sister."

Good grief, what did I say? I've practically joined their family and Bernie hasn't even asked, and I haven't thought the whole thing through. It didn't matter. If it all came crashing down later, at least right now it had almost brought a smile to that thin unlovely face.

FOUR

The large electric fans placed around the edges of the auditorium did little to ease the heat of that first day of June. Amid the audience of women, Lindy longed to rush off into some fresh air, but the sight of her mother on the platform held her in proper decorum, though her handkerchief was sodden from repeated moppings of the brow.

How does she do it? Not for the first time, she marveled at that poised lady up there. Merle Forrest, in a stylish new gold pongee tunic, looked beautifully cool presiding over the chattering group of club presidents and assorted officials who had gathered for this momentous meeting. They were here to launch a great project: a new art gallery.

"As you all know," Merle Forrest was saying, "Mr. William Rockhill Nelson bequeathed his whole estate to the founding of a museum that would be the centerpiece of a rich cultural blossoming here in Kansas

City. He left us his money and his lands, but it is up to us to provide the energy and will to make it happen if we want our city to be known as the artistic heart of the middle west."

As the discussion went on, about architects, curators, the need for an Oriental collection and so forth, Lindy felt caught up, as if she could almost see it happen. *If this museum doesn't top the big one in St. Louis, it won't be for lack of spirit.* So much energy, talent, ideas, these women could have been running the city themselves. Four great organizations had committed to the cause, the DAR, the Athenaeum, the Colonial Dames and the Delphians. Lindy spotted Bernie's mother on the far side of the room. *I must get over there and speak to her before she leaves.*

She was worried about Dolly. It had been such a wretched excuse for a wedding, in the tight little office of the Justice of the Peace. The dressmaker had done a marvelous job of creating a bridal gown in ecru silk, with a multitude of snaps and sashes and bows that could be adjusted to disguise the ungainly figure. Suspecting that no one was going to provide a bouquet, Lindy had brought a small clutch of tea roses which Dolly could hold like a shield across her frontage, to add a touch of beauty to the moment.

She herself had tried to be quietly festive in a pale lavender afternoon dress, but the rest of the guests were somber. Dolly's mother in dark brown velvet, and the father in Navy blue serge, they might as well have been attending a funeral. The illusion was reinforced by the groom, who wore black.

Hereford Romney was younger than she had expected. An ascetic face topped by a flowing mane of pale hair, he could have posed for a sculpture of Saint Sebastian, noble, but cold as marble. Not the sort of man to give comfort to the poor, and yet if he saw that as his mission in life he would be unwavering. There was grim determination in the lift of the prominent chin, the pale blue eyes focused on other-worldly matters as he spoke the vows that duty prompted.

In the weeks that followed the sad little event, Lindy hadn't heard from Dolly. It troubled her, and yet she hesitated to call the Settlement House until it became certain beyond a doubt that the baby must have been born. When she did ring up the office there, an unknown woman had informed her that Mrs. Romney was abed, unable to come to the phone, and yes, the birth went well, thank you, goodbye. That was over a week ago. *I should go and see her.* But the girl was so remote by nature, Lindy was reluctant to intrude.

"In closing," Merle Forrest was suddenly on the offensive now, impatient with the bored disinterest of the men, "let me observe that there is a powerful energy among the people in this room. We are not just a bunch of chatterers, gentlemen." She turned to eye the male contingent on the platform, representatives from the Chamber of Commerce, the Kiwanis Club, Department of Parks, a couple of banks, *The Kansas City Star.* "We have the wits and will, and the cultural education to contribute. We expect our various associations to be represented on your planning committee. We request — no, I will go so far as to say we demand — to have input into this great project. Trust us, we will help bring this dream to life."

Thunderous applause, while the officials looked embarrassed.

As the crowd stood up and began to mill around the auditorium Lindy made her way over to the contingent of Delphians. Mrs. Jones stood out among them, an imposing figure, a half head taller than most of her group, dressed in ultramarine silk with red sequins, topped by a very Victorian hat complete with large silk roses.

"Lindy! My dear! How nice to see you." She was flustered as if faced with royalty.

Impatient, unwilling to be set off as one of the chosen, Lindy gave her a hug that startled the woman and said, "I'm glad you're all boosters of my mother's pet project. And how is Dolly coming along?"

Mrs. Jones slanted her a startled look as if she'd said something improper. "Oh, fine. She's fine, I'm sure. I was there for the — well, you could hardly call it a blessed event."

"Of course it was blessed. That innocent baby is a child of God, as we all are." Lindy blurted it out. *Where did that come from?* It was as if someone had spoken through her. But the plight of the infant touched her heart. To be thought of as a shame upon the family? Stigmatized by his own father, a poor damaged confused victim of an awful war, it was a sad beginning to a young life. Rushing on, she said, "I'm glad the birth went well. I've been meaning to pay a visit down to Settlement House as soon as Dolly feels up to it. Is she ready for visitors?"

"I'm sorry to say I haven't been down there this week. It really is a dreadful part of town. You need to be escorted. And my husband's been busy. I'm always in a rush myself these days. Since Grossmutter left us — she did so much of the work — er — that is to say, she ran our household so well for years that — er —" In a dither of confusion, Mrs. Jones fanned herself rapidly with the small ivory fan she carried. "And I do have so many civic responsibilities, you know — well, of course you do. Your mother, I don't know how she keeps up with all those commitments. I guess what I need is some hired help, in the kitchen and all that — I just never realized how much — Anyway, I'm afraid I have to run, I've got an appointment with the restoration committee. We're trying to preserve some of Kansas City's beautiful old homes. It was nice to see you." She laughed, a high-pitched unnatural titter, and reached out to press Lindy's hand. "I do want to thank you for showing up at the — uh — marriage ceremony. I'll tell Dolly you asked after her when I see her." And she trotted off across the floor, long skirts flowing.

Lindy followed more slowly, bemused by the torrent of confusion and guilt she had just witnessed. Grossmutter must have insulated the family from all the labors of the household. When she reached the car her mother was waiting.

"Well, it was a beginning. I think we got

their attention." Merle started the motor. "I saw you talking to Mrs. Jones. How is that poor baby doing?"

"I don't know. She hasn't been down there lately, and it worries me." The windows were open to the warm breeze that was stirring across the city, but it was more than that, some inner flush that suddenly brought out a trickle of perspiration on Lindy's neck. She'd just had a thought so daring she hesitated to spell it out.

"By the way, before I forget," her mother was going on, "Helen Archer is anxious to have you run for Secretary of our Chapter. You'd be good at it, Lindy, you might have to work on your handwriting a bit, you tend to scrawl, but you could be an important figure in the organization. I know you've been reluctant to join The Colonial Dames, but it's a special group of women. Not everyone can claim a lineage dating back to the days of the Thirteen Colonies. I wish you'd give it some thought."

"It's very good of them to want me." But her mind was racing after this new idea. *If Dolly hates this child so much, why couldn't we — Bernie and I — adopt it? What would he think of taking it into our family, not some stranger's abandoned offspring, but one of his own blood? Especially if it was the thing that made our marriage possible.* Her heart was pounding with excitement at the idea as they came into the mansion through the kitchen, to be met by Clemma, a sturdy woman as warm a chocolate color as the cake she was mixing.

"There y'all are! You had a phone call, Miss Lindy, that Dolly lady you stood up with last month. She all upset, asked would you please to call her back soon as possible."

With her mother hovering, Lindy rummaged in a drawer beneath the telephone. She never liked the new phone, which had to be handled with both hands, unlike the old one that had hung on the wall. Reading off the scrap of paper she gave the number to the operator and waited.

"Dolly? It's Lindy. How are you? What's the trouble, my dear?"

"Oh. Thank heaven you called." The words came raggedly through background noise.

"It's not a very good connection, I'm afraid. You'll have to speak louder."

"Wait a minute, I'll put him down." A baby, wailing. Now it was more evident, but the sound had a mechanical quality as if the cries were produced by a phonograph with a stuck needle. *Wahn, wahn, wahn, wahn . . .*

Dolly was on the line again, her voice thready and distraught. "I'm sorry, but I just don't know what to do. I never had to take care of a — an infant. I feed him and rock him and walk the floor, but he keeps crying and crying. I was up all night. Hereford is out of town, and there aren't any women here at Settlement House, and I don't know where my mother is. I didn't know who to call."

"Well, I'm glad you thought of me. You just hang on. I am coming down there to help."

"Oh, you really shouldn't, it's a bad part of town, but . . ."

"Never mind. I'm on my way. Sit tight." As she put down the phone she was aware that her mother was shaking her head urgently.

"You mustn't drive down to the West Bottoms alone, dear, it isn't safe. And I can't go with you. Your father is bringing home some important people for dinner, members of the state legislature. They may be considering him for the Court of Appeals. I really have to be here."

"Of course you must. Don't worry about me, I'll be fine." Lindy was already on her way out, keys in hand. "There was real desperation in the poor girl's voice. She says

70

the baby won't quit crying. It may be sick. It sounded sick."

"Wait, dear . . ." Merle was searching the cabinet in the pantry. "I'll give you something." She found a small brown bottle marked PARAGORIC. "On your way there, pick up some canned milk. The child may just have colic — not all infants respond well to breast feeding. Get a nursing bottle, mix some of the canned milk with warm water and put a few drops of this in it. Then drape the baby over your shoulder and pat it quite firmly on the bottom, get up the gas which is causing the pain."

Fighting a slight panic, Lindy went on out the door. *I'm about to find out about motherhood, the part that isn't all roses.*

FIVE

The West Bottoms didn't look dangerous. Old frame houses, some of them the earliest ever built in Kansas City, crouched tightly as if under attack. Gaps in the rows were scars of fires or other disintegrations. Porches tilted and paint peeled off the clapboard walls, weeds grew up in the cracks of the sidewalk. But there was no menace in these streets. The only aura was one of sadness and ultimate disinterest.

Settlement House had, in years past, been a travelers' hotel. A large square two-story building without pretense of beauty, its only grace was a large veranda across the front. Once white, it was now the gray of hopelessness. Rows of small windows marked the upper floor. Dolly had mentioned they had an occupancy of twenty or so, men who had been sleeping on the streets. Hereford gave them a roof over their heads and one meal a day, thin comfort but better than starving.

The vacant lot behind the hotel was overgrown by cockleburs, flourishing in the young summer heat. Lindy found a clear spot to park near the back porch. As she got out she noticed a shed off to the rear and, angled against it, a Negro boy of about ten, big ears, wide mouth. Or more like twelve — something unchildlike in the way he leaned there, hands in pockets, billed cap pulled down over a bony face the color of polished walnut.

She made a small summoning sign which brought him ambling over. "Help you, ma'am?"

"I believe you can. What's your name, young man?"

"Will'm Anthony Bickford. They call me Willy."

"Good. Willy, would you like to earn a dollar?"

"What'd I have to do?"

"Not much. Just hang around and keep an eye on my car. Don't let any little kids climb on it. Here's fifty-cents." She had the money out ready to give. "If I come back and find no scratches, you'll get another."

"Sure thing." The words were casual, but the brown hand closed tightly over the coin.

And thank you, Cocky, m'boy, for that lesson in back street savoir faire.

73

Carrying her small rescue sack, she hurried up onto the back stoop past a washing machine and a pail full of dirty diapers soaking. In the kitchen she found Dolly pacing, cradling the infant, which still bawled incessantly. Matthew, they had called him, too grand a name for the tiny creature who squirmed and wailed and waved its miniature fists.

"Oh, Lindy, thank you for coming!" Overwhelmingly relieved, Dolly's thin face was not made for smiling. All through the wedding her natural look had been one of dismay. "I couldn't get hold of Mom, she's so busy all the time. And I don't know . . . I don't have many . . ."

"It's okay. I'm glad you called me. My mother had some ideas which we can try. She says it may be colic. In fact she went through the same thing with me. Some infants don't do well on breast feeding. The milk is too rich for new-borns." As she spoke she had found a can opener in a drawer. In the nursing bottle she had bought, she mixed the condensed milk with hot tap water and added a couple of secret drops of the paragoric. No need to mention that. Dolly might be shocked at using an opiate to quiet the child.

"I never thought of canned. I tried regular

74

bottled," Dolly sounded doubtful. "That just made it worse. Wouldn't you know my milk would be sour. What I get for being such a crosspatch. Poor baby, hush, hush, I'm sorry . . ."

They managed to get the little thing to start suckling and the cries stopped. He went at it hungrily, small hands grasping air, feet kicking.

"You're a miracle worker." Dolly sighed. "Would you like to hold him? I'm about ready to drop, but I didn't want to just lay him down alone in the crib. Anything that little needs human warmth." She thrust him into Lindy's arms and folded into a nearby rocking chair.

The kitchen was obviously the center of their lives. Huge steel sink, a large ice box and in the corner was a big stove on which a vast pot of stew simmered, giving off an aroma of onions and potatoes. In the center of the room a table was a clutter of un-washed dishes and in the corner, a crib. Through the doorway was another room, possibly a converted pantry — it was too small for the big bed and dresser.

Lindy paced slowly, rocking the baby. The cries had stopped, but the bare feet still kicked and the hands struggled to grip the bottle. Marveling at so much compressed energy, Lindy was a little awed at this small package: the raw material of a human being in all its parts. "Pretty lively for one so small . . ." she murmured.

"Yes. Only eight pounds. You wonder where he gets the strength to cry like that!" Dolly lay back with her eyes closed. "I didn't know motherhood would be this hard."

And this might be the perfect time to broach my idea. Except I have to ask, could I manage this? Mother would help of course, we'd ask our doctor for a good formula that wouldn't cause colic. I'd have to learn to cook the right foods . . .

"Would you take a look at the stew," Dolly asked distantly, "just give it a stir to keep it from sticking?"

"I didn't realize — do you cook for all these people?"

"Oh, no. Thank heaven. We buy the groceries but the 'guests' do the work. Several of the men were Army cooks, they fix the meals, and the rest of the fellows do the clean-up afterward. It's good for them, to earn their keep."

By now Matthew had downed the whole bottle of formulated milk and shoved it aside, beginning to fret. Over by the crib, Lindy found a box of folded cloth diapers.

Draping one of them over her shoulder, she positioned the baby and patted it as her mother had suggested until a large belch escaped. Almost at once she felt an easing in the tense little body. He seemed to be falling asleep. *Poor kid, he's as tired as she is.*

"Oh, that felt good — to just sit there for a minute." Dolly stood up and came to relieve her. "I'll be all right now. Thank you for your help."

"My mother's the one who knew what to do."

"I guess I should read some books on the subject of babies and their care. But before he was born, I could hardly bear to think about it. All my family was ashamed — well, not of me, I didn't do anything wrong, but they were embarrassed, you know? I didn't even want the baby. Now, of course, I feel entirely different. It makes you believe in God. Look at the little thing, how perfectly made he is. How beautiful."

"Yes, beautiful." Lindy thought she had never seen a living object that ugly in her life, wrinkled and red, toothless mouth, head almost bald, just a fuzz of black hair. And yet the hands and feet were perfect and the flow of life powerful. *Look at the way she rests her cheek against his head, she's*

77

no reluctant mother. Dolly adores her little illegitimate infant.

"Why don't you put him down for a nap and I'll make you a cup of tea?"

"I'd rather have soda pop. There's some in the icebox out on the porch." She dropped into the rocker and began to rock, cuddling the child. "I don't know why you're so good to me. It's so great to — I mean, are you really going to be my sister? Have you and Bernie set the date yet?"

"He's due home next week," Lindy said cautiously. "He's been working on some project, he hasn't written much lately."

"He doesn't know about any of this, you know. I didn't tell anybody about the attack except Hereford, he had to know. The police had to be called. Poor man, he blames himself for everything. I didn't want that. And I couldn't stand what people would say so I just pretended it didn't happen. Until I got so big I couldn't hide it anymore. Then, of course, it was frightful, the way people talked. Even my own mother couldn't look at me. I thought I'd run away somewhere, but I didn't know where, and I had these dizzy spells. I was scared . . ." the word came out thinly.

"Of course you were! I'd be terrified," Lindy poured two glasses of sarsaparilla and

78

pulled up another chair.

"You don't mean it. I'd bet you never were afraid of anything in your life," Dolly spoke in awe. "You're beautiful and rich and smart — well, I'm fairly smart, I got all A's in school. But I'm not very clever with people. I don't have a lot of friends. It's my own fault, I'm kind of snippety. But when you've got a face like a mud fence and big feet and clumsy elbows, awful hair that won't curl — well, the girls back off and the boys snicker. So you rush in and sneer at them before they can snub you."

Lindy felt a surge of sympathy. She could see whole vistas of loneliness in the dark eyes, and then they softened, actually took on a different light as Dolly bent over the sleeping child.

"So now, it's going to be different. I'm going to learn how to be sociable, for Matthew's sake. Now I've got somebody who will love me, need me. I've never been needed." The baby stirred and whimpered. "Shh. You're okay, sugarplum. Anyway I'll be all right now, Lindy. You should start back before dark."

"When will Hereford be home?"

"Late tonight. He just had to go up to Jeff City and appear before some committee about the segregation thing."

"What — ?"

"Oh, there's some foolish law that says hotels can't house both white and colored people at the same time. We have eight Negro veterans among our flock. Men from the 92nd Division, they fought as hard as anybody over there. The same risks, the same pressures, gas, shell-shock, all of it. Now they can't find jobs and nobody's helping them. I don't see what's wrong with letting them live together with the other fellows. So he's pleading the case that we're not a hotel, we're a charity."

"Who on earth could object to that?" Lindy marveled.

"Oh, lots of people. They come by and yell at us. Our poor colored men don't even sit out on the front porch any more. They say the Ku Klux Klan is starting up again, here in Kansas City. It's a fearful thing when men dress up in sheets and go out and harass these poor people who've lost everything. But if we go on helping them we could lose some of our funding."

"Your money comes from donations?"

"Yes. Several of the churches, the Red Cross, the Pendergast machine. Big Tom's always contributing to the needy. And he has been very helpful to the Negroes in his district. He gets jobs for them. But even he doesn't like us housing them in with the white veterans. He says he doesn't want trouble to break out in his district. Having a machine run your city is very efficient, but if the Boss gets down on you, you get all kinds of bad luck. I know, I worked down here almost a year before this happened." She glanced at the baby, and a weary smile lit her face. "This terrible thing that turned into a miracle."

Lindy reached across and patted her knee. "What you need is some rest. I'm going to go and leave you to take a nap. But if you need me, call. I'll come."

As she walked back out into the parking area, heading for the little red roadster, her troubled thoughts veered in another direction.

"Willy! What happened to you?"

The boy was hip-hitched onto the fender, dabbing at his face with a rag. Cap on the ground, shirt-tail half out, he had a bloody lip. But the car was pristine, shining in the sun. He looked pleased.

"Little dust-up," he said. "That pug-nosed Irish kid from over on the next block thought he'd like to sit in the front seat. I set him straight about that, I'm a fair scrapper."

"You did battle for me! That calls for

combat pay." She got out a five-dollar bill.

"Oh Lawd in Heaven." He accepted it reverently.

"I'll be coming down here again, every few days. Any time you see my car parked, consider yourself commissioned to watch over it."

"Yes, *ma'am!*" Pocketing the money. "And you got that baby to stop crying, you a magic worker."

"We both fight to win," she told him. "By the way, if you save up enough change I have a friend who's a stock broker who will help you invest it."

"That's nice, but I got me a hidey-hole where I put my cash until I get enough, going to buy me a set of drums."

"You mean instruments, as in a band?"

"You bet. I know a guy down on Twelfth Street who's teaching me in his off-time. I'm gonna be a red-hot slammer one of these days. Bing, bang, bam!" He beat furiously on invisible traps. "Bring down the house, make folks yell and whoop. I'm gonna do it."

"I believe you. Good luck, Willy." She meant it fervently.

"Thank y' ma'am. I'll take all of that I can get." He grinned, and it flashed on Lindy that the boy was sharp of mind. Going to make something of himself — she have bet the bank on it.

Her whole world seemed to have come into focus since she held that baby. Trivial things had receded and the wondrous possibilities of life loomed large. It was a moment of truth. Especially about her own future with Bernie, which was looking more hopeless than ever. Obviously Dolly wasn't going to give up her child. And just as clearly she saw what it meant for herself and Bernie not to have one. Because if ever a man was born to have a family . . . it brought tears to her eyes.

He'd make such a wonderful father.

SIX

Bernie. It seemed a lifetime ago that Lindy had first met him. A charity event at the old Coates House, he and his friend, Zoobird, high-schoolers at the time, had stood on the sidelines and watched the wealthy socialites at play. Ballroom dancing was a new fad that had sprung up after a concert by Irene and Vernon Castle. Lindy, only eleven then, had drifted up to his side, as close as was proper. What attracted her was hard to define.

What ever makes you fall in love at first sight? No slickly handsome face like John Gilbert. Not very tall, short of six feet — he had put on a couple of inches in the Army. But that afternoon he still had the angles and elbows of a boy, as he stood there, hands in pockets, cap on the back of his head. It was the air of self sufficiency that drew her like a magnet.

Then he glanced down at her, and the

brown eyes had quickened as if a prim little grade-schooler was just what he was looking for. Asked her to dance. She'd had to decline, she hadn't been to dancing school yet. But when her mother had come to take her in to the other room where she was on the program to give a poem, he had followed. She saw him out there at the far fringe of the audience as she recited — Wordsworth's *The Daffodils.* Odd how that day stuck in her memory as vivid as a page of pictures in a keepsake book.

It was the beginning of everything, though it was years later before they met again at a rally to sell War Bonds. That time they had danced in an intoxication of discovery. Since then he had never been out of her mind. All through the War their letters had gone back and forth as steadily as the uncertain mails allowed.

The Great War. It had ruined everything, a lovely innocent way of life, a sense of beauty that was born of ignorance. When she volunteered to work for the Red Cross, Lindy had never expected the misery, the ugliness of the job. Every day she had seen at first hand the damage to the soldiers that came through this Union Station.

Now as she walked slowly down its waiting room, the ceiling that arched high

85

overhead seemed still to echo with the sounds of wretchedness. The groans, the sobs of the shell-shocked men, the murmurs of the dying, would they drift up there in the dome forever?

With a tremor of nostalgia she walked past the point where her old station had been, a counter set up to offer coffee and dough-nuts, but, as it turned out, much more. Blankets, bandages, writing materials, Bibles, most of all a kind touch and a soft voice.

Now she was the one with the wound. For her, the stitching across her midriff was a kind of battle scar — she hadn't gone down without a fight. In spite of the doctor's stern warning, she had put off the surgery until the hemorrhaging got so bad she was almost out of blood. She almost wished she had let matters take their course. It would have been easier than telling Bernie goodbye.

Glancing around, she tried to spot the Jones family. Surely they would have come to welcome him home. But there was no sign of them near the gates to the train yard. As she wandered over in that direction a crowd of newly arrived passengers came through from the tracks and with them a familiar figure.

The boy she had met at the dance was

still there under layers of hardship and maturity. The brisk buoyant step of an athlete, the cock of head and lift of chin. When he saw her Bernie dropped his suitcases and broke into a trot, dark hair scattering, brown eyes alight. He swept her to him and kissed her hard, enveloping her in a tight, needful embrace.

"Oh boy, oh boy," he was murmuring. "I thought this day would never come."

She clung to him hard. *One last time, give me one last time.*

"Lindy! I love you. I have been dying to say that for years and I'm not going to wait one more minute. Will you marry me?"

Curls tucked tight against his neck, bobbing up and down in assent, she wailed, "Oh, Bernie, I can't!"

A half hour later, in a small tearoom near the Station, they sat across an elegant little Chinese table and sipped illicit brandy from cloisonné cups. The scent of liquor was overlaid by the aroma of incense that burned in a bronze fixture in the middle of the room. As the drink produced a growing warmth within her, Lindy began to come alive again. Or was it the return of hope? The look of love in Bernie's eyes had only deepened during her fumbling revelations.

"For heaven's sake, girl, you aren't going

to let that wreck us? The fact that we can't have a bunch of kids? Dear heart, it's the last thing on my mind right now. Of course, I'm sorry you've had such a rough time. How do you feel? You look kind of pale."

At that point she gave up control and cried, and still his eyes never lost that adoration, as he held her hand across the table, refusing to relinquish his tight grip. "You should have written me. I'd have been here with you. As of right now promise me we will share everything, even the rough spots. You're not entirely over this, are you?"

"I'm okay," she said thinly, "except that I haven't had much appetite. I couldn't sleep, knowing I'd have to break off —"

"I'm sorry you went through all that. It must be kind of devastating to a woman, but as far as I'm concerned it doesn't change a thing. I'd want to marry you if you were, God forbid, totally disabled, or disfigured or damaged beyond repair. You're what I live for, girl." A kind of fierceness in the words, a violence she had sensed in him since the war. "If you want kids, eventually we'll have them. Somewhere there'll be a child who needs a family."

"Well, I did think at one point maybe Dolly would like to give up hers, but she doesn't. In spite of all, she loves that baby."

"Yes, poor Sis. I didn't know she'd been through such a bad time, not until Dad wrote me, after it was all over. Said my mother is too embarrassed to discuss it. But drat it all, this wasn't something Dolly asked for. And certainly not anything to be ashamed of. I'm kind of sore at them, which is why I didn't tell them I was coming home today. I needed to see you first, to say a lot of things I've been holding in for a long time."

Lindy waited. He was obviously having some doubts that made him diffident. Cautiously at last he went on. "Truth is, I'm just as glad we aren't going to plunge into parenthood. My plans are risky enough without tiny tots thrown in. We've got a challenge ahead of us, a chance to determine our own future. If you agree. It all depends on you."

He really isn't going to take "no" for an answer. Again, Lindy felt the tears rising. *What's the matter with me? I hate weeping females.*

To the waitress, he said, "Yes, thanks, we would like some more of that 'tea.' " Then bracing up he went on, "In fact, I realize you may not be totally thrilled about the prospect of living in Kansas. But don't dismiss it, there's a lot to be said for a small town . . ."

Lindy wiped her eyes. "Kansas? What's in Kansas?"

"Well, there's wheat, corn, wide-open spaces, silos, grain elevators, labor disputes right now, an honest Governor, a big newspaper editor in a little burg called Emporia. In fact there are over two thousand weekly newssheets sprung up in the state since the War, and pretty soon ours may be included in those statistics." His excitement was so contagious she felt herself lifted out of a dark place toward the bright light of a new life, one that included Bernie Jones. He was talking faster, something about a partnership?

"Pete Koslow, you've heard me mention him in my letters. He's been a classmate in Journalism, both of us war vets, both want to be newsmen. Pete's been learning the knack of writing editorials, he's good with words. Can't draw worth a darn, but he likes my cartoons. We began to see we'd make a good pair, and now he's offering me a terrific chance. His dad is head of the People's Bank and Trust of Pawnee Bluffs, Kansas. They must be doing pretty well out there, the bank needed more space, so they put up a nifty new stone building. Which left the old one empty, and to get to the point — it's ours."

Lindy struggled to keep up. "What will you do with a thing like that?"

"Honey!" As if it should be self-evident. "We're going to start a newspaper."

SEVEN

Orientation. Lindy had written an essay on that for her English class at Gunston Hall. Though most of her education at the finishing school had concerned the social graces, the Hall did provide a basic curriculum for their rich little charges. And while the intricacies of geometry and chemistry never had imprinted themselves deeply, she had loved her lessons in language and literature.

"Take an interesting word and study its origins, write a short explanation, then use it in a sentence."

Orient — from the Latin word *orisis,* to rise. When the sun rises you know you are facing East and can find the other points of the compass. You know where you have come from and which direction you want to go. Therefore: It is well to have a sense of orientation. (Teacher's comment: Try to compose a more meaningful sentence. B+)

Okay. If your orientation is correct, you

know where you are even if you're heading West. Lindy smiled at the thought — everything made her smile, this week since Bernie had come back. Right now, she wanted to laugh out loud from sheer joy.

Orientation means you know who you are: a girl engaged to be married.

Her heart jumped as she looked across at Bernie. Driving a car brought out the boyish glint of delight in his eyes. The bleak shadows left by the war were in retreat. Today he was like a kid on a spree. He had handed her into his father's old Dodge as if it were a limousine and she was royalty.

Now, glancing at her, he said, "Is it too breezy for you?"

"No, no. I like it." The dry wind smelled rich, as if it came from great distances bearing the scents of raw earth and cow barns and pasturage, green corn somewhere. Right here, of course, the land was brown and stubbly, the wheat already harvested. Summer was rushing in fast now, promising its fierce heat, but today the air was still pleasant.

"Sorry about the bumpy road. Kansas isn't blanketed yet with Tom Pendergast's concrete."

Lindy grasped for a meaning in that.

"Well, you know — you know why Missouri is the best-paved state in the middle west, don't you? Pendergast practically invented Ready-Mix Concrete. Every foot of cement roadway means more bucks in his pocket. Sure, he's the one who pushes the public works program through the City budget every year."

"Is that bad?"

"It's a question of influence. The Pendergast machine . . ." Bernie had to break off, guiding the old truck around some pernicious potholes in the gravel road. Where it wasn't pitted, it had turned to washboard, which made it hard to talk. When they came to smoother going he said, "Did you ever hear of a benevolent dictatorship?"

"Didn't one of the old Greeks invent something like that? Plato, or somebody?"

"I don't know the history, but I can tell you that its practice is right here and now. Eastern Missouri is owned by T.J. Pendergast, ruling from his little cramped hidey-hole up above a saloon over in the West Bottoms. Never runs for office, never gets into the arena, he puts his trusted buddies on the ballot and pays people to vote over and over again to make sure they win. Why do you think it's so easy to get liquor in Kansas City? The Boss is against Prohibition. So he tells his cops to look the other way."

"You mean he runs the police department?"

"Absolutely. His candidate is always elected Mayor, in return for which he gets the say-so on the appointed officials who run the city. I'd say he's aiming at control of the entire state. And you have to admit, a power broker gets things done. If the economy is off, too much unemployment, he makes jobs by hiring workers to pave the bottom of Brush Creek at the city's expense. Some folks say it's good to live under that kind of rule. Me, I'd rather be in Kansas."

They had come up to a crossroads where a sign pointed south with a hand-painted arrow: TO PAWNEE BLUFFS. Bernie put the wheel over. The truck was now bucking along a rutted dirt lane that was barely graded, heading for a group of silos and a grain elevator ahead.

"I don't know," Lindy said, over the rattle and bang, "but I'd say Kansas could use a little concrete about now."

"Bricks," he yelled back. "That's our native wealth — we have a lot of mud here. Makes great bricks. They're already laying a road to Topeka. Look, those are our bluffs." Off to the west, a line of low undulations strung out on the horizon. Maybe a couple of hundred feet high, but on these plains they were noticeable. Lindy laughed. Again happiness swelled inside her like a tide. *"Our bluffs"* and *"our native wealth"* — yes!

"I know this seems a long way from Kansas City," he was saying, between bumps, "but we're on two major railroads. The main line of the AT&SF goes through, plus the MKT. They both stop to pick up passengers, it's only about an hour's ride to the city. In fact, the Katy is talking about putting in an interurban to serve us and Fort Scott and some of the other small towns."

"Does Pawnee Bluffs have a hospital?" she asked.

"Not yet. But there's one in Topeka, only a half-hour's drive."

If the good Lord's willing and the creeks don't rise. Except that Kansas doesn't seem to have any creeks. It was the color of dust, the town spread out ahead. Elderly modest Victorian houses under a few determined cottonwood trees, four or five blocks were grouped around a massive fieldstone Courthouse that stood amid them like a mentor. To one side a brick school building was flanked by a playing field that could be for football or baseball. Beyond, a park dotted by picnic tables made a small patch of green. Bernie veered the other way, toward

96

the depot and its water tank.

"There's the new bank building." He pointed to a brick edifice with a brass railing by the front steps, splintering the sunlight. Beyond it stretched a row of small shops, a gas station with one pump. Near the depot was an eatery sporting the sign: JOE'S DINER. And across from it, looking deserted, a clapboard building bore the weathered remains of words: *Pe pl 's B nk nd Tr st.*

"We'll get that repainted, as soon as we have a name for the paper." Bernie was driving around behind it to park near a large barn, equally shabby. Next to it an unremarkable two-story house looked empty, no curtains at the windows, a shutter hanging loose. "The Bank's assistant manager used to live here. He moved to newer quarters too. So we can have it free of charge — if you think you could stand it for a while. Just until we start making a profit on the paper."

Orientation — lead on. Lindy followed him into the back door of the former bank building. The large room showed signs of recent demolition. The row where tellers' cages had once stood had been ripped out, and an office to one side was empty of furniture. In the middle of all that space stood a hand-operated printing press and a tall rack of shelves, next to a table where a man was inserting type into a frame.

A great hulk, his head frowsy as a frayed piece of hemp rope, muscular arms, he looked like a laborer, but his fingers handled the tiny bits of metal as delicately as a concert pianist. Glancing up, he stopped his work and came to meet them with a wide smile made glorious by two gold front teeth.

"Bernie, you brought your little gal! Welcome, Lindy. I won't shake at this time." He held up his grungy paws.

"Honey, meet Pete Koslow."

"Glad to know you," she said fervently. Something about that big simple face made it impossible not to warm toward the man.

"Of course," Pete added, " 'Koslow' is a concoction of the people at Ellis Island who couldn't spell our real family name. A problem your ancestors never encountered on the Mayflower I'll bet."

Lindy smiled back. "Family mythology has it that the first Forrest stowed away on a tobacco ship that ended up in Virginia. He was running from the law at the time."

"So how's the front page going?" Bernie had gravitated over to look at the framework where large type was already set to create a headline:

"You set the whole paper by hand?" Lindy marveled. "And print them one by one?"

"And we will deliver them in person, we give good service," Pete told her cheerfully. "For awhile there's a lot of scut-work. But there are compensations for being your own boss. You get to say whatever you darned well think of the state of affairs — town, city, the whole country. I just got a new story which I'm going to put on the front page, Bernie. Took it off the wire from Tulsa. They have a race riot going on down there. The Oklahoma State Guard is patrolling the streets with bayonets. I think I'll make up a sidebar about the Ku Klux Klan."

"Want me to do a new cartoon?"

"No, but we need a plate made for this one. Lindy, for now we'll have to get our art work engraved up in Topeka, but some day we'll do our own. Anyway, in this first edition I think we should focus mainly on local affairs. And this is appropriate, wouldn't you say?" He led the way over to a drafting table where a large sheet of paper was pinned.

She recognized Bernie's strong swift strokes, depicting a girl — Dorothy from

99

the Wonderful Wizard of Oz — standing in the middle of a muddy, rutted country lane, clutching a small dog. The words ballooning overhead were, "Yes, Toto, we're back in Kansas." And the caption read: WHAT WE NEED NOW IS A YELLOW BRICK ROAD.

"I love it!" Lindy marveled. "Bernie, you're good!" The slashing depiction of prairies and hills and stubbled fields was done with professional confidence.

"My lead editorial will be on the condition of our highways," Pete went on. "We want to have causes, a lot of them. It makes people buy papers, whether they agree or disagree. The more readers we get, the more we can charge for advertising. Right now, we are thin on ads. We only have one, courtesy of my generous dad. It's a full page welcoming everyone to the new location of The People's Bank and Trust. So we are funded through our first edition. What we need, right this minute, is a name for the paper."

"I think I have an idea," Bernie said. "It came to me as we drove over, looking at those hills where the Pawnees used to hang out. They didn't like having their territory invaded and they pestered the wagon trains. The Cavalry had to be called out, and in those skirmishes the redskins kept in touch with each other by a special whistle. It became the most feared sound on the prairie. Old man Grizzard said the Pawnee whistle would raise the hairs on your neck. He was a codger lived in our neighborhood, claimed he was once a mountain man."

"Those wonderful ancients." Pete was nodding. "My grandfather — mother's dad — was a buffalo hunter. Said he'd brought down buffalo right out there around Dodge. Never mentioned the Indians; by then they probably scattered on up into Wyoming. But I like this idea of the Pawnee whistle. It sounds wild and woolly. An attention-getter, to say the least. And it isn't hackneyed, like all the Stars and Times and Tribunes. Let's see how it looks in type." He went over to the rack and began to hunt through the fonts. "Need something with a touch of the historic elegance, but still modern. How about Goudy Old Style?"

Leaving them to discuss it, Lindy wandered over to the front window and looked out at the little town. A gang of kids was playing ball over on the field by the schoolhouse. Closer by, two little girls were turning a jump rope for a third while their mothers stood in the shade of a tree and chatted. It brought back grade-school days.

House for rent,
Inquire within.
When I move out,
Molly moves in.

The trick was to change places without stepping on the rope.

"And if we do run a little short of operating funds," Bernie was saying, "I may be able to kick in a few more bucks. I've lined up a commission. To paint a masterpiece." He was chuckling, shaking his head. "Bull Durham. On the side of a barn outside town. Twenty-five dollars and lunch, you can't beat that."

Trust Bernie to scout out every angle. Lindy was proud of him. She had never been more in love. But a small doubt had snaked its way into her brain. *What does a woman do around a little burg like this? Unless she has children she'll never be part of the town.*

EIGHT

Bernie guided the car through traffic with innate skill, handling his father's Dodge carefully. He was still shy about driving her little roadster. *Lindy, she's such a beauty, not a scratch on her, it would be my luck to run into a tree or something.* He was a good driver, his touch was firm, even though his expression was troubled.

"I don't really understand why you want to do this. I mean, I'm very grateful you stood by Dolly in her time of need, but this . . . You're not doing it on my account?"

"Absolutely not! It has nothing to do with you. It's between Dolly and me."

"But you must have a bunch of friends hoping to be your maid of honor."

"It's matron of honor. And my other acquaintances can be bridesmaids, they're a silly lot. I wouldn't even ask them if it weren't for my mother. She's got her heart set on this big wedding at St. Andrews, I hope you won't be too bored. The list of guests to the reception at the Muehlebach is three pages long. Her friends and Dad's. Me, I'd be glad to elope tomorrow."

"How about next Tuesday afternoon?" he kidded. "No, it's okay, honey. I can understand the need for all those rich people to show off their beautiful kids. But that's why Dolly is going to look a little out of her element. She's never been used to that kind of society."

"She'll be fine. I just hope she'll do it — she's really very shy, you know. All that aloofness is a kind of defense against being snubbed."

"Never thought of that." He made a right turn and they were on the side street headed for Settlement House, which stood alone on its big lot. "Do we dare leave the car on the street?"

"There's a very nice young man who will look after it. Just turn into that parking area behind the building." She glanced around, didn't see Willy. "He seems to reside in that old shed over there. He's never failed me yet."

"Looks like something's going on," Bernie muttered.

On the far side of the lot a long yellow school bus was parked, driver lounging nearby, smoking a cigarette. As they got out of the car, Hereford came out the back door of the House and headed for it, carrying an ice bucket. Several of the lodgers followed, men in neat threadbare work clothes, a few wearing their old uniforms, stripped of Army details. They trailed across toward the bus, some of the sturdier fellows carrying picnic hampers.

Going on into the kitchen they found Dolly packing another basket with edibles, potato chips, jars of pickles.

"Oh, hello," she greeted them. "Wasn't expecting you, but your help is very much welcome. There's a case of pop in the icebox, if you could maybe take that out to the bus?"

"Sure," he said. "What's going on?"

"Well, it's an outing for the men. Courtesy of Mr. Tom Pendergast — don't scold. I know you don't like him, Bernie, but he's doing this of his own free will, no strings attached. He said he just wanted us all to have a day in the country. We're going down to Swope Park. So you see, he's not all bad."

As Bernie went off to help with the loading of the bus Lindy gravitated over to the crib in the corner where the baby lay, sound asleep. "He's growing fast. He's lost that little newborn look, and he seems to have

105

quieted down."

"Don't let that fool you. He always sleeps well in the daytime." Dolly sighed. "But at night, I swear he turns into a different child. He cries and screams and kicks and squirms, poor little darling. I think he wants something but I don't know what." She came over to stare down at him. "I love him so much, he's so helpless. I hold him and walk with him and rock him and I think he's okay. But when I go to put him down he gets hysterical."

No wonder she looks worn out. Lindy was troubled by the dark circles under the woman's eyes, the new lines in her forehead. "Dolly, you need sleep."

"And that's what I never get around here. I can't nap in the day time," she said. "The men always need something. Mostly, I think they just want a woman to talk to, to fix them little snacks and mend their clothes. Well, you know, you went through it when you were with the Red Cross. It's like this picnic today. I wanted to skip it, but Hereford says he needs me to be there."

"Nonsense. I'll tell you what: Bernie and I will go with them and you stay here and snooze."

"Oh, Lin, you don't know how good that sounds. It's like an angel sent you just at the right time."

"Actually, the reason we came — I want you to be my matron of honor. Bernie and I are getting married the first of September." He said it was going to take him that long to get the house in Pawnee Bluffs furnished and ready. "Will you stand up with me?"

Dolly's plain face warped into a knot of disbelief. Tears welled in her eyes. "You mean it?"

"With all my heart."

"I could wear my wedding dress. I can take it in so it's not so loose, it's such a beautiful gown."

"Good, then I can count on you."

"It's so strange. I was going to call you tomorrow. We're going to have a christening for Matthew next week. I was hoping you and Bernie would be his godparents."

"We would be honored!"

Dolly was learning to smile. It did wonders for her bony face. "It's like we had mental telepathy. Our family and yours, we will really be connected. It's the nicest —" Awkwardly she clutched Lindy in a hug.

"I'm glad we'll be sisters. Now you go in and snuggle up under some sheets and don't worry about the picnic. I think they're getting ready to leave."

Hereford was coming back across the

yard. Going past the kitchen he said distantly, "Hello, Lindy. Ducks, I'll help you bring the baby out in a minute. I've got to make sure all our fellows are aboard." He went off up the stairs.

"Ducks?" Lindy repeated, bemused.

"He calls me that. He says I'm good at keeping all our ducks in a row." Dolly went to the icebox where a half-dozen nursing bottles were stashed in the cold water at the bottom. "I got everything ready for a long day. All I have to do now is warm one whenever Matty wakes up. I can feed him and just go back to bed. He'll sleep all afternoon. That canned milk is a miracle — he loves it."

Hereford had returned. "That's everybody. Come along, Ducks. I'll carry the child, you bring the basket . . ."

"She's not going," Lindy told him. "This poor girl is exhausted from lack of sleep. I'm coming, Bernie and I. We'll provide you with all the help you need."

"Oh?"

Dolly turned, nervous. "If that's all right with you, Hep?"

"Fine. The more the merrier. Well, we'd better get moving. The fellows are starting to sing the old war songs."

When Lindy went back out she found Bernie caught up in conversation with one of the veterans. He beckoned her over. "Honey, I want you to meet an old friend from the killing fields. Hobby Carter."

One of the lessons of finishing school: never show shock. Her face was under perfect control as she rapidly took in the fact that the man had no hair on him at all, head, eyebrows, eye lids. It's as if he weren't finished. "It's nice to meet you, Hobby."

"And you, ma'am, are a perfect lady." He shook her hand, the blue eyes full of humor. "Most people at least blink a little. Bout of scarlet fever when I was a baby."

"Hobby's been staying here, temporarily down on his luck," Bernie told her. "We've got to persuade him to let this picnic go, so we can catch up on old times."

"Darling," she told him, "I'm sorry to break it so suddenly, but I volunteered us both to accompany the boys out to the park. Dolly is just about done-in. She's been walking the floor with that baby all night. He's asleep now, and I just put her to bed for a nap. We are going to be Hereford's assistants."

"That's great," Hobby nodded enthusiastically. "I really hate to leave him in the lurch. Most of these fellows aren't up to much lifting. Or they think they aren't. I personally believe they're pretty spoiled. It's easy being taken care of. Me, myself, I won't stay here long, I've got a life to live. All I have to worry about is some shrapnel in my shoulder. So I try to help out with the chores. This picnic, I can do a lot of shepherding and serving and so forth."

"Well, at least you don't have to ride the bus," Bernie said. "Come with us in the car, we'll talk as we go."

They took up the rear of the procession, Hereford leading the way in a seedy Model A. As they wound through back streets, Hobby was going on with the story of his fortunes since he left the Army.

"Like I was saying, I did pretty well selling insurance. The trouble was, the company offered too many benefits and the outfit went broke. So then I sold magazine subscriptions, but this last year there hasn't been much money in it. So I was low on cash when I got arrested. The cop said I was speeding. It couldn't have been more than a couple of miles over the limit, but he didn't care. Just yanked me out of the car and, when I couldn't pay the fine, sent me off to the County Farm. I understand that's one way Boss Pendergast keeps in pocket money. He gets paid to supply food to the lockup, and whatever is left over feeds his own kitty. We got one bowl of oatmeal in the morning and one bowl of soup at night. I never had it so bad in my life. You don't move fast enough the guards slam you with a two-by-four. Latrine's a hole in the ground, one for fifty fellows. You can imagine. Sorry, Ma'am, this isn't polite conversation for a lady." He glanced back at her.

Lindy had taken the rumble seat so the men could sit together and talk.

"Just confirms what I've heard about old Tom," Bernie was saying. "Then he does something nice, like arrange this outing for the fellows. I guess that's how he keeps his popularity in the Bottoms."

"This time maybe it's a guilty conscience," Hobby said. "A week ago he sent his boy — lieutenant, I don't know exactly what Voorhees is — but he came to see Hereford with a demand that he get rid of all the colored men. He said there was talk of the Klan coming back. They're spreading through Texas and Oklahoma, now, wearing their sheets and burning their crosses. The Boss doesn't want any trouble like that in the West Bottoms. Lots of Negroes down here, but they don't live in the same rooming houses with whites. That seems to be the sticking point for Settlement House. Hereford may look kind of light-weight, but he's stubborn. Told Voorhees to stuff it. So next we know, Tom sends his apologies and wants to give the boys a day out in the country, bus, food, the works."

"I'm sure glad we happened along," Bernie told him. "I don't have a lot of loose cash myself, but I bet I can find you some work over in Kansas. We're setting up a newspaper in a place called Pawnee Bluffs. Nice little town, they must have jobs for a fellow with a college degree in agriculture. Maybe you can sell them whatever it is they spray on the potato plants."

"Nicotine," Hobby laughed. "Tobacco juice right out of the old spittoon. Dilute it with a little soapy water and it'll get rid of aphids and most grubworms. And I'll bet your farmers know that already."

"Well, Pete can tell where you fit in. My partner, Pete Koslow, lived there all his life. I'll take you over. We can find a room for you until you get squared away. Our house isn't furnished yet, the one we're going to live in. And by the way —" he turned to Lindy — "as a wedding present my father is going to give us a whole new kitchen, including an electric refrigerator. He gets these wholesale, he's in the real estate business."

"Why, that's wonderful!" she said fervently. *I've got to take some cooking lessons from Clemma.* It was coming clearer every day the reality of being a house wife.

"I never lived in a little town," Hobby was saying. "Grew up in Philadelphia. Couldn't wait to get out, I was happy that the war came along. See the world and all that. I never figured how bad it would get."

Bernie turned to Lindy. "Hobby lost his best friend in the Argonne. Abe Peters. Played the banjo like Kreisler plays the violin."

"I had to hock the banjo," Hobby said on a sad note.

"We'll get it back."

"And my car's been impounded."

"We'll take care of that too. Somehow."

Hobby was silent a moment, wondering: "You always struck me as a kind of high-tuned sort of guy, I mean, you know, mettlesome. You sure did settle down fast."

"Just needed a center point." Bernie looked over his shoulder at Lindy and she smiled back. "Like Zoobird used to say — you recall him?"

"Who could forget that harmonica?"

"He was big on the Bible. He had this verse he used to recite, about how there's a time for everything. Only one line I never understood: 'There's a time to cast away stones, and a time to gather stones together.' Begins to make sense now. There comes a time when you need to start taking responsibility, set goals, consider the future."

It wasn't the interpretation Lindy would have given, but then she never had understood the quotation. Today at least was a time to enjoy. A golden gloss seemed to be laid over the world like a gift. The simple food tasted better outdoors. Impromptu baseball game in a weedy field. Songs from wars past. The men took on a look of wonder, as if they had forgotten what life was about. A beautiful day. Lindy would come to think back on it as the last day of her youth.

Driving back to town Bernie was singing "Tipperary" and Hobby had made a kazoo out of a comb with a piece of paper over it. The school bus was lumbering along a few blocks behind as they turned into the West Bottoms where a soft haze hung over the streets.

"What's that?" Lindy peered ahead. "Looks like smoke."

Hobby said, "Probably another one of those tenements burned. Old frame buildings, they go up like tinder."

But Bernie's foot came down on the accelerator. He spun the car around the last

114

corner, an awful premonition shattering the day's easy grace.. Heavier haze lay ahead where fire engines blocked the way, a tangle of hoses. Pulling into the first open space, Bernie was out of the car and running.

"Good God!" Hobby muttered. "It looks like — where's Settlement House?" The building was a blackened pile of smoldering wreckage. "Thank the Lord we were all out."

"Not all." Lindy choked on the words. *Not all. Dear Lord . . .*

NINE

They'll be all right. They've got to be all right.

Lindy was trying to step over the fire hoses in the tight skirt, *silly dress, silly shoes.* A hand beneath her elbow steadied her across the cluttered yard — Hobby Carter, nice man. *But where's Dolly?*

She looked around at this unfamiliar place with its smoking wreckage, caved in roof, the washing machine on the back porch. *That didn't burn. They must have got out.* And then over to one side she saw the truck with its stark black letters: JACKSON COUNTY CORONER. *The baby. All that smoke. Poor little thing . . .*

Bernie was ahead of her, already talking to the Fire Chief. A haggard middle-aged man with trickles of sweat making tracks down his grimy face, he was saying as she came up, ". . . it was smoke inhalation, she didn't feel a thing, sir. I doubt she was even awake. We found her in that bedroom

116

behind the kitchen."

Lindy seized his arm. "But there was a baby in there, too!"

"No, ma'am. We didn't find no baby. I can vouch for that."

"In a crib, in the corner of the kitchen."

And then a voice piped up at her elbow. "Y'all looking for this maybe?" Willy had come across from the shed. Brown face darkened with soot, he was carrying a dingy bundle of blankets from which muffled wails emerged.

"Oh thank God!" Lindy breathed.

"Heard him crying in there. Couldn't see anything, it was too dense. Just felt around until I got him and ran back out. I'm sorry I couldn't go look for Miz Romney too." He eyed Bernie nervously.

"Don't apologize, boy," the Fire Chief told him. "You're a hero. Saved that child's life. It's no daisy-chain to go into a burning building, and that one was a furnace from the beginning. Dad-ratted Klan! Think they can come into our town and burn things down . . ."

Gray with shock, Bernie struggled with the news. "You mean somebody deliberately . . . ?" His face took on a fierceness that shook Lindy. "This was the Klan?"

"White sheets and all," the Chief said.

"Lots of witnesses, it being Saturday afternoon. Everybody agrees, they came in an old Dodge touring car, side curtains on the windows. Had their gas cans ready and went straight at the building, four, five of 'em. They had it torched in minutes. Piled back in and drove off."

The baby's cries had become more insistent.

"Let me take him." Lindy held out her arms, but Willy held back.

"Get you all dirty in that pretty white dress, ma'am."

"No matter about that. The child's hungry." Lindy had a sudden inspiration. "And there's — there were — bottles of milk in the icebox inside. Maybe it didn't completely burn up?" She started for the charred building.

"No, ma'am, you stay here." The chief put a restraining hand on her arm. "I'll go take a look. That wreck is not done collapsing yet." He left them, and Bernie turned to Willy.

"Did you get a look at those bozos?"

The boy straightened up, stared back at this angry man whose fierce eyes looked so lethal, and swallowed hard. Then the Chief was coming back with a handful of nursing bottles.

"Amazing. That old icebox is made of tough wood. Outside got singed, but these are just about the right warmth to feed an infant."

Lindy took one and turned to Willy. "You know more about this than I do."

He accepted the job, easing the nipple into the wide-sprung mouth. "I been taking care of him some, when she was too busy. Him and me are buddies, aren't we, fella?" He juggled the baby gently.

"You folks go on home," the Chief advised. "There's nothing you can do here. The lady's body will be released to a funeral parlor tomorrow, after the Coroner does his job. Got to make everything official. Probably be an inquiry. Don't any of you go near that building, please." And he left them to return to where his men were still mopping up.

"Where's Hereford?" Hobby looked around. The school bus was parked on the far side of the fire scene.

"He took the men into the Bar-B-Q Pit over yonder," Willy told them.

"Does he know about Dolly?" Lindy wondered.

"Yes, ma'am. He was talking to the Coroner." Willy was watching the death wagon pull away.

"You'd think he'd care a little about the child," Bernie muttered.

"Well, he has all those fellows to look after," Lindy said. "Why don't we go over and join them, let him know that Matty's all right."

As they made their way toward the street Hobby said, "It might be the best thing ever happened to those guys. They've been lying around, taking it easy. Now, maybe they'll get on with their lives. They're all good men."

Bernie didn't answer, his thoughts in some very dark place. Lindy couldn't straighten out her mind to accept the fact that Dolly . . . *but the baby's all right.* He was going at the bottle with an appetite. She kept close to Willy and clung to this one reality.

When they went into the restaurant the crowd of refugees was handling the shock, beginning to clamor for answers. Hereford was trying to reassure them, his face emotionless, but stretched tighter over the bone as if he were exerting a massive effort to keep calm.

"I will make sure we all have a place to sleep tonight. Just give me an hour or two. Stay put here and —"

"No worries!" A strong voice took over, coming from a man who had followed

Lindy and her group into the café. The picture of efficiency, he looked out of place, in a well-tailored dark suit, blue tie to match the piercing eyes, and silvering hair. "Everything has been taken care of by a friend. We heard about this disaster an hour ago, and T.J. got right on the phone."

"He means the Boss," Willy whispered to Lindy. "Old Pendergast. This-here's Voorhees, his bully-boy."

"You will all be housed by the Salvation Army. They are putting up cots right now in their big meeting hall downtown. The bus is at your disposal to take you there." Voorhees had an overriding manner, not to be questioned. "Meanwhile, you folks sit here and eat all you want, it's taken care of. And if any of you need jobs, just go over to Tom's office tomorrow and you'll get a slip that will guarantee you some kind of employment."

They sent up a ragged cheer. Close beside Lindy a small derisive snort. Willy said, "Reckon the Boss done got a little nervous, didn't expect nobody to get theirself killed."

Bernie heard and gave the boy a sharp glance. As the men were on the move to catch the yellow bus that had parked out front, he waited until Voorhees had followed them out into the street, then drew Willy aside.

"What do you know about this, son? I really want to hear it, and I won't ever let on who told me. But it seemed to me there was something fishy about us being carted off to a picnic just when the Ku Klux Klan decided to make their move."

The young brown face under its smudges took on a bitter expression that rendered it years older. The boy lowered his voice to a murmur. "You axed me did I see who lit the fire? I reckon I did. It was him, that Voorhees. Not personal. He got thugs that he trots out for the dirty work. Anybody can throw a sheet over their head. Sure I seen 'em. Tom wanted the House shut down, so they did it."

"It's what I pretty much thought when I put two things together. The cheeky buzzards, pretending to be such benefactors. And Hereford's falling for it."

Romney was ushering his tenants out to climb aboard the bus.

"He knows the truth," Willy said glumly. "He just can't do nothing about it, so he rides along, you know? Ever'body rides along with the Boss."

"Pendergast. I knew he was a power in the city, but this is murder." Bernie's face took on that bleakness of the battlefield. "When I get done with him he won't be the boss of anything but a prison cell. I swear I will get that man, or die trying."

Lindy shivered, a long frisson that ran down her backbone and into her knees. She could hear Clemma saying: *Somebody just stepped on your grave.*

By then the place had cleared, they found a table and Hobby removed the dirty plates from it. Lindy peered down at the baby in wonder. Matty had gone off to sleep as if nothing had ever happened. It suddenly struck her full-force: the child had lost its only parent. What now?

As they settled at the table the proprietor came over with chili dogs all around. "On the house, thanks to good old Tom," he told them cheerfully.

They sat there immobilized for a minute. Then Hobby picked his up and began to eat. To Bernie he said, "It's not going to make any difference to the Boss if you don't stoke the furnace, old pal. You look ready to cave in."

"At least have some coffee," Lindy advised. "We all need a little stimulant after this day." The only thing that bolstered her was the sight of the baby cradled in Willy's arm. "Are you okay?" she asked the boy.

"You've outdone yourself, my friend. And you're not out of danger. I hope they didn't see you?"

"Oh sure, they did. They know I know 'em. Reckon it don't worry 'em much. Figure nobody gonna listen to some nig—"

"Please don't use that word. I hate it. And you mustn't count on them not caring. You can't go back and stay in that shed tonight."

"No, ma'am. I already packed up my things. Stashed my bindle out behind the woodpile. Don't worry none about me. I can be gone in a hurry."

"But where?"

Willie hesitated. Hereford had returned. Coming over to them he looked pale, but still under iron control. "Thank you, William, for saving the baby. I'll take him now."

"You?" Bernie eyed him grimly. "What will you do with him?"

"I've called the Sisters of Mercy. They'll take him in. They have a special wing for foundlings. They know how to care for infants."

Bernie was on his feet now. "That child is not some foundling! I won't have him farmed out to strangers. What's the matter with you? You're his father."

"Oh no," Hereford shook his head, "I'm not. I was glad to take care of them, Dolly and the boy, until we can make things right, eventually . . ."

"Right?" Lindy echoed.

"Yeah, I don't get you," Bernie bristled.

"Well, Tyler Puckett — the boy's real father — is in jail. He'll be there for another seven or eight years with time off for good behavior. But by then he'll have straightened out, I'm sure. Tyler's not a bad man, he just had some mental problems due to the war. As soon as he regains perspective and the pressures ease, he'll get back to his natural self. He won't have access to liquor in jail. And time is a great cure-all. I expect he'll want his parental rights."

"What rights?" In growing rage, Bernie looked ready to attack the man bodily. "That guy raped my sister and you talk about rights?"

"He was drunk, he went a little crazy, I can't go into it all now. But he's very sorry for his acts. Eventually he hopes to take responsibility for them. Meanwhile it's my duty —" He reached for the baby.

Lindy was ahead of him. With one quick step she was at Willie's side — the boy transferred the bundle of smudgy sheets to her arms so adeptly Matthew hardly stirred. Then facing Hereford she drew herself up in a stance of authority that had served a long line of Forrests from Valley Forge to Bull Run.

"You don't seem to feel any grief, that a woman is dead. And you obviously have no compassion for the child. But I can assure you that Dolly would want this baby to be cared for by a loving family. Her last wish was that Bernie and I be Matthew's godparents and I promised her we would. It was almost as if she had some premonition of disaster. She wouldn't want the boy handed over to strangers, in a cloistered environment detached from the world. He is going to grow up to shoot marbles and swim in a swimming hole and have fights and lose and win and learn about life. So you go on back to your damaged homeless ones, you can't do them any harm. Just leave Matthew to us."

Hereford seemed startled, not by her argument but her fury. "Excuse me, my dear, but I don't see how — I mean, you and Bernie aren't even married."

"We will be. Within the week. We'll have a quiet wedding and that baby is going to be there with us."

Bernie was quick to pick up her lead. His arm around her now, he said, "And forget about inviting that brute of a criminal to ever come poking around in our lives."

Hereford looked a little dazed. "I only wanted to do the proper thing . . ." Outside, a horn tooted. "The men are very tired." Turning, he headed for the door, but when he got there he paused and looked back. "I do feel sorry about Dolly."

In the silence Willy whistled softly. "Now that," he said, "was some speaking, Miss Lindy. Wisht I could peel off the big words like that. You was purely powerful."

"That you were," Bernie said softly. She glanced up and saw something new in his eyes. Beyond the love there was a different appreciation.

Lindy fought an impulse to laugh. She suddenly saw herself in the mirror beyond the lunch counter — dress grungy with soot, arms full of a helpless, odoriferous little being that she had just acquired, pre-empting a job she knew nothing about. And she had never felt more ready for the future.

"Did you mean it, about the wedding?" he asked.

"It just makes sense," she told him. "We can't have a fancy reception now, with a death in the family."

Hobby stood up, stretching. "You folks go on and regroup. Me, I got to catch a bus if I want a bed to sleep in tonight."

Bernie held up a hand. "Hold on, I've

been thinking. What we need is a plan. I say we all head for Kansas. The press building has a big basement under it, we can put up cots like a dormitory, have an all-night bull session, the way we did in college. Pete's going to appreciate some new help. Willy, you can sort type from the last edition, that's a big job needs doing. And Hobby, I had an idea: maybe you could sell newspaper space. We need ads, takes time going around to the little towns, hustling business. We'll take turns feeding the baby . . ."

"Dearest," Lindy interrupted gently, "Matthew's a bit young to rough it. I'll take him home with me. My mother will know what to do. He needs a bath and — other things."

"You right about that, ma'am," Willie grinned, his snub nose wrinkling.

"Okay." Bernie was coming up out of his darkness fast now. "You get started on your mothering. The rest of us better dig in on our next paper. Willy, if you like words, you'll be hip-deep in them at *The Whistle*. And I've got a cartoon to draw, about some dopey little guy on the staff getting married to the most wonderful woman in the world!"

THE WEDDING PICTURE

In the garden behind the Forrest mansion the rose arbor is covered with pale green tulle. Posed in front of it, from left to right: Mrs. Jones in a voluminous black taffeta dress with a sprinkle of sequins, small jacket with puffed sleeves, and a ponderous gray bonnet with a cluster of dark red taffeta roses. Next, her husband in a business suit. His square-cut face is troubled, sad, but putting on a smile for the occasion.

Continuing on down the row, Mr. Forrest is wearing his gray gabardine cutaway with golden weskit and a conservative dark four-in-hand. He could be about to preside over a swearing-in. Merle is lovely in a gray silk gown, small veil falling from a white pillbox hat. A single rose is her one touch of color: after all, it is the only wedding her daughter will ever have.

There are no guests except Hobby Carter, his bald head looking as if it were newly polished for the occasion, and halfway behind him Willie in a new suit. It having turned out that the boy was fourteen and a half years old, Bernie had pronounced him ready for long pants and dress shoes, which had produced obvious delight, though he was trying not to show it. He's half hidden by his bundle, a baby enveloped in a handsome fringed shawl.

The central group is solemn, but happiness beams from their eyes. Bernie and Pete Koslow in tuxedos, Lindy, looking as if she could fly, in a flowing white gown, its bodice is bright with embroidered rosebuds. She carries a modest bouquet of daffodils surrounded by lilies-of-the-valley and green fern.

The daffodils were a special request from Bernie.

■ ■ ■ ■

1929

■ ■ ■ ■

TEN

The tires vibrated on the surface of the road, bringing a frown to Cocky DeMille's cheeky face. "You hicks need a good cement plant. This magnificent machine is accustomed to smooth surfaces." With an elegantly gloved hand, he fondled the wheel of the new Cord. "Whatever prompted the citizens of Kansas to pave their highways with brick?"

"We pretty much had to," Lindy told him. "When the State turned down Tom Pendergast's bid to take over the road surfacing for the whole of eastern Kansas, lo and behold! no other Missouri contractor even wanted the job. So our Department of Roads decided to do the job using our own native materials. Bricks are an improvement over gravel. And we don't have to kowtow to the Boss."

"Ah yes, Bernie's favorite nemesis. You know, Lin, he's asking for trouble, making war on the Machine. Even if you do live in Kansas, you're not that far from old Tom's dominion. When your newspaper was in its infancy nobody gave it a second thought, but now people are beginning to take notice of *The Whistle.*"

"Isn't it grand? Our circulation is over 3,000, we're selling papers as far away as St. Joseph and best of all, we're making money. Advertising revenue is way up — Hobby Carter has turned out to be a wonderful salesman. And Pete Koslow is a great promoter. He's gotten to be a leading figure in Pawnee Bluffs. Of course, it helps that his father is the owner of the bank, but the old man never was active in civic affairs. Pete is tireless in organizing events, Pioneer Days, Indian Powwows, mule races, he even calls the square dances at the Grange Hall. It doesn't hurt a bit — draws people in from Olathe and Fort Scott and the other little towns around. And in the long run sells more papers."

"You sound as if you're in hog-heaven," he teased. Same old Cocky, boyish in spite of a slight increase of waistline. The DeMilles always did like their beef steak. By now Austin had noticeable jowls and their father was verging on obese. "I must say you look as if Kansas agrees with you,"

134

he went on. "Have you formed a reading club, or started a theater troop lately?"

Lindy laughed lightly, a chuckle that spoke of joy. "I'll have you know that I am well-known for my cross-stitching, and my bread won a red ribbon at the County Fair last year. Cecilia Wiggins beat me out by a half-inch. Hers rose beautifully, I must say. In my militant moments I have campaigned for shorter skirts, at risk of being called a 'flapper.' Of course my neighbors would shake their heads gravely if they ever saw me like this." She glanced down at her dress, a narrow sheath of gold that failed to cover a shapely knee. Delicate white stockings descended into orange ankle boots.

"No rolled hose?"

"Can't stand them. That's one look I don't intend to promote. And I'm not about to start smoking, even if it does look rather devilish, with the long cigarette holders. Actually, I'm happy with my gingham house dresses, believe it or not. I like being part of a community of good sturdy capable women who don't get the mimsies at every crisis, and support their men in all the wifely ways. But I must admit it's fun to escape to the city. Once a month I dress up and sneak onto the early train to go shopping at big stores where I am elbow-to-elbow with people I don't know. Of course, sometimes my plans run aground. I am so grateful you were free to drive me home today." Glancing over her shoulder she felt a small flip of elation at the sight of the bright red bicycle angled into the rear seat. "It was on sale. I couldn't resist. Matt's birthday is tomorrow and we couldn't find the right bike in Topeka."

"How old is the tiny tot by now?"

"Eight. And not exactly tiny — he's almost as tall as me. Can you believe it's been eight years?"

"How's he doing?"

"Oh, fine. Just fine." Lindy knew it came out too emphatically. It drew a look from her companion.

"Ever hear from Hereford?"

"We see him a couple of times a year — we make it a point to take Matty in, have a sort of family dinner. Hep's still working the Bottoms. He's set up a Mission there and gives out meals to the vets. He gets a big donation from Pendergast, so long as he doesn't try to start another settlement house. At least not a desegregated one. And he won't have a shelter unless it's open to colored people too. I'll say this about Hereford, he sticks to his principles."

"Doesn't pester you about the boy?"

"No, but he's still keeping in touch with the father, due to get out of jail any day now. One more thing I don't need —" She broke off and bit her lip.

"Trouble in juvenile paradise?"

"Matt is — complicated. I suppose all children are at his age," she said. "I'm never sure what posture to take — firm and parental, or soft and friendly. Neither works very well. Only Willy seems to have the hang of it."

"Ah yes, and how is that young man doing in this extremely white environment?"

"He's the town mascot," she laughed. "Everybody likes him. He can do anything with any sort of engine, he's really gifted at fixing cars. And his drums make him very popular. He plays with the Pawnee Ragtime Band, does all the parades and so forth."

"What sort of education does he have?"

"Well, he was too old to go into third grade when we moved here. That's where he belonged, his schooling had been almost nil. So I taught him to read and write and after that he took off on his own. He's got more books down in his basement hideaway in the press building than I have in my living room. Gets them from everywhere, whatever the library discards, the attics of people who are cleaning house. The school gives him their worn out textbooks, and the church passes along whatever people donate. Willie knows more about early Christianity than I do."

"Doesn't he miss companionship of his own color?"

"Every Saturday he loads his drums into his old jalopy and heads for 12th Street in Kansas City. Doesn't come back until late Sunday night. I think he has plenty of girl friends."

"And *The Whistle* lets him live there free?"

"Oh, he earns his keep. After the paper is printed he puts the type back in the job case. And today, being Friday, he'll be out delivering papers to the town. Everybody in Pawnee Bluffs gets a copy — we are the official record for the County, all the legal transactions, land sales, foreclosures, births, deaths and marriages, everything gets published in our pages. We get paid a nice sum for that. In fact it saved our bacon in the early days of the paper. But in return we have to deliver a copy to every house in town. So Willy and Matt are out there in his old heap, spreading the news and . . ." she broke off. "Oh, my lands! Cocky, step on it."

They had topped a slight rise and saw ahead far out across the rolling land a sight that had become all too familiar on the prairies — a thick wall of dust rising a hundred feet high, boiling toward them kicked by a strong wind. Cocky made an inarticulate sound of anguish.

"That grit will strip the paint off my expensive little toy in seconds." He sent the car spinning forward at a headlong pace that racked its sleek body. The Cord was a gleaming beauty, glossy black with a tan canvas top, wire-spoke wheels and brilliant chromium exhaust pipes bursting out of the engine. In the advertisements it was promised to do 85 miles an hour, and now the speedometer was pushing seventy, the tires making a high whine on the brick highway.

Lindy sat tense, staring ahead at the seething cataract of dust. Too dense to breathe, it had become a menacing phenomenon of the drought, especially in Oklahoma. Pictures showed farms down there half hidden under the drifts of fine sand, fences buried to the tops of the posts. Kansas had fared slightly better. There had been some rainfall last spring, but not enough and a storm like this could stifle the knee-high corn.

Things had been getting worse for several years, bringing foreclosures, land sales, bankruptcies. Lindy had heard the sound of fear in the voices of her friends around the sewing table. Their husbands all ran the small businesses that made the bulk of Pawnee Bluff's economy. Everyone was feeling the lag of sales. The Bank had extended more credit to those in trouble, but Pete's father had warned there was a limit to that.

As the car swept into the little town Cocky breathed an audible sigh of relief. The dust wall was only a few miles from them now. Lindy had her door ajar and was out before he'd quite stopped. She ran to shove open the doors on the barn behind the press building. The huge structure was empty — Willie's Chevy was still gone, and Bernie had the roadster today, delivering *The Whistle* to Topeka. Pete would have taken his truck to Kansas City to drop off the paper at the newsstands there. He always left before dawn, only minutes after the last bundle was tied.

With the Cord safely inside, she hauled the big wings shut and set the bar across just as the wind hit. It seemed to rock the building on its foundations, the power of the blast thrusting through the cracks, filling the air with a fine haze. In a screech of nails a board was ripped from the roof, to reveal a roiling darkness above. As they stood there silent, holding their breaths, a flash of lightning hit somewhere nearby, a

140

spatter of rain fingered the building, and then the wind began to ease off.

"I wonder where the boys are." Lindy peered through the window in the smaller door beside the big one. It had been a horse barn, but the stalls had been torn out and the hatches nailed shut. A generous space to house all their vehicles, it still bore an aroma of hay and neatsfoot oil and leather. They'd had to remove the ladder to the hay-mow above after Matty had climbed up there at age three.

He had always been overloaded with energy — that was the hardest thing for Lindy to deal with. Even as a baby he'd been as difficult to hold as a twenty-pound sack of Mexican jumping beans. Never wanted cuddling, fought off fond arms and blankets and the shelter of his crib. By the time he was two he was in constant motion. At four he had run away. In an instant's flicker of distraction, she had looked around to find him gone. They had spread out in all directions, but by the time Pete caught up with him on the wagon road to the Bluffs, he was almost two miles away. Bernie had given Matty his first licking and Lindy had gone to bed with a monstrous headache.

At six, the boy had come home to dinner one night carrying a writhing creature that turned out to be a prairie rattlesnake.

"Where did you get that?" Bernie tried to keep his voice even as he took the thing.

"Mick O'Malley showed me how to catch 'em." Matty scowled ferociously. "That was *my* snake. You didn't have no right to take it away."

"Any right," Lindy corrected faintly.

Afterward, comparing notes with the women at the sewing club, she saw them exchange looks and hedge the truth. "Oh, that's what all children go through." "He's just a very smart little boy who's interested in everything." "Curiosity is part of growing up."

But a few quiet inquiries revealed a whole side of Matty that she hadn't realized. She discovered that the boy didn't have any friends at school, that he never was asked to join the teams that were formed and re-formed throughout the years. His teachers were lukewarm in their appraisal. "Matty could make all A's if he wanted." They all agreed the boy was not good at taking orders of any kind from anybody. Except Willy — Matt did seem to respect Willy, thank heaven.

Through the haze outside she saw movement, a familiar silhouette against the dust. "There the boys are now." She went to un-

142

bar the barn door. Over her shoulder she said to Cocky, "You'd better get between them and your car. Matt will make a run for it, don't be afraid to grab him. That's the only way to stop him."

Cocky frowned, puzzled. "I've never been afraid of an eight-year-old child in my life."

And then the battered jalopy was bursting in out of the wind and she shut the door again quickly. Before the beat-up old Chevy had come to a complete halt it ejected a sturdy little boy like a projectile.

"Gee whillikers!" It broke out of Matty in a modified yell. Stocky, square-cut, a hundred pounds of concentrated energy, he launched himself toward the Cord.

"Hold on, partner. No hands on the polish." Cocky intercepted him firmly.

Willy had followed along, almost as radiant with delight at sight of the gleaming vehicle. "Good thing you didn't get caught out in that trash storm. We made it to the gas station. Not much protection, but we put up in the shed where they change the oil. Except the wind blew the top off the shed. We was okay, though, in the cab with the windows shut. Little sand can't hurt old Bizmo much." He had never explained why he called his car that.

"Well, thank heaven you're both home

safe," Lindy said. "Let's go in and get something to eat."

But now Matty had torn himself from Cocky's grasp and was plastered against the window of the Cord, peering in at the bike. "Mama! Is that for me?"

"Oh dear, it was supposed to be a surprise for your birthday tomorrow."

"I want it now!"

"You can't ride it now. There's still too much dust outside."

He turned and faced her with those blazing eyes. They had always been too deep a shade for a child, the color of green turquoise, fringed by thick black lashes. His rampant hair was almost black, too. No sign of resemblance to his mother. The whole Jones family had agreed on that, with some dismay. Matty was undoubtedly the spitting image of the father who had begot him so savagely.

"You gimme the bike now or I'll . . . I'll kill you."

Willy was the one who stepped in. "That's bad talk, cut it out." The curt order made the boy flush and lose his tense posture. "You go tell your mom you're sorry and you love her. Who else would buy you such a great present?"

Glum-faced Matty scuffed over to Lindy

144

and gave her a quick perfunctory hug. "Thanks. I really wanted a bike, but could I look at it now. Please."

"Okay, I guess we can do that." She kept an arm around him as the men opened the rear door and angled the bicycle out, with care to the car's gleaming paint job.

Thank heaven for Willy. How many thousand times had she thought that? Lindy wondered. He hadn't changed much since she first saw him. Taller now, more mature, but then he'd always had a knowing look about him. The impish grin could flash on occasion, but most of the time his dark face was shining with intensity. If life was a challenge, Willy loved it.

Matty had climbed on the bike, teetering precariously around the vehicles to ride to the far end of the barn and back. Lindy tried not to watch. There were so many things that could impale — the raw nails where the horse stalls had once been, the splinters on the rough boards of the tack room which still occupied one corner. *I'm being one of those over-protective mothers.* She said, "The men will be home soon. I'm going over and fix us some supper."

"Let me do it, I'll make us an omelet." Willy gloried in his cookery. And never more so than when there was a good crowd around the table. With sundown coming on, the absentees trickled in — first Pete Koslow. He had heard about the storm and left the truck in Kansas City, coming home on the train. A few minutes later Bernie arrived, looking windblown.

"Don't worry," he told Lindy, "the car is fine. I was delayed in Topeka and the worst was over by the time I got on the road." He was still reluctant to use her roadster, but she had convinced him they didn't need to baby a ten-year-old car. And certainly not to buy a second vehicle that was beyond their means.

"Anybody heard from Hobby?" Pete asked.

"He went up to Kansas City." Willy flipped the giant omelet expertly. "Get a new head for his banjo. Somebody stepped on it last week at the jam-bo-ree. We had 12th Street jumpin' that night. You ought to come hear us some time."

"Wish we could," Bernie said. "Maybe when Matt's a little older." They had settled around the kitchen table. Lindy brought them coffee.

"I hate omelets," said the subject in question, muddling the food on his plate. "It's got onions."

"Made you some hotcakes," Willy told

him. "Right over there on the stove, hold on."

"Well, I love omelets and this is the best I just about ever ate," Cocky announced. "Had no idea you were a blue-ribbon chef, Willy. You could get a job at the Muehlebach."

"Not me," the boy said, setting down a plate of flapjacks. "I got my future all set here, the fastest growing paper in Kansas. Ain't that — isn't that right, Pete?"

"Absolutely. We're making so much money, I think we'll be able to buy a linotype machine one of these days." The big man had cleaned his plate. "Where are your eggs, Lin? I need more nourishment. Oh, I see 'em."

"If you folks are really doing that well," Cocky said, "you should incorporate. It's better for tax purposes. You could even sell stock."

"We're doing fine without a bunch of shareholders telling us how to run the paper." Bernie shook his head. "Lot to be said for total freedom of speech."

"Well at least you should have a partnership agreement in writing. In case something happened to one of you, the other should be able to take over and keep the paper going. Why don't you go in and see my brother, Austin. He's great at making things legal."

"Not a bad idea." Pete was scrambling eggs. "We're not financial planners, I'm afraid. We're just happy when more money comes in than we spend. Lindy, is that a new dress?" He was teasing.

She was still wearing the stylish yellow sheath, the orange boots. "Yes it is. I bought it with the check my Dad gave me for my birthday. Don't worry, I'd never bankrupt us over a silly set of clothes."

"I wouldn't call it silly." Her husband grinned with a gleam in his eye. "There are better words."

"And there's something to be said for helping the economy," Pete added solemnly.

"Excuse me, I hate to belabor a point, but you could increase your funds by investing in the market. It's going up like an elevator. You could double your worth in six months. Or less, if you buy right." Cocky's enthusiasm was genuine and personal. "I bought General Electric back in the early years for pennies, and now look at it — right over there in the corner, a refrigerator in every home. You are helping my assets. It doesn't even take much cash if you buy on margin."

"Elevators go down, as well," Bernie reminded him cheerfully. "I'm keeping my money in a bank, thank you."

"And as for *The Whistle,*" Pete added, "our goal is quality first, then quantity. Subscriptions will increase if we put out a good paper. You did give me an idea, though, Cocky. Why don't you write a financial column for the paper? We couldn't pay you, but we'd give you a nice spot of free advertising."

"I'll think about it. Thanks for the offer."

Bernie's look sharpened. "Hey, that's a great idea. I mean to diversify, put in some weekly departments, golf tips, maybe. Automotive advice. Lindy could do a woman's column with recipes and sewing patterns. Encourage the wives to read the paper, take an interest in civics."

"That's a very dangerous suggestion," she told him lightly. "You might find us all out picketing Kansas Feed and Grain for lower prices. Flour has gone up two months in a row."

"And the farmers are still starving. No, that's something the men need to take up at the Grange meeting. But maybe you could find a crooked politician to picket. Not here, Kansas is safe under our good Republican leaders. But there's plenty of corruption across the border."

"Aha," she laughed. "I knew we'd get

around to Tom Pendergast." To Cocky, she added, "Bernie loves to irritate the Boss. His cartoons are hilarious."

Curiously DeMille asked, "Don't the locals object, to your going so far a-field with your pen?"

"No, they kind of enjoy it," Bernie said. "Many of them moved here from Kansas City because they didn't like living under a machine."

"And it makes money for us," Pete added. "We sell advertising to stores over in Kansas City. Lot of folks can't stand The Boss, but they also can't afford to stick their necks out over there."

"Anyway, I consider it a public duty to try to bring that crook down," Bernie said. "I have a series going, once a month, I call it the Nasty Neighbor Next Door cartoons."

"Could get you in Dutch," Cocky told him cynically. "That last one was verging on libel."

Bernie had drawn a wicked sketch of a burglar with Pendergastian face robbing a store labeled "Kansas City" and making off with a sack of jewelry. The caption had been: WE NEED TO PAVE SWOPE PARK. "Next year I'm going to do my best to get the electorate to vote against the machine when they go to the polls," Bernie went on.

"You know what my sources tell me? The word is out to the underworld: Come to Kansas City, you won't be bothered by the law."

"Which is why the old man is dangerous," Cocky insisted. "The mob is not contained by city limits, old boy."

"My friend, you can't instruct me about the Boss. Remember, he burned down Settlement House with my sister in it."

The room went silent. They all glanced at Matty, who seemed unaware of the discussion. Wiping up syrup with the last of his pancake, he shoved back from the table and headed for the door.

"Aren't you forgetting something, son?" Bernie said.

The boy stopped in his tracks. Without looking back he said, "Can I be excused."

"Certainly dear," Lindy said. "And happy birthday, as of tomorrow."

Matty glanced over his shoulder then. "Thank you for the bike."

She smiled. The kitchen door slammed. "He's off to the barn to look at his new possession, I'll bet." But she wondered, *Why doesn't the child ever smile back?*

151

ELEVEN

In those long-ago days when she had first moved to Pawnee Bluffs, Lindy had looked with dread upon one aspect of married life. She had always hated sewing. In her childhood, learning the womanly skills, she had tried embroidery with such pricking of fingers there had been more blood spots than rosettes on the fancy little handkerchief. So it was with gritted teeth that she had accepted the invitation of her neighbor wives to join their quilting circle. Only grim determination had kept her at it until, by sheer practice, she had learned to use a needle.

Now it had become a welcome moment, a respite from the home chores, to sit with the girls and make a thing of beauty. Today it was Cora Pegg's first effort stretched on the quilting frame, a simple double-wedding-ring pattern which she had executed very neatly. Spaced around the edge the women sat in tribute, their hands fluttering over the multicolored design in a graceful dipping movement as they laid in the top stitching to bind the three layers of the quilt together. Lindy felt a warmth of pride as she kept pace with the others, though she could never outdo Maisie Stark when it came to gossip.

"And what I heard was that Penelope Riffkin had a big fight with George and the two aren't sharing the same bedroom." She giggled. Plump as a doughnut, honey-blond hair in fat braids around her head, she was dressed primly as a pastor's wife should be. But there were secret facets of Maisie's soul that sparkled when her husband wasn't around.

"That kind of news is best left unrepeated." Gertrude Koslow had, by right of seniority, the last word in what was acceptable around the circle. "Especially if it was divulged by someone in the privacy of the rectory."

"Oh, shoot, Gertie, I'd never spill any of those kind of beans. Absalom always closes the door of his office when people come in to get advice. I heard this from —"

"Never mind!" The admonition was sharp and final. The lady at the head of the table was small, brittle as thin steel, and capable of the same kind of edge. It was hard to picture her mothering a hulk the size of Pete, but he often said she had raised him with kisses and switches. It occurred to Lindy that she really should ask Gertrude for some advice about Matty.

Agatha Hackman stopped to thread her needle. "The trouble with Penelope is that she doesn't know how to handle a man. You don't just go head-to-head with them, or they'll win every time. You have to plot a little, use strategy to get your way. My Johnny has big shoulders, but beneath that he has the softest heart in the world. Whatever I want I just say it's for the good of the children and he melts." A tough angular woman, she went at the quilting again with cocky little dips of the needle, the fastest and best of the sewing circle. Her dark hair and eyes and olive skin testified to her Greek ancestry in which she took a good deal of pride. Her three girls were in the third, fourth and fifth grades at school. Now there, Lindy thought, was another possible source of advice. And yet, through the years, she had never felt close enough to the ladies to open herself to them, to divulge her insecurities.

"I have an idea. Let's give Penelope the job of handing out the hotdogs at the

Fourth of July picnic. It does wonders for a person's confidence, you feel so popular." Cora laughed, a lovely sound straight from the cornfields. A pretty pink-cheeked child she was glowing with the joy of a pregnancy which was becoming more evident day by day.

Lindy said mildly, "I thought the refreshment table was my assignment." For two years it had been. She was puzzled by the swift exchange of looks.

"Oh well, we just thought you ought to be free this year to enjoy the festivities." Agatha's cheerful tone was patently false.

So this was something they had talked over. Lindy tucked the end of her thread under and snipped it. Her silence provoked an uneasy pause among the group. Without starting a new needle she looked squarely at Gertrude, waiting for a true explanation.

"To be frank," the older woman said finally, "we were going to ask you to keep a little sharper eye on Matthew. We quite understand that he's a difficult child, and we'd be happy to help in any way. But the fact is, he was very disruptive last May Day."

"Began doing cartwheels and somersaults right in front of the audience when the girls were trying to get the maypole started — it's not entirely simple you know, weaving those ribbons in and out," Agatha explained. "They practiced and practiced. And then this frantic little boy comes galloping around and showing off and they got distracted and Susan Powell went the wrong way and my Diane tripped and fell down, not her fault, I might add. It was just very upsetting, is all."

Lindy sat quietly taking it in. She knew there had been a fuss over at the maypole, but she had been putting cake on the paper plates and hadn't paid much attention. It embarrassed her to think that nobody had mentioned all this before now.

She began to nod. "Frantic describes Matt perfectly. He's always in motion. I don't know what drives him. I am sorry he disrupted things, and I'll do my best to see it doesn't happen on the Fourth."

"Well, boys will be boys. But there's just so much that can go wrong when they all get to playing with fire crackers and so forth." Gertrude seemed to regret her position as mentor, but not enough to retreat.

"It's not just that." Maisie spoke up hesitantly, all pastor's wife now, grave and apologetic. "I have worried about telling you: in fact I asked Absalom last night and he said it was my duty."

"Tell me." Lindy made it an order.

"Well, you know Ab goes over to that bunch across the tracks, to counsel those poor fellows." A collection of hoboes had set up camp beyond the depot, waiting for the corn crop to come in, hoping for work. "They're not really bad, most of them are share-croppers with nothing to share this year. But any time you get men who are down on their luck, living in cardboard boxes, and right over here in plain sight are people who are able to buy food and . . ."

"Maisie," Gertrude said firmly, "get to it."

"Well, all I'm saying is, it isn't a safe place for a ten-year-old boy."

"Matthew's only eight," Lindy said automatically, trying to absorb the unspoken. "Do you mean he's gone over there?"

"At night. Ab has seen him more than once, hanging around their campfires where they play cards and tell rather earthy jokes and so forth."

"You didn't know?" Gertrude stopped stitching to eye Lindy with sympathy.

"Lately he's been going to bed early," she said. "At least that's what we thought. Bernie would never allow such a — Excuse me, but I need to go home right now and talk to my husband about this." She put her needle down and shoved back from the table.

Nosy biddies! Lindy let go her inner anger

157

as she walked back up Main Street briskly, fists clenched. One thing about small towns she detested, the fact that your family life was public property. And Absalom Stark would do well to keep what he sees to himself. Except, of course, he couldn't — not if he thought Matty was in danger.

The little devil, must have climbed out the window. But I can't watch him every minute of the day and night!

The gold-edged red letters were fading on the side of the building. *The Pawnee Whistle.* It seemed like only yesterday that Bernie had painted them there, but the Kansas sun is fierce. And after a few more dust storms like the one last week, they'd be unreadable. As she let herself in at the side door of the building, Lindy hesitated. Over at his easel Bernie was frowning at a blank sheet of paper. The floor around him was littered with wadded up discards. Not a good time to spring new problems on the man. And yet, with dark hair tousled and a shadow of beard on his jaw, Bernie looked every bit as tough as those drifters across the tracks.

I've got to tell him. He'll know what to do.

Glancing over, he beckoned her in. "What's happened? You look upset."

"I am," she admitted. "We had a quilting bee this afternoon and the women were talking — I guess everybody in town knows more than we do about our own child. Apparently Parson Stark has been going over to the hobo camp across the tracks these evenings, to offer counseling to the men. It seems he has seen our Matty over there hanging around those bums."

Bernie gave a short laugh and shook his head. "That kid! What won't he get into next?"

"He must have been sneaking out after he pretended to go to his room."

"I thought it seemed pretty early for him to be so tired he had to hit the sack. At eight o'clock in the evening?" Bernie chuckled. "I should have been suspicious. It's exactly what I used to do at his age. That's when the gang was building the tree house. My mother would have had a conniption if she could have seen that, a platform forty feet above the street in a giant walnut tree. We rigged a sling from a nearby hillside to get the lumber across to the top of it. One of my favorite childhood memories, meeting the gang there after dark."

"At eight years old?"

"Oh, I suppose I was more like ten or twelve. Sometimes I forget, Matty's so big for his age. Look, Lin, don't fret. It's all part of the growing-up process. You learn

159

by trying things out."

"But those men are rough. Homeless and angry and desperate, what do they think when a child wanders into their midst dressed in nice clothes and smelling of beef stew?"

"They might steal from him, or cheat at cards with him, but they're all solid country fellows. They wouldn't harm a kid. However, I will have a word with Ab Stark. It's bad enough when women gossip, but for a man of the cloth it's not seemly. I will go to his church, but I'll be damned if I let him tell me how to run my family."

It was pretty much what Lindy had been thinking. For all that she had accepted neighborhood customs when she moved to Pawnee Bluffs, she was still a woman of the city, where people were independent of each other.

"Still, it worries me," she insisted. "A little boy roaming around out there in a hostile world."

"Well, it's natural for mothers to worry." Bernie glanced back at his new sheet of paper. "It's a woman's way. But don't say anything to Matt. I'll handle it. If there was one thing I used to hate it was my mom saying 'Be careful.' "

By the time she reached the door he had

picked up his charcoal stick, beginning to make a bold outline on the new page. Even a few strokes and it looked like Tom Pendergast.

Obsessed. He's obsessed with the Boss. That rotten man is a cloud over our lives. Of course, she understood. The memory of poor Dolly was still as fresh as if the fire had happened yesterday. *Maybe I should tell Willy about the nightly excursions across the tracks.* But she decided not to. Evenings were the time when the boy played those drums. If he wasn't at some gig over in Kansas City he practiced lustily in the basement of the press building. The joyous tympani would reach them distantly on warm nights when the windows were open. *We've already asked too much of Willy.*

Back in her own kitchen with the afternoon only half spent Lindy went to the refrigerator and took out the jar of lemonade that she kept there for the family. Matty loved the stuff. She could see him now, down the block, pedaling his bike furiously, going away. *I'll bet he saw me coming home and took off. Do I look so forbidding? What kind of mother am I?*

It wasn't the first time she had asked the question of herself. Sinking down at the table, she considered the drink — what was

161

that age-old question: is your glass half-full or half-empty? Bernie had sounded the least bit condescending when he said, "Go ahead and worry, it's a woman's way." Did he mean it was a woman's way to be weak?

Inside everything went stock-still, the way it did when she had a moment of discovery. An idea. The thought was daring, she would be risking rejection, at the very least criticism. Did that matter? At the moment, no.

Abruptly she got up. In the living room she rummaged in a drawer and found a notebook, one of Matty's school tablets, red, with a picture of an Indian head on the front. A pencil. It was dull, she found a sharpener. Taking them back out to the kitchen she pulled up to the table and began to write.

A Woman's Way

It has been said that women have a different outlook on life . . .

Scratch that.

It has been said that a woman's outlook on life is different from a man's. Not only is that self-evident, but it is a good thing, one that ought not to be taken for granted.

In this column, I want to . . .

Scratch "want"

I will discuss some of the ways in which our wives enrich our community, and I thought I would start with bread.

Men plant the seed and reap the wheat, they thresh it and mill the flour. But how many men know what it takes to bake a good loaf of bread? I suggest that it would do some of them good to knead a lump of dough. Not just an exercise in patience, they could ponder on getting the right texture. They might discover that yeast is a very humble ingredient but without it the bread won't rise, no matter how you order it to.

Men are great at giving orders. They are born to be leaders, and nobody could deny they're formidable in action. But the other half of living is the sustenance a family receives from its womenfolk, especially the subtle ingredients of emotion, sympathy, understanding, all in a certain proportion. To make good bread you need a recipe.

By the way, here's mine:

163

To a half cup of warm water add one cake of yeast. When it tests out add it to three more cups of water. Put in three teaspoons of salt, three of sugar. Add enough flour to make dough . . . and now we get the moment of creativity. The more flour you add, the lighter the bread, up to a point. Too much and it gets dry and tough. The baker experiments. Judges. Senses. Feels for the moment when it is exactly right.

This is the art of the cook. And of the wife. The feeding of the family's inner hunger — this is a woman's way.

Lindy Jones

Putting the pencil down she sat and reread her neat handscript. It gave her a secret bump of joy. The little essay had a kind of unity, a theme. Flowing quickly from her impulse, it had channeled feelings she had hidden away, unspoken, with a clarity that startled her. Not great writing, but it was short and to the point, and she knew instinctively it would strike a sympathetic note with every wife on the block.

Before her resolve could falter, she tore out the pages and took them, across the yard and into the press building where Bernie had just crumpled another unsatisfactory cartoon. He slammed down the charcoal and it broke. In frustration he turned to her. "Yes?"

She tried not to retreat under his ominous look. "Do you remember when we were all talking the other day and you said I might do a column for the paper?"

It took a minute for the new subject to engage his mind. Then he eased off and said, "Yes. And it's a good idea."

"Well, I tried one. I mean, I wrote a draft. It isn't all that great, but I wondered if you'd look at it. Tell me how to improve on it." She held out the pages.

Bernie glanced over them quickly, then went back and read slowly line by line. "Lin, this is good. You have a nice literary touch. Not to carry the bread metaphor too far, but I believe you can give the women more to chew on than idle gossip. Emotion, sympathy and patience are only the beginning of all the ingredients our gals have when it comes to running a home. If you want to you can make it a regular feature. This has great potential. Sweetheart, I'm proud of you."

Lindy felt the slight chill of hurt fade away under his warm words. She had hated that sense of inferiority she sometimes got when men — especially Bernie — treated her like

165

a mere spectator to their lives. Now, or at least a few more columns from now, she thought she might earn a little respect from the forbidding world of male superiority. Not to mention from certain ladies of the community.

Oh I'm sorry I can't come over to quilt, she would say casually to Gertrude Koslow, *I am busy writing my column for the paper.*

TWELVE

There are many ways to celebrate a holiday. Just sitting in the shade with nothing to do was one of the most delightful. Under the stirring branches of a great sycamore tree, Lindy leaned back on a park bench and reveled in the moment.

For July the weather was marvelously pleasant, not too awfully hot to commemorate the Fourth in traditional pursuits. Bernie was umpiring a game of softball a few hundred feet over on the diamond behind the Grange Hall. It, like the rest of City Park, was festooned with red-white-and-blue bunting. Over by the bandstand Willy and a couple of others were setting up chairs for the patriotic concert to come later. In the yard behind the school teams of girls were running a race with spoons full of water. The younger boys were playing tag around the statue of William Jennings Bryant, who had dedicated the Park when it

167

was first laid out, though few people remembered his Cross of Gold. Ancient history.

The world seemed to spin faster than it used to — or else, Lindy thought, she was slowing down. It felt incredibly good to sit here while the rest of the women set out the picnic food on a long table, Gertrude Koslow presiding. The women were casting glances in Lindy's direction, and the town matriarch looked a little flustered, as if she regretted wielding her powers unwisely.

In an impulsive dash Cora Phillips came over to sink into a seat beside Lindy. "You know they're all talking about you over there," she chattered. "We really wish you would come join us."

"Thanks. But I think I'd rather just sit here and relax."

"It was wrong to take the refreshments away from you. You were so good at it, and Penelope is bungling the hot dogs. She can't keep straight who wants sauerkraut and who wants relish."

"She'll learn. We all have to learn some time." In her mellow state Lindy didn't even mind pontificating. Felt good.

"We finished quilting my quilt — it's beautiful. I — we missed you after you left that day."

"Mmm. Well, there are some things that

can't be shrugged off. Criticisms of Matthew are a first priority to a mother. You'll discover that it's a handful, trying to keep track of an eight-year-old."

"Oh I'm sure of that! Where is Matty?"

"He's at home. He's forbidden to leave the house today. His father is very angry with him." And her tone discouraged any further discussion of the matter.

Cora dithered nervously. "Bernie's a very — very — I don't know, he's a sweet guy but there's a kind of toughness that comes over him."

"The War." Lindy knew exactly what she meant. "It inures a man, to face death on a battlefield. After those months at the Front he never shrinks from a challenge."

"Neither do you," Cora blurted. "I mean, to write that marvelous column for the paper — how did you find the words?"

"Thank you. That's a compliment I very much appreciate. I never tried my hand at it before, but I've been asked to make it a weekly feature, and I think I'm going to enjoy it. In fact, I was just sitting here, trying to figure a way to work this holiday into my next attempt." Lindy had been toying with the theme of fireworks. The need to explode something, to signify patriotism. Symbol of war, purely a male phenomenon.

How would women celebrate the Fourth if left to themselves? Maybe make a giant quilt of stars and stripes and raise it on a flagpole over the Park?

She watched Cora's return to the picnic table, slightly pleased that she would be the subject of their discussion. For years she had been considered a bit of an outsider because of her wealthy Kansas City connections. She had tried to play it down, but now, all at once, she felt comfortable in becoming her own person with no apologies.

If she could just find some magic words that would reach a certain little boy. Lindy glanced across the fields to the house behind the press building, a trifle uneasy at the thought of Matty over there alone. Or was he? Surely he wouldn't dare defy his father's orders, not after that scene last night.

When the boy had gone off to bed early again, Bernie laid down the book he was reading and moved to the window. After a minute he muttered, "Yep, there he goes." But this time the amused tolerance was gone from his voice. "I'll give him a minute or two to get ahead of me . . ."

"You mean to follow him?"

"I think I owe you an apology," he said,

170

still staring from the window. "I was over at the station this afternoon to pick up a shipment of paper. When the train came in from Kansas City the whole top of it was populated by bums. These were no farmers down on their luck — they looked tough, mean. A bunch of them dropped off and went over to the tent camp across the tracks, so I followed. Kept an ear out as they gabbed along. They were heading west for Nevada. It seems there's a rumor going around about a big dam going to be built on the Colorado River. They figured to be in line to pick up jobs out there, construction workers, cement men who were kicked off Pendergast's teams for one reason or another. When I mentioned that the corn crop was about to come ripe, they laughed. Wouldn't know a cornstalk from a beanpole. The reason they dropped off here, I gathered, was to relieve the yokels of some small change at poker, see what sport they could find around a camp of rustics. They were disappointed there weren't any women." He headed for the door. "I'll be back shortly."

Taking no pleasure in being right, Lindy stayed by the window as night deepened until a half-hour later she saw a pair of familiar figures trudging home. When they came in Matty was dirty and grim, Bernie tousled, red in the face, angry as she'd ever seen him.

"You will stay in this house tomorrow, young man. I don't want to catch sight of you at the picnic. If I do, I'll take away that bike and it'll be Christmas before you see it again." He was talking to empty air by then. Matty had gone off clomping up the stairs.

"What happened?" she asked in a low voice.

He waited until the door slammed above. "The little bugger talked back. Said there were men over there in the camp who had been places and seen things, who had good stories to tell. When I ordered him to go home, he swore at me in words I didn't learn until I was in the Army. I moved in to grab him and he fought me off with his fists. Eight years old? I can't believe it. So what could I do? I never hit a child in my life. I wrestled him down, held him there with his face in the dirt, and described to him in detail what a mean city thug could do to a young boy. I hope it demonstrated that he's not as tough as he thinks he is."

And just maybe it had worked. Matthew had looked subdued at breakfast this morning. Silent, but hardly contrite. The underlying resentment had still been there in his scowl. She wouldn't be surprised if — another glance toward her home brought her upright. The barn door was ajar, just a thin black crack, but it hadn't been there earlier. The bicycle was locked in the tack room, but the boards were old. As she watched, the crack widened, boy and bicycle eased out and were gone from sight around the barn in an instant. A few seconds later she caught sight of him pedaling off furiously in the direction of Kansas City.

On her feet now, Lindy hesitated. Bernie was deeply involved in calling balls and strikes. Pete Koslow was helping set up the merry-go-round. Willy was marshalling his musicians; he had become the unofficial leader of the Pawnee Bluffs Band, though an elderly trumpet player was their conductor. All of them enjoying the day.

But that wasn't her main reason for heading to the house on her own. Sooner or later there was going to have to be a showdown between her and Matty, one that fortified Bernie's stand and established her, too, as a person of authority. It might as well be sooner, she thought with a small shiver of trepidation. Getting into the roadster she drove slowly over the rutted barnyard and out to the street which evolved into the state secondary.

It was only five miles to the main highway. In a few minutes she spotted the red bicycle ahead. Without a clear plan she put down the pedal of the car and came up past the runaway, braking a hundred yards ahead. When the boy didn't stop, she felt her own inner clutch go to a different gear. Ready to tackle the bicycle bodily, it must have showed because Matthew came to a halt twenty feet short of where she stood on the shoulder of the road.

"Get off!" she ordered.

"I don't have to!" he yelled. "It's my bicycle."

"Not any more. You just forfeited the right to ride when you disobeyed your father. Now get off."

He stood there, still straddling it, fuming.

Adrenaline surged. Lindy moved. At that instant she felt as if she could throw bike and rider down into the ditch with one hand. But the boy resisted, clinging to the handlebars fiercely. As they wrestled for it he lunged forward. Lindy felt the edge of his boot on her shin, and she slapped him hard, rage overriding everything.

At that point she was joined by an ally. Hobby Carter came up beside her and yanked the bicycle out of Matty's grasp.

"You're too nice a person, Lin," he said in

hard tones. "I'm not. I will explain to this brat that he is the luckiest kid in the world to have parents like you and Bernie, he's just too dumb to know it. Stupidity isn't a crime, but for fighting with his mother he ought to be licked within an inch of his life, and unless he apologizes I will do it. Right here and now."

Matty stared at Hobby transfixed. With that hairless head, the bald eyebrows and lashless eyes, the man looked hard as polished ivory. Finally, in a hoarse croak the boy said, "I'm sorry."

"Get in the car," Hobby said curtly. "You will not make any further trouble because I'll be right behind you. Go ahead, Lin, I'll bring the bike." His Chevy was parked on the shoulder across the road. He had been on his way home from the city.

Lindy got behind the wheel, seething with frustration. Even though she knew she had needed the physical strength that Hobby provided, he had preempted the showdown she must have with Matty. All the way back to town the steam built up inside her, like a boiler ready to blow. When they parked in the barnyard, the boy was out and into the house in a flash. She waved a thanks to Hobby. *I'll take it from here.* Going up the stairs quickly, she tossed open the door of

Matty's room. As they faced each other, she didn't choose her words. They came streaming, out of months of desperation.

"Matthew, I don't know what it takes to get through to you. Maybe you'll have to be terribly hurt on one of these escapades before it will dawn on you that you are too young to be on your own. I don't believe you are stupid. I think you are capable of understanding, if you took long enough to listen and think. So let me tell you this, young man — no, you are not a young man, you're a child. A juvenile, with no rights whatever. I can promise you that if you had got away and gone on into the city, without money or family or friends, the police would have picked you up as you begged for nickels so you could eat. Or maybe they would have hauled you out from under a loading dock when you tried to find a place to sleep. They wouldn't give a hoot about your feelings and they'd laugh in your glowering face if you tried to talk back to them. They would chuck you in the County Orphanage where you would stay for the next ten years, behind locked fences with the other strays, eating oatmeal for breakfast and scrubbing a lot of bathroom floors. Now think on that picture hard, because the next time you pull a stunt like this I will not come after you. I will not bring you back. I love you dearly, but it's not a one-way street. A mother needs to feel some return of allegiance. If they were to ask me whether you're my son, right now I'd have to tell them I don't have a son."

The boy's eyes had changed color, from that electric blue to a clouded green, impossible to read, but the shade of his face had faded from red to ashen white and his lip was slack with shock.

Maybe I should have spoken like that before, Lindy thought in a spasm of anguish as she went back downstairs. *At least I got his attention. But at what price?* With sore reluctance she went out of the house, leaving the door wide open. The bicycle was propped by the barn — purposefully she left it there, completely available if he cared to make another run. Aware that she was watched, she headed briskly across the fields toward the Fourth of July gaiety and the shouts from the stands around the baseball field. The anger was fading, but its dregs made her a little nauseous.

Worst of all, she dreaded what it would do to Bernie when she told him about it. Because obviously the crisis wasn't over.

THIRTEEN

After the Fourth the temperature flared up like an oven turned on HIGH. A dry, bleaching, withering sun seared everything it touched. Leaves hung limp on the corn stalks, wheat stubble turned almost white. Trees held very still as if to conserve the sap inside them, the pale sycamores motionless as a tableau. At midday the streets were deserted; it was only toward late afternoon that the town stirred, voices filtered in on the quiet. A burst of talk broke out somewhere around the railroad station that reached Lindy through the open kitchen windows.

Some agitation in the sound alerted her, scraped the nerves of fear as if she had been expecting it. Matty had gone out a half hour ago. No reason he shouldn't. Since the Fourth, he had been in a muted state of obedience. She hadn't told Bernie about the attempted runaway, and for his part the

178

boy was doing his chores, helping with the dishes, sweeping dust off the porch, hardly saying a word. But he always had been a silent one, never babbling like other toddlers. As he grew older his reserve seemed to intensify. He mumbled to himself sometimes, but to his parents he only responded to questions, and then with perfunctory indifference.

Since the showdown, first with Bernie and then on the Fourth with her, the boy had withdrawn even further from the family. It worried Lindy night and day. When she watched other children with their parents — the mutual love, the smiles, the giggles — she wondered whether Matthew was born lacking some seed of happiness. *He used to kiss me, didn't he? Or was it just that I kissed him. A lot. Maybe too much. What have I done wrong?*

Now he stayed in his room all day, listening to the Victrola his grandfather had given him for his birthday. *Though why did Dad pick out that one record?* Well, there weren't a whole lot of phonograph records to choose from, but it made her nervous to listen to "The Road to Mandalay," sung over and over in a mournful baritone coming from the upper regions of the house. The reverse side was even worse: "They're Hangin'

Danny Deaver in the Mornin'."

And yet when the music went silent, she found that even more disturbing. She seldom knew when the boy left the house. There was an easy exit from his window onto the roof of the porch and down the cottonwood tree in the side yard. Though why he would want to go out in that heat — ? And yet some hunch seized her when she heard shouts over by the depot. Pulling off her apron Lindy ran for the door.

As she headed for the station she was met by Maisie Stark, her round little body jiggling as she ran across the field. "Lindy, come quick. Matthew's climbed the water tank."

And now Lindy could see him. It was a big tank that loomed over the station a good forty feet high. Drawing water from a deep well it supplied both the town and the trains that came through. On it were the painted words: PAWNEE BLUFFS and under the "W" a small figure sat on the catwalk, feet dangling, black hair glossy in the blistering afternoon sunlight. Posture rigid, his hands gripped the iron track that circled the tank. A horrifying thought raced across her mind — he looked as if he might just launch himself into space. It shook her to the core. *Children don't commit suicide!*

Bernie . . . Willy . . . no, they were both out on their paper deliveries. Pete was in Kansas City. Hobby would be covering Wichita. It was publication day, Friday. *The boy planned this! He waited until all the men were gone. This is my fault. I should never have been so hard on him. I should have waited until the anger died down.* But she knew in her heart that it hadn't been a flash of temper. The fury was deep-seated by now, ready to burst loose at any time. Lindy could hardly believe that she, a grown woman, could harbor such feelings for her own child. *(Except he's not mine. He's never been mine.)*

The crowd had opened to let her through, waiting expectantly. *But what can I do? I certainly can't climb the water tower myself. And if I did, what good would that do? Try to talk to him?* What could she say that would bring him down?

A train stood in the station, the engineer aware of the predicament. An old man, he wasn't in any position to come to the rescue, just stood there discussing it with a couple of codgers from the town.

"Somebody call the Fire Brigade."

"They're already on a call. Brush fire out near Chisholm's farm, they been trying to bat it down all day."

"I'll get Absalom." Maisie went trotting off down the street toward the church. The picture of the pastor climbing that height sent a wave of hysteria over Lindy.

A man who had got off the train wandered over now to join them. Lindy was vaguely aware that he was taking off his coat. Laid it across his suitcase and headed for the ladder — a stocky figure in a porkpie hat, neatly trimmed black beard, he appeared to be middle-aged, but agile. Without any hesitation he began to climb swiftly, moving as if he did this every day of his life. In awestruck silence the crowd watched, murmuring, as he reached the catwalk and made his way almost casually toward the small figure. Without fuss, he sat down beside Matthew as if they had both just chosen the same park bench.

Having a conversation, first on the part of the stranger, but the boy was answering now. Hard to imagine what could make the man laugh and Matthew could be seen to grin a little. The tenseness of his body eased and his dangling feet began to kick idly. The talk went on, minute after minute. And then a sigh went through the crowd as the rescuer stood, gave his hand to help the boy up, and the two of them made their way back to the ladder. The stranger started down first, then got Matthew to follow closely, so that the man's arms were braced on either side of him. Still talking in conversational tones, he kept them moving steadily.

"Thank God."

"Now that took some doin'."

"The kid ought to have his backside tanned."

Maisie had returned with the parson. "Well, I'll be darned." She hugged Lindy. "They're going to make it just fine."

"The Lord has provided." Sweating profusely in his pastoral weeds, Absalom nodded as if he personally had called down help from above. "Excuse me, but I have a sermon to prepare." He headed back the way he had come.

The rest of the crowd surged forward to meet the two as they touched ground, then drew aside as the stranger kept going, arm around the boy's shoulders, heading straight for Lindy. And she knew him.

The blue eyes edged in turquoise were the prototype of the eyes that looked back at her across the breakfast table. When he took off his hat the tousled black hair was a match to the crop on the boy at his side. Matthew had seized an elbow and was propelling him forward faster.

"Mother! This is Tyler. He works for a

circus!"

"How-do. Mrs. Jones?" The little bow was almost courtly. Or was it stagecraft? The demeanor of a ring master?

Seeing the crowd about to close in on them, Lindy said quickly, "Let's go back to the house. Mr. Puckett, I believe?"

"At your service." He matched her pace and they out-distanced the onlookers.

"How did you know his name?" Matty demanded.

"We have a common acquaintance in Hereford Romney." Tyler Puckett was a smooth operator. He had been careful in his preparation for this meeting, though he could hardly have foreseen the fortuitous event that launched it. "He suggested I stop by and say hello. Sends his best wishes and so forth."

"Oh, him." Matty made a face. "He's a crab. Tell Mother about the trapezes."

"Later, maybe." The man was easy-going, but there was no room for discussion. "Right now we have some business to attend to, Matt. Would you please go along to your room for a while, so your mom and I can talk."

The boy stood there, staring now at their visitor, wheels going around visibly behind those strange eyes. Then, with a submission

184

that was completely uncharacteristic, Matty trudged off upstairs.

Lindy had got out the pitcher of lemonade from the refrigerator along with a dish of ice cubes and set the sugar bowl on the table. Pouring two glasses full she set one before her visitor wondering that her hands didn't tremble. For years she had been bracing herself for this, rehearsing various speeches. And yet she couldn't remember any of them and her heart was skipping around like a bird in a gooseberry bush. She sat down opposite him and waited.

"First off," he began quietly, "I want you to know I didn't come here to make demands or start trouble. I wanted to see my son, just once. Hardly expected it to be in such a dramatic way, but I feel a little as if the Lord had arranged for me to turn up at the right minute."

Bernie would agree with that, he believes in Divine guidance. Cautiously she said, "Maybe we should hold off on this until my husband comes home. He's due shortly."

"Fine. I hoped to talk to you both. But in a way I'm glad it's you first. As Matt's mother you must have had a hard few years. If the boy takes after me at all, he's a little scallywag. I'm grateful you are so patient. And I want to assure you that if you say so,

I will go back to the station right now, pick up my suitcase and vanish on the next eastbound train. I won't be back. I'll never meddle in my son's good fortune, to have such a solid loving family."

"I don't think — I mean, it wouldn't be civil to let you go without having supper with us. Of course, you might have a touch of trouble with my husband. He's — Dolly was his sister."

Tyler bowed his head. "That shameful business. He's got a right to be bitter. I'm willing to take whatever blame he wants to lay upon me. That's why I'd really appreciate it if you could let me stay long enough to meet him. Maybe it will do him good to empty some of his anger. I hurt a fine woman, and the fact that I don't remember any of it is not a mitigation. I was sick, after the War, I had black-outs. But a lot of men went through the Hell that I did and came home with their senses intact. So I'm making no excuses."

"The fact that you saved our boy today ought to go a long way toward easing his resentment." Lindy hoped it was true. Because Bernie had just driven the roadster into the barnyard.

He looked tired and hot and windblown. Plainly irritated. "What's all this about Mat-

186

thew climbing the water tower?" he began before he took in the fact of the stranger in his kitchen.

"News travels fast," Tyler said quietly.

"How did you hear about it?" Lindy wondered.

"I stopped for gas and George Phillips told me." But by now his mind had veered off toward recognition. "My Lord." He stared in disbelief.

"Bernie, this is the man who brought Matt down off the tower. Meet Tyler Puckett." Lindy put a glass of cold lemonade in his hand, pulled out a chair at the table. "Let's all sit down."

In obvious ambivalence Bernie sank into the seat and took a long swallow of the drink. "Man, it was hot out there today. Must have been scorching up on that tower. What got into the kid, to pull such a stunt?"

"I don't know," she said. "I haven't talked to him yet. Mr. Puckett, did he tell you why he was up there?"

"I didn't ask. It didn't seem like a good moment to probe his state of mind." Puckett shrugged. "I just began to talk trivialities. About the great view from up there, and how I have always enjoyed heights, which is why I went to work for the circus. That got his attention," he added with a short laugh. "Somehow I knew it would. Good God, he resembles me so much I'm still in a state of shock. I came here to get a brief look at my son and find myself on the edge of a volcano."

"That's a pretty accurate description of Matthew." Lindy tried to converse normally. She could see that Bernie needed time to get oriented. His reluctance was plain, his natural warmth lost in the confusion of actually meeting the shadowy symbol of evil he had been hating all these years.

Tyler seemed to understand. Almost as he must have talked the boy down off the tower, he went on in an easy tone, "It wasn't just that I recognized his features as mine, I saw the same emotions that racked me as a child. I was an incredibly wayward kid. It was as if there was some demon inside me demanding that I try out wild things, go close to the edge in dangerous situations. Drove my poor mother to distraction. I must say, I admire you folks for bringing up such a bright undiminished boy. My father wasn't so patient. His solution was to use his belt frequently. When I was Matthew's age I had already run away twice. The second time I got into bad company, would have been dead if strangers hadn't helped me. A circus troupe. It was my salvation."

Bernie had got himself together by then. "Mr. Tyler, I guess we owe you a vote of thanks —"

"Mr. Jones, you don't owe me thing-one. I am the culprit in all of this, I can only beg for your Christian forgiveness. It will always be a source of great grief to me that I hurt an innocent young woman. I don't recall any of that — I was severely damaged by shell shock in the War. I began to drink a lot of bad hooch, trying to drown out the noises in my head, the red visions of the battlefield. If Hereford hadn't taken me in I would have probably been carted off to an asylum somewhere. He gave me sanctuary and brought me to a state of prayer. I was making headway, but then something happened. I blacked out. Went kind of berserk, I guess, from what they told me. It doesn't excuse what I did, but it may help to explain it."

Lindy was taken back to those days in Union Station when the men were coming home from that terrible war, so ravaged and confused some of them could hardly function. It touched her heart to see the man's humility. Nothing that happened over there was his fault.

"Where were you stationed?" Bernie asked, still struggling.

"I was in the Infantry on the Meuse."

"I was Artillery. The Argonne."

Puckett sighed and shook his head. "I heard that was even worse than what we got."

A small sound intruded on the silence, a tiptoeing downstairs. "Come on in, son," Bernie called out. "You ought to be here."

"Do you think — ?" Lindy caught her breath.

Bernie had thrown her a look of warning. *I'll handle this!*

Tyler started up. "No. I don't want to confuse the boy at this point. I never intended to reveal —"

Matthew came in hesitantly. "I just wanted a glass of water."

"Here, sweetheart, a good cold drink of lemonade." Lindy poured it.

Bernie said, "I hear you had quite an adventure out there this afternoon."

"Yeah. I'm sorry." The boy looked at them solemnly. "I know it was wrong to scare everybody. Tyler explained how you shouldn't get up that high until you trained for it, like they do in the circus. They start out on the low rope, only a little bit off the ground, and they practice and practice until they can walk across the wire without a net, right up in the top of the big tent." His voice

190

quickened with the thought, his eyes bright with imaginings.

His parents exchanged startled looks. Lindy had never heard Matty speak like that, with excitement, long sentences that poured out of him as if they'd been pent up for a long time.

"Tell 'em about the elephant, Tyler."

"Matty, I don't think your folks want to hear circus tales right now. And I have a train to catch. I'm on my way to join the old gang under the big top. After all these years I can't do the acrobatics, but I can still be a clown, and they've offered me a job, so it's important I get going. The last train east will be through here at six-thirty, I checked. You see, I never intended to hang around. It was just a compulsion to see —" he looked at Matthew and smiled in evident satisfaction.

The boy looked dismayed. "You can't go now!"

"Matthew . . ." Bernie began.

And Lindy said, "Honey, there are things . . ."

"But he's my father!"

Out of the stunned silence Puckett said, "Now how did you get an idea like that?"

"Well, it's true, isn't it? I remembered Hereford talking about Tyler. And then I

191

knew: *You look like me!*"

"Seems there's no doubt here," Bernie said grimly. "And I believe it's a good thing. The boy should know who his natural father is, and the circumstances seem right. You wouldn't want him to grow up imagining —"

"I agree," Lindy put in. "Maybe the past can stay buried."

But Puckett shook his head. "Now that he's halfway there, he's got to know it all. Matthew, for the last eight years I've been in prison. It was because I hurt your mother, Dolly, your dad's sister. I didn't mean to, but that's no excuse. I'd like to put it behind me, but I can't until I ask your pardon — all of you."

"I didn't even know her," Matty said, in practical tones. "Anyway, tell how you had to shovel elephant manure." The idea seemed to delight him.

A natural affinity, Lindy realized, as she went about preparing supper. From the front room she could hear Tyler's voice, speaking in that light self-deprecating tone, answering the boy's high-pitched questions. She had never known Matty to be so animated. From Bernie there was silence. And in the distance came a train whistle — the

192

six-forty-five heading east had come and gone.

FOURTEEN

Midnight. Lindy lay motionless next to Bernie in this familiar bed where for years they had loved passionately, laughed together in friendship, talked of the future, ironed out the day's emergencies, spoken in the dark of what they believed. The best part of marriage was a closeness that prevailed over all problems. But this night she felt more lonely than she ever had before. With a decision to be made they should have been discussing it, as always in hushed voices. Even in the sweltering heat they should have been holding each other. She knew he was awake too. He would be playing back the scenes of this evening, just as she was, reliving the moments, at supper and later.

"This is great potato salad . . ." Puckett was a very polite man, smooth, asking about where the traveler might find a hotel in this town, and so on. ". . . train in the morning . . ."

"There's one at six-forty-nine." Bernie knew the time tables by heart.

And then Matthew's abrupt cry. "I want to go with you!"

It left Lindy speechless, but she could see that Bernie was not that surprised. And Puckett was very fast on the reply.

". . . no place for children, Matt, the circus is a hard, tough life."

"I want a hard tough life!" The boy was building up heat, his eyes alight with determination. "I hate these kids, playing their dumb baseball! I want to learn to walk a tight-rope, I want to feed the elephant."

With a sigh, Puckett said, "You don't know how much an elephant eats."

"I don't care, I want to go!"

Puckett frowned. "Matt, I am glad to know you, and I envy you the good life here. Better than I ever had. You've got fine parents and a chance at an education. Take it from me, that counts out there in the world."

"I don't want an education!"

Watching the storm build in Matthew's face, Lindy struggled to find a way to quiet it. "Let's ask Mr. Puckett for breakfast tomorrow morning *so you can say good-bye!*"

Bernie hadn't approved, his look was very

dark now. But Puckett understood what she was doing.

"All right, I'll see you tomorrow. But Matthew I want you to think about something. You are certainly mature enough to understand that this is a great place to grow up, right here with these good people. If you keep on with your schooling you have a bright future ahead. This was something I never was given. My life has been a failure from start to finish. I don't want that to happen to you."

After the boy had gone trudging upstairs, Puckett turned to them apologetically. "I seem to have kicked over a hornet's nest, and that was the last thing I wanted to happen. I would slip on out of town without seeing you again, but I'm afraid that would provoke a bad reaction in the boy. Against you. I certainly don't want that. I know so well what fires are burning in him down deep, where voices can't reach. It's like having a fever, you can't talk it away. But I'll come over in the morning and try again." He put on his porkpie hat and picked up his suitcase. "Unless . . ."

Now, in the darkness, that word echoed in Lindy's head. Everything upside down, a lot of tightly contained emotions overflowing. *Was it such a crazy idea?*

196

". . . it would be just for a few weeks, until school starts in September . . . nothing like hard reality to take the edge off a buzz-saw of imagination . . ." Puckett, obviously, knew from experience. "The circus is all about discipline. The children who grow up in it learn early that life is demanding. There's no regard for tender years, we all pull our weight according to our various strengths."

Lindy wished she could read what was going on behind Bernie's poker face.

". . . not the least benefit would be that you two would have a brief respite from the burdens of parenthood. By September you might find Matt an easier person to deal with. But I don't want to press it. The decision has to be yours entirely. One way or another, as of tomorrow morning I'm gone from here."

Left alone, Bernie turned to his wife with a flash of anger. "Why did you do that? I mean, to prolong this by asking him to breakfast? He could have been out of here by seven in the morning."

Startled by the reproach, she said, "I did it for Matty. He was ready to explode. He's been so keyed up all day, I thought it would give us a chance to cool down by tomorrow."

"Or was it me you wanted to put a cork in? I'd have liked to take the kid to the barn for a licking, to put us through all this, leave us vulnerable to that man's coming into our home. If he'd planned it, Puckett couldn't have worked a better scheme to ingratiate himself."

Quietly Lindy cleared the dishes from the table. "You weren't here —"

"But you were. Where were you when the boy was climbing the damned water tower?"

For her husband to use a profanity jolted her to a halt. She turned and faced him. "I was darning socks. He goes through them so fast . . . For heaven-sake! I can't follow him around all day to make sure he doesn't get into something. I can't manhandle him physically. And I can't keep him locked in his room. Bernie, be reasonable."

"You're too permissive. I noticed, the other day, you let him ride the bicycle after I told him he couldn't."

"No, that's not what happened!" She raised her voice just slightly. "He went out and stole it from the tack room and was headed for Kansas City when I caught up with him in the car. Even then, I couldn't take it away from him — he's getting strong, Bernie. I was struggling when Hobby Carter came along and lent a hand. He got the

198

bike in his truck and I got Matty in the car and we came home. I was angry, I gave him a talking-to such as never before. I told him if he ever disobeyed again he was on his own, that I wouldn't help him when the police put him in an orphanage. That's what I said. I said, 'I'll tell them I don't have a son!' And I left the bike out in the yard so that he'd know I meant it. I wasn't going to prevent him if he wanted to run away again. I was at the end of my rope. And it seemed to have worked. Only today, when I saw him on that water tower — oh Lord, Bernie, I thought he was going to jump!" Tears were streaming now, an aftermath of memory. She yearned for him to take her in his arms, to tell her it was all going to be okay.

The fire had gone out of his face. He sank down at the kitchen table, slumped in a posture of frustration. After a while he said, "What worries me is, this — this encounter with Tyler Puckett is going to make things a lot worse. With this bee in his bonnet about the circus, he's going to be harder to live with than ever."

Lindy had already thought of that. And a wild fire had raced across her mind: *maybe it would be the making of the boy if he did go with Puckett, spend a couple of months learning about discipline and the chill of being around strangers, the falseness of all that glamour, the weariness of traveling the road.*

"Bernie . . . what if we did go along with it?"

He stared at her as he would at a stranger. Then, without a word he got up and left the house.

He'd been gone a long time. For hours Lindy sat staring at the pages of a book she couldn't read. Fragments of emotion slivered across her mind, frustration, embarrassment, guilt over a small secret wish that she could have a few weeks off from being a mother. Followed by a rush of love for the boy and sorrow that she understood him so poorly. *Why couldn't I think of something that would turn him suddenly into this eager, lively person?*

By the time Bernie got back she was ready to beg his forgiveness for even harboring the thought of respite. His face was stony, but he seemed to have made some sort of peace with the situation.

"I've been on the phone — I used the long distance wire over in the press room. Called my father. He has connections all over Missouri. He did some checking at the lockup in Springfield. They say Tyler was a model prisoner, good behavior all over the place. Got two years knocked off his sentence.

200

Pete came in then and suggested we check out this circus — Featherton Flyers and Wild Animal Acts. It's been around for thirty years, started at the turn of the century, good reputation, pay their bills, never create any trouble apparently. One tent, a few side-show acts, travel around in wagons from town to town, the Carolinas, Georgia. Winter in Sarasota, no bad marks."

She waited silently.

"Then I called Hereford," he said. "Don't frown, he's got a right to put in his two-bits' worth. Invited him out for breakfast tomorrow, but he's got other demands on him. Said he trusted our judgment. He just wanted everybody to be fair with each other. Cold fish."

In earlier days Hereford had tried to interest them in giving Matthew religious instruction, getting him confirmed in the church, but Bernie had argued he was too young to understand a decision like that and Matty had resisted furiously. Since then Hep had lost interest in the boy.

"Fair? I don't know what that means. What is the fair thing to do?" she pleaded. "Tell me, Bernie."

"Darned if I know. Let's sleep on it."

So here they lay, braced for what was to come, and Lindy wasn't even sure what she wanted that to be.

Her worst fears were confirmed when she found Matthew already in the kitchen a little after five-thirty next morning. He had packed his suitcase. Hope bulged from all his seams. There was only one person who might stem the tide of all that desire.

Willy. During the long night hours it had come to her: Willy should have a say-so about all this. She'd heard his step on the back porch yesterday evening as they ate supper, and then he'd gone away. It often happened, if he thought they were in the midst of a family problem. But now she wished she'd called to him. Of all people he had a right!

"Matty, will you watch the biscuits," she said as she headed out. "I'm going to ask Willy to join us for breakfast."

"I already went over there," the boy said. "He's gone, and so's his drums. I reckon he got a gig in Kansas City tonight." Then he added, "I wanted to tell him goodbye."

Lindy sat down across the table. "Matty, I have to say something: I'm sorry I came down on you so hard the other day. You know I would never desert you if you were in trouble."

"Yeah, I know. You didn't mean it."

"I doubt if you have any idea how worried

I get when you pull one of your wild stunts."

"They're not so wild." He eyed her calmly. "Not near as wild as getting in a cage with a tiger. Hi, Poppa, didn't you ever want to swing from a trapeze?"

Bernie had come to join them, moving slowly. His eyes looked heavy, as if he couldn't quite get them open. There were sheet wrinkles on one cheek; when he had finally dropped off he'd slept hard. Hadn't shaved, his beard was like sandpaper, coarsening his jaw line.

"Matthew, I know what it's like to wish you could grow up in a hurry. Comes a time we all feel we can't wait to be an adult. But wishes don't make it so. And the more you struggle against it, the more you miss some of the good times that you could be having as a kid."

"Like what?" Matty wasn't being sassy. He was asking a genuine question. "You mean playing marbles? Or mumblety-peg? Or pinching girls? That's what the other guys do. I don't get it, but they think it's fun."

Lindy marveled. They were actually having a conversation, not a diatribe, not a rebellious rant, not a fuss — they were talking around the table. If just a visit from Tyler Puckett could accomplish this kind of miracle, what would it do for the boy to spend a couple of months with him? Just until school started?

A slight rap on the back door, she went to let him in. Neatly groomed, Puckett left his suitcase on the porch, and came in with an air of deference. "How's it going this morning?"

"Good!" Matthew squirmed with an impulse to go greet him, not knowing how. "I'm all ready to leave."

"Oh, boy." Tyler bit his lip.

Bernie said, "Matt, did you ever stop to think: you haven't actually been invited?"

Lindy kept busy with the omelet, stirring in left-overs of chopped ham, scallions, cheese, and *please help us, Lord!* It was rare that she ever prayed. She knew Bernie did, but it had nothing to do with church. Their Sunday visitations were merely a show of respect. It occurred to her now that she really did believe in Somebody up there, because she was fervently begging for guidance.

Matty, never one to skirt an issue, was facing his natural father squarely. "Don't you want me to go with you?"

Tyler accepted a seat at the table shrinking down in it as if to lessen himself. It only accentuated his blocky muscular shoulders.

"I want what's best for you, buddy," he said bluffly. "And that I leave up to your parents. They're a lot smarter than I am."

"No, they're not. You've been in jail!" the boy said proudly.

"Exactly. And smart people don't get put in jail. I never had any education after the sixth grade. All I know of life has been from the school of hard knocks. But I have learned to survive, and anybody who travels with me has to be willing to accept some tough rules of the road."

"I will. I promise!" The earnest young face looked older than its eight years, more determined than Lindy had ever seen it before.

Tyler looked helpless. Embarrassed. "I'm sorry it has put you folks on the spot. But I accept your decision, and so must Matthew."

Lindy was swept with a feeling of inevitability. Bernie sat silent, he seemed to be waiting for her to speak. In a strained voice, she said, "I think it's what our son needs. I vote yes."

FIFTEEN

A patchwork quilt, fashioned out of left-over scraps of old clothing, cut in neat shapes and matched, piece by piece, with loving attention to design and contrast and color, to make a thing of lasting beauty — that's a woman's way. Lindy stirred the big kettle of peaches, trying to get a handle on the thought, sure that it could lead to a good column. A quilt could be a powerful symbol.

And for the recipe to end the essay — her readers loved the recipe part — she could give them Clemma's jambalaya, a dish handed down from the old woman's bayou-born ancestors. A great way to use leftovers, with a variety of herbs that gave it character. Should she reveal those secret spices? she wondered.

As if in answer to her question a car drove into the yard. A long-lined Cadillac, sleek, white with modest brass trim, it fit the stylish woman who stepped out. Lindy set the preserving kettle off the burner, pulled off her apron and rushed to greet her mother with a fervent hug.

"I was just thinking about you! How great of you to drive all this way!"

"It was fun. I read the Burma Shave signs: 'Rip a fender off your car and send it in for a half-pound jar.' How do they think of silliness like that?" Merle chuckled. Like a priceless art object in her beige suit and matching Empress Eugenie turban, she looked totally inappropriate to the dusty little farm town, but never seemed aware of it. "And those big advertisements on the barns are beautiful. Does Bernie still paint them?"

"Yes, once in a while. He did the big Red Rooster Feed and Grain sign on the road east of here. It brought him offers from all over the County. His old boss at Kansas City Bag wanted to hire him to design logos for their grain sacks, but he wouldn't hear of it, of course. He loves his work at the paper."

"I hear the cartoons are causing quite a stir around Kansas City," Merle said. "Is that peach preserve?"

"Uh-huh. Bernie loves peach jam. Which reminds me: do you think it would be wrong of me to put one of Clemma's recipes in the paper. She takes such pride in not revealing certain secrets."

"It's good of you to care." Her mother looked in the refrigerator and got out the bottle of lemonade that was always ready there. "My, I worked up a thirst driving over these dusty plains. As for Clemma, I don't think she'd approve, but there's no reason she'd ever know."

"Well, I'd know. I guess I'd better not do it. I'll give some of the herbs but not all. I think I have to put in the saffron."

"You're talking about her jambalaya. Yes, you need the saffron. And the red pepper. Leave out the mustard and the bay leaf. No, you really need the bay leaf. Omit the cinnamon, nobody will ever miss that. You're actually writing a weekly column for the paper. How delightful!"

"It's fun. And the women around town seem to like it. I think they respect me a bit more than they did. In a place like Pawnee Bluffs, being from a rich family is something of a stigma, even though we don't have much wealth ourselves."

"How's Bernie doing?"

"Very well!" And Lindy realized she had spoken the words too emphatically. "We're both a little disconcerted not having Matty around. It's funny, I thought I'd be relieved not to have the worry, but I actually miss it. I miss him. Strange little boy, he's never been affectionate, he's not even much of a talker, but for eight years my life has revolved around him. To have that focus removed — it leaves me sort of aimless. Bernie is absorbed in his work, he doesn't feel it until he comes home. But these evenings have been almost too quiet, you know?"

"Was he in favor of the thing, to let the boy's father take him off to live with the circus?"

Cautiously Lindy said, "I think he's convinced it was a good decision. Matty needed some outlet for all that pent-up energy, something he couldn't find in our quiet life here. I've been very afraid he'd run away. At least now we know he's not wandering lost somewhere. Tyler has been very good about writing to us, giving us progress reports. The man is poorly educated, his spelling is atrocious, but he says Matty is learning some lessons about work, practicing acrobatics and feeding the livestock. I hope he's right. Mainly I hope the boy will start to open up with people, not to keep himself so tight and solitary." She held up a spoon and watched the hot preserves drip off it. "I think this is ready for the jars." They stood in a row, gleaming glass fresh out of the boiling pot. "Mother, will you put that pan of paraffin on the burner, please?"

"This tickles me." Merle smiled. "You've turned into quite a housewife."

"That's not the amazing part," Lindy told her. "What's more incredible is: I love it. I love Pawnee Bluffs."

And yet she had to admit she missed the close contact with her family. As she watched her mother drive off that afternoon, it was with a pang of regret that the day had gone so quickly. And a touch of guilt. She hadn't been totally honest.

All was not well with her marriage, and she knew it. Bernie had undergone some kind of shift in disposition. It was subtle, he still was agreeable, but detached. He had been studying some of his old college texts, mostly about printing techniques. A shop up in Topeka had acquired a rotogravure machine which turned his charcoal drawings into finished plates — a technique that enhanced them, but one that he couldn't do himself. He preferred hand engraving them, a perfectionist, demanding the most from each cartoon. Everyone liked them, it was one of the paper's biggest selling points. But he never discussed his ideas with her any more. Never asked her opinion.

Or expressed one about her work. Last week when she had written a column on peach conserve, a recipe that had intrigued the wives of the community with its subtle quirks, to dry the peaches overnight, and so forth, she had been rather proud of the way it tied in to her message: preserving the summer's bounty to sweeten the lives of a family all winter. In other words, a woman's way. Even Pete had congratulated her, but Bernie hadn't said a word.

In fact they didn't talk much now that Matt wasn't there to argue about. *Is that all we ever discussed?* She just knew that he had changed since that morning. With the boy jumping around in a state of high excitement, Tyler giving such resounding assurances, and her own heartfelt agreement, Bernie had simply stepped back and let it happen. *He had no idea how close to the edge I was. I should have talked to him more about that. He probably thinks I'm weak, and maybe I am.* But the end result was a growing gulf between them. Or is something else bothering him?

As she was clearing away the dinner dishes she saw Pete Koslow heading across the lot between the press building and their house. It had proved to be a convenient arrangement for them all to live close by each other.

Pete had fixed up an apartment in the loft over the press room, but he was so active around town he seldom could be found there. In fact she got a touch of concern as she watched him come up onto the porch — very casual, sort of strolling, which didn't go with his usual abounding energy.

"Come on in, Pete." She was about to put away the remains of an apple pie. "Cut you a slice?"

"Not tonight, thanks. I have to go in to Kansas City, can't hang around long." He gave her his brotherly grin, garnished by those gold front teeth, and went on into the living room. "Hi, G.B., I'm off to the city. Wanted to have a word before I left."

Lindy smiled to herself. Pete had always been tickled by the fact that Bernie was named for George Bernard Shaw. He said it was the ultimate literary compliment. She finished putting the dishes away and took the trash out to the ash pit. It was a beautiful evening, the sun hanging like a golden coin above the Bluffs. There had been wind again today, dusting the sky with a pale dry overlay, but it was quiet now.

As she walked back to the house a fountain of grasshoppers burst from her steps in all directions. They had turned into a real pest this summer, even eating the corn stalks. It had been a poor harvest. Not enough to stake the desperate men who worked the fields. Certainly nothing to tide them over a long winter. They had migrated back to their camp across the tracks, only now there was nothing to wait for. *They really ought to go out to the West Coast where crops come in all year around. If they stay here they'll starve and freeze and then what will we do?*

Like an extension of her thought, she heard words coming from the living room. "Those poor devils are desperate." Pete's hearty voice carried like the boom of a double bass viol. "It's not just my father, Bernie, it's the men at the Grange meeting. By the way, we missed you there the other night. They wanted to make a suggestion, so I guess I got appointed as their spokesman. They would appreciate it if you would do some cartooning about the hobos. A lot of people would like to see that rag-tag lot just run out of town, burn the camp down. But most of us feel that the Christian thing to do is to give them a ticket to ride a train off into the sunset. Dad suggested we hold a fund-raiser, but we need to rally public opinion behind the idea. So we thought a cartoon might spark the humanity in our society. What do you think?"

Lindy held still, curious to hear what her

husband would say. His words were so low she couldn't make them out. "I've already . . . two sketches . . . the Boss."

"Well, hell's bells, Bernie, this isn't Jackson County. We owe our own people some help here. We're their newspaper."

"We're more than just local now. One reason we're doing so well financially is that Hobby is selling ad space over in Kansas City like a house-afire. He's doing it on the basis of our position against Pendergast. The papers over there don't dare lift a finger against him. Even The Star tiptoes around the man. Somebody's got to blow the whistle."

"But not all the time. Not every edition. All I'm saying is that the fellows would really appreciate some of your talent to be turned toward our own problems."

"Any time you don't like —"

"Don't say it, old friend. Don't even think it. I'm just the messenger. And I'm on my way out of here." The front door slammed and she saw Pete striding back across the lot to the press building.

Slipping inside, Lindy finished up in the kitchen and went to the living room to sit near Bernie. He looked angry and frustrated and weary, staring at her without seeing. "I don't know what I'm doing in this job. You think you're going to crusade against evil, you see yourself as a hero. I should have known that was a mistake — that was the word which ruined Ookie."

A childhood friend, member of the old gang, the thought of Ookie always brought a grimness to Bernie's face. "Hero. So busy flying above the clouds, shooting down fighter planes, he lost sight of the war below, what was going on down in the mud. I told him the word 'hero' is booby-trap. Ought to listen to my own advice. Truth is, nobody really wants some smart aleck to step in and save the world. They'd rather play it safe, have a fund-raiser. That's more your department." He turned to Lindy suddenly. "Why don't you volunteer your services. Show 'em how it's done?" And thrusting up out of his chair, he headed upstairs. The sound of his footsteps was heavy, slow. It reminded her of Matthew.

SIXTEEN

Paper plates — Lindy didn't like them, but at least you don't have to wash them. She gathered the lunch trash and put it in the barrel nearby, then set out five new plates on paper doilies around the wooden picnic bench. Spoons or forks, which is better for eating watermelon?

"Lin." A timid voice. Cora had come up softly, as if a misstep might waken the bundle in her arms. A large, husky boy, her baby was deep in dreams. "Lin, would it be okay if my sister Katie sort of wandered over, maybe she could sit with you guys? She's got a terrific crush on Pete Koslow."

And Katie was getting almost too old for the bridal veil. Nice girl, she'd make Pete a good wife, but . . . "This wouldn't be a good time. The fellows are discussing plans for *The Whistle.* Why don't you bring her around tonight at the square dance and I'll see that Pete is primed to give her a whirl?"

Lin marveled at herself. *I must be getting old, to turn matchmaker?*

Then she almost wished she had agreed to a social interruption. As the men gathered at the table they were joined by a paunchy, balding stuffed shirt, Robert E. Lee Whiteman — he always used the full name — the town's elected Mayor. As usual, he was in a mood to complain.

"What the devil, Bernie! Are you in the real estate business now? Going to sell us out to the Kansas City developers? You got such a fondness for that place, you should never have left there."

"What's your beef, Whitey?" Pete deliberately used the nickname the Mayor hated most. "All we're doing is celebrating Labor Day. Why can't you just lean back and have fun like the rest of us?"

"Not when our town is in dire danger, sir. I am referring to your promotion of this expansion of our boundaries to include a bunch of Show-Me Democrats who'll just bring their crime and meanness with 'em."

"Ah-ha." Pete smiled his broad, ingenuous grin. "You're afraid they'll vote in our city elections and you'll have to really run to hold your office."

"We don't need outsiders to come in and change our way of life. That cartoon of

217

yours was practically an invitation." The Mayor was still targeting Bernie, who had helped himself to a chunk of watermelon and was digging in, as if there were no discussion. "Could it be that your father offered you a nice little bonus if you can pull his chestnuts out of the fire?"

"Now you're really stepping over the line," Pete said, irritated. "It's editorial policy, to expand our community. It will improve our economy, and if we choose to be happy about the new interurban train we intend to say so."

"Well, the interurban is okay," Whiteman admitted grudgingly. "But I'll be damned if I want to see a whole new town popping up on our doorstep, elbowing in on our territory."

"Only reason the railroad sold the land was because it was promised that there would be customers for the interurban," Bernie put in, without bothering to turn around. "Dad was simply doing what real estate people do — opening a door to the future." Hiram Jones was the president of the development company that was planning to build a whole new suburb only a half mile from the Pawnee Bluffs limits. Bernie's cartoon had suggested that the town cut through the red tape and broaden

218

its boundaries to include the newcomers.

Hobby looked up with a frown. "Mr. Whiteman, the development's going to be an asset. Those folks will be paying taxes, patronizing our stores, it's going to be good for business."

"Or they'll get on that nifty little train and trot right over to shop in Kansas City where they always have." The Mayor refused to be placated. "You can brag about your freedom of speech, Koslow, but the rest of us got certain freedoms too, like the freedom to not read your paper."

They watched him march away stiffly, as if he were on a parade ground. Sitting close on Lindy's left, Willy fiddled with his watermelon. "They won't stop reading *The Whistle*. Fridays, I go around the town folks are waiting on their front porch for it. Lin, is there any pie over there?"

"They ain't seen nothing yet," Pete chuckled, quoting a popular entertainer. "Bigger community means more readership, not less." Then casually he added, "And a bigger newspaper. I just bought us a new linotype machine."

Bernie went on eating, he was in on the decision obviously. But Hobby was electrified. "You what?"

"Got a chance to get a good used one.

219

Little paper over in Independence went under, had to sell off their equipment. We got it for a good price. It's a monster, you're going to love it."

Willy was the only one to show dismay. "But you get that machine, what am I gonna have to do around the pressroom, if I don't put away type and all that?"

"There'll be plenty of work for you, m'boy, no matter what. This will lead to even more presswork, more folding and delivering," Pete told him. "This — as soon as I get used to the crazy keyboard — will make it possible for me to set up to seven lines a minute. We can go to two sections, Hobby can sell more ads, and we can put in more illustrations. Hey, that's something for you, Willy. Learn to use Bernie's camera and go around taking pictures of the news as it happens."

Lindy saw her husband glance up sharply at his partner. He obviously hadn't been consulted about this. Pete had a tendency to over-reach and he delighted in surprises. The ruddy cheerful face was innocent as a child's. But she could almost read Bernie's thoughts: *If anybody takes pictures it should be me — I'm in charge of the paper's artwork.*

Over on the bandstand the orchestra was tuning, tuba getting its breath, fife running scales. Willy picked up his plate and half rose, then settled back down in a tense watchful attitude, his look fixed on a man who was approaching across the park.

It brought back a memory in a rush — the afternoon of the fire. Lindy remembered him well, the fellow with the smarmy smile who had come to offer assistance that day. Pendergast's man, a strutting lofty type with the smell of power about him, what was his name? Voorhees. He looked out of place in this rural setting, with his expensive pongee suit, wing-tipped shoes. In that narrow face his jaws were hardly mobile enough to accommodate the smile he assumed.

"Afternoon, everybody. Just the folks I wanted to see."

"Voorhees, this is a private gathering, and I don't recall anybody inviting you to join us," Pete said with an edge of metal under the casual words.

"But I'm the bearer of the good news," he said. "The Boss wanted you all to know that he has plenty of work for those poor guys over there in your tent camp. He'll even send buses to take them in to the Bottoms. Find them places to live . . ."

Bernie gave a disgusted snort. "In those roach-traps along the river? And it's just a coincidence that there's a city election coming up. He'll be needing extra hands to circulate around and vote, early, late and often. What's the going rate these days, used to be two dollars."

"Oh come on, that's a vicious rumor. We need these good men for a big project, going to build a new City Hall."

"Those boys are farmers," Hobby said. "They wouldn't know an I-beam from a cement truck."

Voorhees eyed him with a predatory curiosity. "Don't believe we've been introduced."

"And you're interrupting a private discussion," Pete insisted.

"I do know you." Voorhees gave him a grin. "Editor of the famed *Pawnee Whistle*. I noticed it as I drove in, pretty big building for a pint-sized paper."

"And no big bad wolf is going to blow it down," Pete said, without returning the smile. "I just mention it in case old Tom's got notions of stepping out of his bailiwick to go hunting Jayhawks."

"Come, come, an editor mixing his metaphors?" Voorhees laughed, just short of a snicker. "People, I just came over to take a look at a little town that's making quite a name for itself over in the big city. Seeing you folks together takes me back, it does, to a time when we all met once before, a long time ago, a sorry day at that."

In one move Bernie was on his feet, facing the man. Voorhees was a half head taller, and yet Bernie managed to tower. His face wore that bleak look as if he were heading up Vauquois Hill with the fire of battle all around him. "Stop trying to be subtle. You came to scout the territory, see where you could make trouble. Your boss doesn't care for my cartoons. They must be hitting close to the mark for him to send you out here. So you think you'll scare us with references to the damage you did to our lives eight years ago. In case you've forgotten my sister was killed in that fire."

"I remember. It was very tragic," Voorhees said gravely. "The Ku Klux Klan, if I recall. Thank heaven we don't see them around any more."

"Anybody can put on a sheet," Bernie said grimly. "I did some detective work after that arson. Found people in the neighborhood who saw the faces of the firebugs, and they weren't Klan after all. What a surprise — they were Pendergast goons. I have affidavits swearing to their identities. I have eyewitness accounts and people ready to give evidence if they can do it without being threatened."

"Oh, come on, man, that was a long time ago."

"There's no statue of limitations on murder. All I've been waiting for is a change in the laws that would take the case out of the local courts. We all know who owns the Kansas City legal machinery. But now," Bernie's voice was building as he went, "we have a new government agency called the Bureau of Investigation. Maybe you've heard of it. Man named J. Edgar Hoover runs it. He has a lot of tools up his sleeve, the tax department, the interstate commerce boys, the prohibition people, all independent of local bullies like Tom Pendergast. He hates political machines like death in the morning. In fact he just put Al Capone in jail for carrying a concealed weapon. You better find a better place than your pocket to put your little derringer."

Voohees had gone silent and very narrow. Lindy thought she'd never seen a more dangerous looking man.

"So here's the deal," Bernie said flatly. "If I ever see your face around this town, I'll call out our local law to arrest you. We don't hold with guns. And if anything happens to the paper or Pete or my house or me or my family, some strange 'accident' maybe, my lawyer will go straight to the Federal government with all the documents and accusations and claims against the Machine. Plenty of suspicions, too. Doesn't matter if it doesn't all stand up in court, just the fact that the Bureau is sniffing around the Bottoms, that the hunt is on, will be the beginning of the end. So tell Tom if he doesn't call off his dog he'll find himself face-to-face with the United States of America. Now git."

As they watched Voorhees saunter off Bernie sank back onto the bench, elbows on the picnic table, visibly shaking with the dregs of rage. Pete gave a low whistle.

"That was powerful stuff, G.B. How much of it was bluff?"

"Not all. Some, but not all." Bernie glanced at Willy.

The boy gave a short nod, then stood up. "I got to go be with the band now. Lemme know if you need me."

Lindy wondered at the look of understanding that had passed between them. *Of course. He means to use Willy. That day of the fire the boy was on the scene. He saw the goons. He knew who they were. Bernie's counting on him, and William Anthony Bickford is ready to stand up and testify if it kills him.*

"No. Not Willy." She hardly knew she

spoke aloud.

They all looked at her, none of them comprehending except her husband. Bernie tightened as if clamps had been applied, somewhere out of sight. Without a word he got up and walked away, heading for home.

In a panic of regret, she started after him. "Wait. I just meant . . ."

"Lindy," a voice called across the park, "we need you. They're ready for the drawing, you know, the door prizes."

"Uh — okay." Reluctantly she turned back. The drawing was an honorary function, usually assigned to Gertrude Koslow. The old girl must be trying to make amends for those hot-dogs last Fourth of July.

Lately Lindy had been staying away from most of the neighborhood gatherings, though now with Matty gone she had plenty of time. This had been a peace offering and she knew she'd better take it. But she was seething with impatience as she followed Cora across to the bandstand where the crowd had gathered. There were a half-dozen door prizes, plus the ribbons for the races to be handed out.

Afterward the girls had cornered her to ask her to be on the school board, another humble admission that they missed her presence. If she wanted to live here in harmony, she couldn't afford to hurt their feelings. So it was almost five o'clock by the time she was able to break away and head for home, into the face of the late sundown.

Even this first week of September the heat still hung over the Kansas plains. Lindy was perspiring, not feeling too well. Something had been amiss with the potato salad. Or maybe it was just a case of guilt. She knew she had spoken out of turn.

As she went in the door her stomach skidded. Bernie was sitting at the kitchen table fingering a glass. In front of him was a bottle of Coke, but the smell was of liquor — he kept a flask of rum on the top shelf of the closet. Just for emergencies, he always said. Glancing over his shoulder, the brown eyes were muddy with inner pain.

"Ah, the lady bountiful. Did you get all the doodads handed out, blue ribbons for the little kiddies and kind words for the founders of the feast?"

"I can't imagine why they asked me. Gertrude usually handles it."

"Oh, but she's not th' voice of womanhood in Pawnee Bluffs any more."

How much of that flask has he had? Going to the refrigerator she got out a tray of ice cubes and dumped them in a bowl. "Can I refresh your drink?"

"You can stay 'way from my drink." He downed a swallow with a gulp.

"Hey, I sympathize," she said lightly. "This was a very disturbing afternoon. I wouldn't mind a shot of rum myself."

"Naaa-naa. Not the little debutante. No cheap booze. She drinks brandy with her pretty friends when she goes to Kansas City."

"What are you talking about?"

"Matter of fact, you were seen with a certain Mr. DeMille at the Muehlebach last month."

How on earth — ? It had to be Agatha. She had been in the tea room that afternoon, came over to the city with her mother to buy school dresses for the girls. She had looked curious, so Lindy had introduced them to Corky.

"Never mind. I know it was all very in'cent. He tell you how to make big bucks in th' market? Fix you up with a por'folio?"

"He knows better than to try. Cocky asked me there to persuade me to set up a trust fund for Matthew. It's something I never thought of, but I've been meaning to discuss it with you."

"Mmmm. Used to discuss things." Bernie nodded sadly.

"We don't seem to spend much time

together any more. It's as if the gap left by Matty has created such an emptiness in this house we can't get to each other." She decided they had to bring it out in the open. "I miss our boy, but I miss you even more." Reaching out she laid a hand on his and he jumped as if the touch was red-hot.

"Well, it's what you wanted," he said bleakly. "Wanted to get away from him. Wanted to get some rest, have time to write those col'mns, have a li'l fun."

"I won't argue with you on that," she said quietly. "And I have regretted it practically every minute since. Now it's fall, school's about to start and he isn't home. We don't know where he is, and I'm scared, Bernie. Not a word from Tyler last week. I called Hereford . . ."

A snort. "Stiff-necked do-gooder."

"Well, it was he who sent Tyler to us, I reminded him. It's up to him to locate the circus and find out what's happening."

"Handled that, did you? Waste of time. We're never going to see our son again." He spoke in tones of deepest defeat. "Maybe jus' as well. I'm a hell of an excuse for a father."

"Bernie! That's not so. You mustn't sell yourself short —"

"Is that an order?" He stared at her with

his mouth at an ugly tilt that changed his face to that of a stranger. "You're pretty good giving out orders these days. 'Not Willy!' No, no, mustn't put Willy in harm's way. Make all the decisions. Next time we get the catalog from Monky-Ward, you better buy yourself some breeches." Thrusting up from the table he caught himself on the edge and steadied, enough to stalk out of the room. She heard the uneven steps go upstairs into the bedroom. A door slammed.

Lindy went out onto the back porch, leaned over the railing and threw up.

Seventeen

Across the barren fields the newly risen sun was already laying a thin heat, and it wasn't yet six o'clock. The town of Pawnee Bluffs was moving slowly to recover from the Labor Day revelries. The square dance had gone on under the stars until after eleven — Lindy could hear the music from three blocks away as she lay sleepless on the couch in the living room. Bernie hadn't come near her. She doubted if he had even wakened during the night. No sound came from upstairs this morning. She imagined he'd have a terrible hangover and she didn't want to be around for that. It was no time to try to talk things out. It was time to act.

She didn't even want to go into the bedroom to change her dress — the gingham wraparound from yesterday would do fine, she thought defiantly as she headed for her car. Only to be waylaid by Pete Koslow who emerged from the back door of the press building, tousled and sleepy-eyed.

"Where y' off to, sis?" His fond look was troubled. "How's G.B. this morning."

"I don't know. I just know I have to do something about — everything."

"Yeah. That was pretty much what I wanted to tell you. It's a lot of stuff weighing on him, and then to have your dad kind of shame him . . ."

"My father?" she frowned blankly. She hadn't talked to the Judge in over a week.

"Didn't you know? Your esteemed parent arranged for a friend at the *Kansas City Star* to offer Bernie a job. Nice desk, reporting on national affairs, take the news off the wire services and write it up, so forth. Brainless assignment. But it would get you and family back to Kansas City and pay enough to situate you in a 'proper' house out there in the Country Club. The fact that it would waste the talents of one of the best political cartoonists I have ever met, that was not a consideration. Of course Bernie turned it down, at least I think he did."

Lindy took it in, confused, turning angry. "I believe I'd better have a few words with my father. I'm going in to Kansas City this morning . . ."

Pete flashed those gold front teeth. "Well, I'd say you're not exactly girded for a showdown. That dress is for baking biscuits, girl."

"Cooking comes in all sizes," she said obliquely. "Listen, Pete. When he gets up, will you sort of give him a pep talk. He was very low yesterday, and I'm not sure why, but a lot of it has to do with Matthew. He never was keen on this vacation with Tyler Puckett. Now we've lost track of our boy, and I'm going in to find out exactly what's going on. Meantime, if you —"

"Gosh, Lindy, I'd do it, but I have to go over to Fort Scott this morning. I'm the guest speaker at the Kiwanis Club lunch today. Probably won't make it home until three o'clock or so. Don't worry about your fellow. He's a tough one. He'll be okay."

"He hasn't been happy with the way the town's after him all the time, people like Whiteman telling him to do local cartoons. I can understand why they want him to address their own problems, but they nag, Pete. He might not take a job on another paper, but he told me he was tempted to go to work for Kansas City Bag where all he had to do was design logos for their flour sacks. I think he was kidding, but —"

"Any chance he'd turn to real estate? With his dad buying up that railroad property, there's going to be a lot of construction soon. Somehow I can't see Bernie building

233

houses, much less selling them."

"Neither can I. All he ever wanted to do was draw. But he can't think straight until we get our boy back, so I'd best be on my way to the city. I have an idea where to begin."

Hereford. He's the one who sowed thorns in our garden, dragging out the past, keeping Tyler's hopes alive, nosey old man. He'd darned well better know where that circus is!

She drove fast, the warm wind lifting her hair which was a mess. She couldn't wash it this morning without going upstairs and maybe running into Bernie, and she didn't feel up to that yet. Her stomach was still queasy, must have been the potato salad, sat out in the sun too long yesterday.

No, not entirely. Her whole life was turning sour. She felt as if the fabric of her marriage was coming unwoven. That's what was making her heart heave with spasms of guilt and regret and impotence. For the first time in years she could feel the empty space inside her where the fountain of motherhood was supposed to rise. It had been foolish to suppose she could overcome the loss of those natural juices by simply wishing it. Somewhere in the nine months of creating, by some miracle a woman becomes prepared to react to the needs of her child.

And that's where I failed. I never did know what Matthew needed, loving him wasn't enough. He never did love me. Us. He knew we weren't the real thing. That's why he rushed to be with Tyler. The highway before her blurred suddenly. She missed the prickly little boy with such intensity she had to pull off the road for a minute and let the tears flow. *Is it even right to insist now that he come back?* Right or wrong, she braced up to the fact: she was going to do it, find him, bring him home. For Bernie's sake. For her own. She got the car in gear and drove on.

Cruising slowly through the downtown area she thought briefly of her father and an ember of resentment flared. No matter how well he meant, it was a cruel thing to make a man feel he'd not lived up to his wife's needs. *Too long a judge, too much power to make decisions that govern other people's lives. Too fond of his only daughter. Go easy, go easy. Think, before you say words that can't be taken back.*

Then she was past that part of the city and making her way through the back streets of The Bottoms. Pulling in to the curb opposite The Mission, with its modest sign and simple cross, she parked and sat, trying to get her temper under control. Sternly she told herself that Hereford had only acted as he saw his Christian duty. He was basically a good man, in the sense that all martyrs are, giving their lives to the poor in spirit. Poor in cash, too. The houses along the block were dilapidated, lacking paint or trim or dignity.

On the front stoop of one several doors down a youngster sat, a boy a few years older than Matthew. Dirty clothes, dark hair sprouting from under a grungy baseball cap, one black eye, sticking plaster on his cheek, he had obviously been in a fight. Probably lost it, and yet there was bravery in the grim determination with which he got to his feet, sturdy kid —

She was out of the car and running. "Matty!"

He whirled and stared a second, then ran to meet her, came into her arms with a lunge and held her in the desperate grip of a drowning victim. As they clung together she felt the weeks of misery melt down into a flood of tears, didn't try to stop them. *Is he crying, too?*

Tentatively, incredulously, she drew away a fraction. "My dearest son, I thought I lost you, and I was afraid. I came down here to speak to Hereford, to make him find you. Only how did you get here?"

"On the train. All by myself." He spoke

the words into her neck as he still held on tight. "I was pretty scared, too."

"Well, it's okay now. You're safe, everything's going to be all right. Are you hungry?" Silly thing to say at a time like this, but it must have been appropriate. She felt him ease up, sniffling, and loosen that desperation grip.

Grinning at her he said, "I'm about starving to death. The meals on the train are too high priced. I ran out of money."

He's as tall as I am. He's grown a couple of inches! "Does Hereford know you're here."

"No. I was going in there. I didn't want to, but I didn't know what else to do because I didn't know how else to get home."

"We're not exactly dressed for a fancy restaurant." She heard herself giggling, a silly high-pitched happy sound. "I seem to recall a diner on the next street."

As they rounded the corner she was transported back in time, to the night of the fire, the smell of the smoke, the smudged faces of the men. Willy with that squalling bundle. Now, there was a vacant lot where Settlement House had stood. She thrust the memory aside. "This little greasy spoon used to serve good smoked ribs."

"I could eat a good smoked elephant," Matty said, with a return of bravado that was more like him.

Still entranced by the feel of that hot body pressed against hers, not stiff and resisting, but full of need, Lindy was walking on air as they went in the Bar-B-Que. "Order anything you like, tell them to bring it to the table." That same corner table where she and Bernie had laid the beginnings of a whole future. *What would those nuns have done with this complex little boy?*

Matt didn't look like a child any more as he dug into a huge platter of barbecued ribs. "It's not as good as yours," he mumbled. The waiter brought her a cup of coffee and a plate of doughnuts. An old man he seemed to understand their needs.

Lindy prayed she would do as well, have the right intuition to handle this homecoming properly. *Should I call Bernie right now?* No, better to surprise him with the fact accomplished. It would only be another hour until they were home. All sorts of reconstruction can be done in the moment when a tragedy is reversed.

Seeing the ravenous hunger diminished a little she said, "I guess you came to know an elephant in your travels."

Matty picked up another biscuit and crammed it in his mouth. "On both ends."

Lindy wanted to laugh, to cry laughing.

She had never realized that the boy had a sense of humor. "By the way," she said casually, "I suppose the circus people know you've left them to come home?"

"Yeah, that's how I got the money for the train. They took up a collection. Vonda Starr did. She's a trapeze arteest. She liked me, she bought my ticket. Only it was for Kansas City, and I needed some more to get to Pawnee Bluffs."

Thank God for the kindness of strangers. "Uh — what about Tyler? He must know that you're gone?"

"I don't know." The young face took on a grimness that lent it a sudden maturity. "He's in jail again. The show's moved on. The circus takes care of their own, like they always say, but this time when he just about killed me, I think they got sore at him."

"Tyler? Almost killed you?" Lindy tried to picture it. "He's the one who did all this battering, those cuts and bruises — ?"

"Uh-huh. Could I have some ice cream maybe?"

She beckoned the waiter over. "What flavor?"

"Strawberry, please. Yeah, he went kind of crazy, Momma. We were in a little town in Georgia last week and they were having a festival about some battle where they won a

239

fight against the King of England. I never heard of it, must have been hundreds of years ago. But every September they shoot off the cannons. They've got a whole bunch of these old guns. They shoot cannonballs out over an empty field, so nobody gets hurt. It was great, except it made Tyler go nuts. He began to wreck things, he threw a chair at the Master of Ceremonies and when the strong man tried to stop him he pulled a knife. They got it away from him, but then he saw me and began to hit and bang my head and punch and kick and stomp on me. You ought to see my ribs."

The shellshock coming back. Cannon fire breaking through the membranes of control. "Thank the Lord you weren't permanently damaged."

"Yeah, I'm okay." The rate at which he downed the ice cream confirmed it.

"I'm glad you decided to come home."

"Well, I couldn't stay with the circus, and anyway I didn't want to any more. I was tired of sweeping up. It's kind of boring to carry water for the elephant. Elephants need a lot of water. And I never did get in the Show. I learned some clown tricks from Tyler, but I wasn't good enough to go into the ring yet. He kept saying 'By next year . . .' Only I told him I thought I should go home, school was about to start. But he just said, 'There's good schools in Sarasota.' He wasn't going to send me back to Kansas. And all of a sudden I missed everybody. I just wanted to come home. I wished I could ride my bicycle, you know?"

"Yes. I do know," she said earnestly. "Matthew, you're still a growing boy. You need to enjoy this part of your life. There'll be years to come when you will have a job, one that you choose. But right now I wish you could be happy just to hang around with us."

He yawned. "I missed my bed."

"Why don't you take a nap on the rumble seat of the car while we drive home?"

For the first time in ages Lindy felt a singing inside, a wordless chorus of happiness. It seemed to be filling up the tight corners that had been so full of shadows. The hum of the brick road under the tires that had sounded so grim on the way to town was warm with promise now. Every so often she glanced back to reassure herself — it really was their boy stretched out in sleep, mouth ajar, hand dangling. A bruised hand. *Poor Tyler, God help him. But please don't ever let him show his face around me again.*

When she turned into the lot behind the barn it was almost three in the afternoon. Pete had just come out of the press building

— still in his good clothes, fresh from the Kiwanis, she judged. He looked hot and worried, carrying a piece of paper, one of Bernie's large drawing sheets.

Braking gently, she eased out of the car leaving Matthew still hard asleep. As she went to join him Pete paused.

"I'm glad you're back," he said. "Look at this!"

It was a cartoon, of a scrawny beaten man, with stubbled jaw and frowsy hair, sprawled over a drawing board and below it the caption: I QUIT.

Frozen, Lindy stared at it, then turned to head for the house to find Bernie on the back porch, waiting with haggard eyes in which there was dawning surprise. "You came back."

"Of course I came back. Did you think — ?" And remembering last night's drunken scene, she realized exactly what he had thought. She approached him cautiously, wanting to run and throw her arms around him but afraid of that dead stare. "I should have left a note. I'm sorry."

"You're sorry? What do you have to be sorry about? I'm the one who —" He seemed to become aware of Pete standing near. "What do you want?"

"I just came home and found this." He

242

waved the cartoon.

"Yeah."

"Bernie, we've got to talk about this. I never — I still don't understand —"

Lindy interrupted. "I believe I have something to show you that will change everything." And now her joy came rushing up into a surge of triumph. She led them over to the roadster where a sleepy boy was just coming awake, staring around. Matthew saw them and burst from the car full-steam.

"Poppa!" He threw himself at Bernie in that same frenzy of affection that had boosted Lindy out of her depths. She saw the shock of relief come over her husband's face, grimness gone, a look of marvel as he hugged the boy, staring across at her.

"How did you pull this off?" There was a trace of awe in his voice.

"I didn't. I went to see Hereford, I was going to bring down the wrath of the Lord on his head. But before I got there I ran into Matty. He was about to go into the mission, looking for a way to get home. He came all the way across the country on a train alone, it's a long story." She was laughing as she moved in to add her embrace to the mix. "He came back of his own accord. He missed us!"

The three words were transfixed with joy.

Waiting a few yards away, Pete looked at the sheet of paper in his hand. "If nobody objects I'm going to get rid of this." And he tore the page in two.

THURSDAY, OCT. 24, 1929

It was a time of confirmation, those days after Matthew returned. Sundays, when Lindy went to the little Presbyterian church she found herself fervently sending up a prayer of thanks to the strange faceless power she had once doubted, but did no more. Any Supreme Being that could take her to the place where her child stood in need was as omnipotent as they claimed He was.

After that awful day when the world had hit bottom, a potent optimism rushed in, drawing them together. Not just as a family, but as a team, her men. She looked out across the pressroom with a flood of affection for them all. Willy folding the pages as they came off the press, two sections this week. Pete's linotype, a huge, awkward machine with an outlandish keyboard, now officially known as "The Monster," had turned out to be a miracle of efficiency. Bernie was making bundles for the outlying markets.

"I'll take a couple of those up to St. Jo." Hobby had the glow of a proud father. He had just sold a half-page ad to a new store over in Kansas City, something called "Gamble's" that promised to be an emporium of marvelous kitchen equipment, hardware, everything down to can-openers. "I'm going to use last week's edition to sell some of the other merchants on an ad campaign over here."

Lindy felt the great gift of peace as she moved around, passing a tray of sandwiches. The big coffee urn stood nearby, each man with his own mug. As they gathered at the composing table they were full of the ebullience of a happy family. *The Pawnee Whistle* had just completed its first run of five thousand copies.

Willy's photos were spread before them. He had turned out to be a natural with the little Brownie camera. "This one's worth enlarging." Bernie picked up a shot of the hobo camp across the tracks. "They say a picture is worth a thousand words. We'll blow it up and post it on the door of the City Hall. If this doesn't get our merchants in step to donate to a fund to get those poor devils out of here, then nothing will."

"It was pretty cold the day I took it," Willy said. The men were hovering around makeshift fires, women and children in the background. "Some of them already hopped trains for California, but you can't ride the rails with three, four kids in tow."

"It's not pretty," Pete said soberly, "but they're our own folks once-removed. Any of us could be walking in those shoes. It may take some persuading to raise a fund for them, though. My father says every business in town is in debt, he's reached his quota for loans and passed it. The rest of the country may be booming like a brass band, but out here on the plains we've got thin pickings and have had for years."

"Thought old Herbert was going to give us all a chicken," Willy said, with one of his skeptical grins.

"He's trying," Hobby assured them earnestly. "Hoover's an economist, he knows how money works. When the fat cats on Wall Street are thriving it trickles down to the rest of the country. You'll see. The Stock Market is at an all-time high. We ought to be getting the benefits any day now."

Pete Koslow shook his head. "If you ask me, it's too high. The *Times* industrial index has gone up eighty-five per cent in twenty months. That's too rapid an appreciation. A lot of those transactions are just paper, people buying on margin. It's like building a house of cards. Reach a certain height and it can't sustain itself."

Investments in paper promises didn't sound like a good idea to Lindy. She was glad Bernie had stashed their savings in the People's Bank and Trust. Her own little hoard, the dowry she had gotten from her parents when she married, certificates that she had converted to cash, was locked away in a Safe Deposit Box over there. Bernie wouldn't touch it — he said that was her insurance policy in case of emergency.

"Willy, what do you do with your hard-earned dough?" Hobby asked genially. "You must have quite a little wealth, all that music you make."

The boy's dark face lit with a strange amusement, as if he knew better than all of them. "I got it stowed. Not saying where. But I'll tell you this: it's in gold. That ain't — won't never go out of style."

"Good man," Bernie nodded. "You're absolutely right. Gold is the basis for all our currency."

Over at the city desk the phone was ringing. Koslow went to answer it, as the discussion went on. Hobby was talking about exchange rates, foreign markets . . . But

Lindy was watching Pete as his big good-natured face turned ashen.

"Can somebody take this down," he called over his shoulder. "And you fellows, open up those bundles, we have to change the front page."

"Go ahead, Pete." Lindy had found a notebook, a pencil. "I know some shorthand."

Into the receiver he said, "Will you repeat those figures. Standard Oil down ten points, U.S. Steel down six, AT&T . . . so far a loss of nine billion dollars, got it. Got it. J. P. Morgan, okay. Thanks. Where's the ticker tape? I see, hours behind, yes. Thirteen million — you said 'billion' with a 'b'? Thirteen billion shares traded as of right now. Thanks, Joe." He put down the phone. "It's happened. The market has gone over the edge, it's headed for rock bottom, everybody trying to unload."

A billion shares? The word was hard to grasp, Lindy kept adding zeroes, a thousand times a million . . .

"What was that about J. P. Morgan?" Bernie asked. By now the others had come over to gather around.

"He's formed a syndicate of bankers to try to plug the sell-off. They're throwing every cent into it, maybe they can reverse it.

But right now our banner headline is: STOCK MARKET PLUNGING.

■ ■ ■ ■

1930

■ ■ ■ ■

EIGHTEEN

Lindy had put on a black wool dress; now she took it off. This was no time to indulge in personal mourning. It had only been six weeks since her father died, heart failure, followed by a bleak November funeral. She would grieve for a long time, not just for him, but the whole happy world of the 1920's. He had only been one victim of that final tragedy when, four days after the initial dip, the Stock Market had — the word they were using was "crashed." Black Tuesday. Whittaker Forrest had lost everything he owned. A powerful man, but he was not invulnerable to such a shock. Merle was more viable; she bent with the ebb of her lifestyle, but still clung to her roots. She would survive, but she moved through these days like a lovely wraith.

Helplessly Lindy had given her support, even while trying to hold her own family together in all the confusion. They had no stocks to lament, but there was no doubt of the massive damage that had been done to the country. Christmas had been almost mournful.

Today they started a new week in a new year in a new decade. It was important to throw off the old and meet the future head-on, and for that she dressed in a brisk blue gabardine suit with a white ruffled blouse and plenty of pink added to her winter-wan cheeks. She brushed the ruddy curls vigorously, relieved that there were no more gray hairs. She'd found a couple last week and yanked them out.

Bernie had gone downstairs ahead of her. She found him now at the window, which was frosted with ice crystals, framing a town imbedded in snowdrifts, sparkling under a bright sun which blazed above the horizon, hardly making a dent in the deep cold.

"Thermometer says ten-below." Bernie glanced at her. "You look nice."

"I thought I should perk up a little."

"Darned right. This mustn't turn into a wake. What did you tell Matt, about staying home this morning?" Sounds from upstairs meant the boy was getting dressed, though the school was still in recess the Monday after New Year's day.

"I didn't tell him," she said slowly. "Yet."

Stepping carefully around the uncertain areas of authority these days. "I wanted to discuss it with you. Bernie, shouldn't he be in on something this important?"

"I'm just worried he'll be scared."

"I know. I'm scared myself. But I'd be more frightened if I were sitting here at home, wondering."

Slowly he nodded. "You're probably right."

And there was no more time. Matthew had joined them, in his new long pants. Fulfillment of a Christmas wish, they made him look older. The boy was bright-eyed with excitement. There had been no disguising the fact that a moment of decision had come in their lives. Putting on coats, without further words they trooped across to the press building.

The others were already gathered there — Pete pacing the room, Hobby pretending to examine the linotype machine, Willy making coffee.

"Looks like the gang's all here." Pete led the way over to the big composing table where chairs were set around. Willy brought them mugs of boiling java, setting one in front of Matty which widened the boy's eyes even further.

"Watch out, it's hot."

"Well, folks, it's time for us to make plans." Pete didn't beat around bushes. His business-like tone and the jut of his jaw, the stiffness of posture, lent gravity to the proceedings. "We need to take stock of what the future holds. The economic situation in the country isn't going to get better for a while. I've talked to people who are in the know. My dad is friends with several New York bankers, and I have a buddy from college who's a broker with Goldman Sachs. He confided to me that his company lost half their value overnight."

"Aren't they speculators?" Hobby asked.

"That's true. But even the conservative houses took a beating. The market was way over its head. With the Dow Jones averages at 452 points, an increase of over 80 per cent in twenty months, it was asking for a correction and it got it. A lot of that overselling had been done on margin — the Street's word for credit. There wasn't any capital behind the face value in stocks, so when all those speculators tried to sell, nobody was buying. Not even blue chips. A number of corporations have folded. Let's not dwell on the details; I am just recapping to underscore the fact that this market isn't going to recover right away. It means that a lot of little businesses are having a hard time. Out here in the boonies we already know what bad news looks like, now the cities are learning it. Point is, can we — I mean *The Pawnee Whistle* — survive? Where are we fiscally, Bernie?"

Having been chosen as treasurer for the company Bernie was ready with the accounts ledger. "Thanks to Pete," he said, "we have always operated on a debt-free principle. We paid our costs as we went along. Then whatever was left we divided: set aside a small amount for future emergencies, and split the rest between us. Lately, that's been a pretty good cut. Hobby has brought in new advertising and we've got a good circulation going throughout the area. We still print the official records for the County, which helps pay for the initial run, so our local customers get the paper free. But last fall we went to two sections and more rotogravure and that has reduced our profits. We expected to make up for it in increased circulation, but with the Market down that hasn't happened. In fact — well, Hobby, you tell us. What's our future in terms of advertising?"

"As of right now it went south," he admitted with a shrug. "When people tighten their belts it's the first thing to go. The small businesses, even the large ones, are cutting their costs to the bone. Pete, even the Bank has dropped its ads, and they have always been the backbone of the paper's income."

"Dad's sorry about that," Pete nodded. "But he has been more than generous with his help to us, giving us the building and providing the house behind rent-free. He has also been liberal in granting loans to our local citizens and giving out second mortgages on the farms around us. The Bank is feeling the pinch just as much as the rest of the country. He's counting every penny. So we can't go to that well again."

"Won't people still read newspapers?" Lindy asked. "Surely life will return to some kind of normality in the new year."

"To some extent." Pete agreed. "In a few weeks or months the economy may pull up out of this, at least find a break-even level where we can all live, even if it's on a tight budget. Right now, though, everyone's in shock. Business as usual has shut down. And we'll be shut down too if we don't find some way to pay the electric bill. I want to apologize for buying The Monster. That was a bad idea. It ate up our reserves just at the wrong time. We don't really need two sections and we can't afford the rotogravure. Photo journalism will have to wait a few years, at least around here. So it's back to basics, but right now there isn't enough money to pay for even those. After last week's run we are low on ink and out of print stock. So I'm opening the floor for suggestions. I can kick in my savings, which only amount to a couple of hundred bucks. What I need is ideas from all of you."

"Well, we can donate two hundred to the kitty," Bernie said. "That's what savings are for. And that still leaves me enough that my family can get by for at least three months without any income."

"I can go longer than that," Pete agreed. "I live free over the press room, and I don't eat much. The only expense I have is gas for the truck, to take the paper up to the Kansas City newsstands and I can handle that."

Willy said, "We don't even need that, Matty and me. We got our bicycles."

"Didn't you just buy a new truck?" Hobby asked. "Or else what is that wooden thing out there in the barn?"

It brought the first smile of the day. They had all gathered around the curious sight of a wooden body on a Ford Model A — the company was calling it a "Station wagon" — the pride and joy of Willy's life. He said, "I got that to haul my drums around. I figure it'll pay for itself in gigs as far away as St. Joe and Jeff City. Fact, I been thinking: if I could start out on Thursday night and take some papers with me, maybe I could find us some new markets out there. 'Course, that would leave the local deliveries to Matty and Lin."

"I can do it!" Matthew asserted loudly. "All by myself."

"Not on a bike in this snow. You need your mother to drive you. But if I can get out into the small towns, early Friday mornings, I might drum up some new connections. I know quite a few folks in them little burgs where I got gigs."

Hobby sighed. "Wish I could go with you. It's good to think that people are still making music in spite of all our troubles."

"Well, they better had," the boy said. "Jazz is the only fun thing left, and it just costs a dime to get into the dives where I hang out. You welcome to come any time, Hobby, you play a right fine banjo, m'man. Anyways, I can get along on what I pick up, long as I can live in the basement here. But you close down *The Whistle,* where'm I gonna go? So what I think is, I better do more than just hang around and look handsome. I got me some savings, I can help you out with that electric bill." He took a sack from his pocket that jingled. "This-here's a hundred dollars in gold."

They stared silently at the offering on the table. Then Hobby reached in his pocket and drew out a wallet. "I can sure kick in a hundred myself. Don't need it where I'm heading."

"You're not leaving us?" Lindy was dismayed.

"No, no. Just moving out of the boarding house. I never did get much for my money in that old Victorian ruin. The bed's lumpy and the landlady's a rotten cook. I'll get me a tent and sleeping bag and move across the tracks."

"In shanty-town? In sub-zero weather!" Bernie protested.

"I don't mind the cold. I'll get along. I know those folks over there, a lot of them were in the Artillery, not far from us, Bernie. If I can park my truck in the barn, I'll be fine. Mainly, I want to see the paper come through this. It's the best job I ever had, and you are all the family I've got." He swallowed hard and shut up.

Lindy felt a welling of fondness that she blinked away. "I know what you mean. I feel the same way. That's why I want to dip into my dowry money, Bernie. That was a wedding present from my father, and I think he'd want me to use it toward our future."

"No, my dear. Not yet. With these contributions," he waved toward the money on the table, "we can go on for a while. I had an idea which I'll try out on you all. Suppose we run a full spread of ads, free of charge to our old customers. It will make *The Whistle* look like it's on solid footing, won't cost much except in paper and ink."

"And it might bring in new business," Willy added, "in these little towns I go to."

"Good idea. Let's do it." Pete's face was beginning to lighten. "We'll keep this rag running if we have to scrape the bottom of the barrel . . ."

"Well, I've got something!" Matty's high shrill voice burst upon them. "If you want it." And from a pocket he produced a coin that gleamed as he laid it on the table. Anxiously, he glanced around at them, awkward with the sorrow of sacrifice and yet proud to be able to make the gesture.

Koslow leaned across and picked it up. "This is a brand new silver dollar," he said in tones of respect.

"A man who came to see the circus gave it to me. I kind of did him a favor, I introduced him to Vonda Starr. I told her he was my uncle, only she knew he wasn't. But she gave him her autograph anyway. So he gave me a reward."

Pete shucked the coin in his hand. "You know what? I'm going to have this framed and hang it right here over the composing table as a talisman. A good-luck piece to remind us we can do anything. We can get through this if we all hang together."

They stood up and raised their coffee cups. Matthew held his up, too. Lindy and Bernie shared smiles. In her husband's eyes she saw dawning admiration. He tipped his cup to her and drained it.

Pete went on briskly, "Now, it's up to you G. B. to draw us a peppy cartoon to start off the new year."

Bernie looked amused. "Already done. I worked on it in my spare time last week. Just in case we decided to keep publishing." Going to the tall draftsman's chest of shallow drawers he took out a sheet of paper and held it up.

On it a wild Pawnee Indian in full feather seemed to be doing a war dance while blowing on a large, umpire's whistle. The caption was:

PLAY BALL!

NINETEEN

Austin DeMille's office was dark with walnut paneling, heavy blue draperies edged in fringe that looked tarnished in the bleak light of a morning in March. The leather chairs were designed for more massive users. Lindy fought a temptation to squirm and Bernie was visibly edgy in a starched shirt. Hereford wore black, of course, animated as a stick of firewood. Matty sat rigid, looking at the knees of his best pants. If he raised his eyes, Lindy thought she would see fear in them.

So could we please get this over with!

Austin perused the papers soberly as if he had never seen them before, probably a gesture to impress his clients. He was turning older, heavy in the jowls, slight pot belly, imposing, but he didn't strut any more. In fact he looked weary. "This seems to cover everything. You say the boy's natural father still can't execute a release?"

Hereford sighed slightly. "That's correct. Poor Tyler is in a state facility in South Carolina; the doctors agree his condition is probably permanent." Which was a polite way of saying that the man was consigned to an asylum for the criminally insane.

"And you are the legal father, mmhm. Hereford Romney, husband of Dorothy Romney, deceased. Mmhm. All right, then, if you will sign here —" He turned the document toward the preacher and offered him a pen. Took a new folder in a blue backing. "You two need to sign this one." He handed it across to Lindy, who affixed her signature and passed it along to Bernie. He scrawled his name and gave it back to the lawyer. "I guess that about does it."

"Do I get to sign anything?" Matty broke in, still intent on the pattern of the carpet.

"You have to be eighteen years of age to execute a legal document, my boy," Austin told him gently. "Your wishes were declared at the hearing last month. They're on record. This proceeding is officially closed. Congratulations to you all."

"Then I must be on my way." Hereford put on his coat. "I have a food kitchen to run. Poor devils, they line up around the block these days for a bowl of soup and a slice of bread."

"And I noticed," Bernie said, "that there are a good number of colored men in that line. Does the Boss ever object to that?"

"No," Hereford told him flatly. "Pendergast and I have an understanding."

After he had gone Austin said, "Bernie, could I have a word with you in private?" He included Lindy. "Matthew, this is grown-up business. Would you wait in the car, please?"

The boy stood up, raised his head to Lindy for the first time, a look of cautious optimism. "Are you my real folks now?"

"Legally, and every which way, we're yours and you are ours," she told him with a smile, and Bernie clapped him on the shoulder.

"Welcome to hard times, son."

When the three of them were alone, Austin sat down on the sofa under the bookcases. Massive legal tomes — how books could seem so ominous. Lindy shied away from them and took a seat near the window where she could look out at the bleak vistas of downtown Kansas City.

"Bernie, I've been asked to convey to you that we — a lot of us over here in the city of mean streets — have been aware of your cartoons." Austin had a small smile that he used sparingly. "I've been asked to enlist you in our cause — namely, to rid Kansas City of the Pendergast machine."

"Give me the recruitment papers, I'll sign up," Bernie said, instantly.

"There's an election coming. Tom's going to try to take over the State House, put one of his pets in as Governor."

"I'll certainly be rooting for his opposition," Bernie said. "Of course, being a good Kansan now, I don't have the vote in Missouri."

"I know. But you are in a unique position to influence our politics. If we happen to come into possession, occasionally, of information on the seedy side of the Bottoms, we'll be glad to help your crusade against the Boss."

"Anything you can tell me will be appreciated. And in return, there's something that might come in handy for your people to know," Bernie added. "Were you aware that the fire which killed my sister was not set by the Ku Klux Klan, as was claimed. The arsonists were Pendergast's men, hand picked by Voorhees, and I have an eye witness who can attest to that."

DeMille was instantly alert. "That's very interesting. It might be a good idea to get his statement and keep it on record."

"I thought I might pass the information

along to the new government Bureau of Investigation. I hear this man, Edgar Hoover, is going to mount a campaign against racketeering. I have to think they'll include our Tom in their plans."

Austin was nodding. "It would be a big help if the government would set up a federal program. The city doesn't have the will to go after the Machine officially. Old Tom knows the law and side-steps the traps we set. He has so much influence that the courts look the other way, even though there are dozens of crimes linked to him. Trouble is getting anyone to testify. It's dangerous, right now. But once a deposition has been taken the information is on record, and if anything happens to the witness then . . ."

"Nothing must happen to this person!" Lindy spoke up fiercely.

"Understood. We aren't considering any immediate action. We intend first to enlist public support, get people so outraged they will rise up and take a stand. If I recall correctly, that arson incident was linked to racial hatred. The Democratic Party is going to be putting forth candidates that will appeal to all segments of the social order, including Negroes. We may be able to reawaken some interest in it."

"Our witness happens to be colored," Ber-

268

nie told him. "I imagine he'd be pleased to help your cause."

"Good. And don't forget that you and Lindy can bear witness too, even if you weren't on the scene at the time. Meanwhile, my boy, keep those cartoons coming. No words can say it better than a clever sketch."

Bernie shook his hand. "I learned that a long time ago."

As they headed for the door Lindy paused. "What do you hear from Cocky? Since he closed his brokerage firm I haven't seen him."

"Poor guy," Austin shrugged. "He's out there selling stocks door-to-door. The man's a hopeless optimist. Of course he's right, the market will come back eventually. But no matter what great bargains are available right now, nobody is going to risk a cent, not even on blue chips. When I see him I'll tell him you asked after him."

They found Matty waiting in the roadster. The boy looked — Lindy searched for a word — he looked happy. An unusual expression for him. She would feel it too once this next hour was over. The truth was, she dreaded the rest of their trip.

Pulling up to the imposing house on Walnut Street she noticed that the first crocuses were beginning to open — it had been a warm week. When she was a child she used to run around looking for them, more fun than an Easter egg hunt. *Stop it! You are not going to cry!*

On the front porch a man stood waiting, gave them a wave of his hand. Bernie's father was a comforting figure. Simple and earthy and full of hard experience in the world, he exuded confidence, which was in rare supply these days. She hoped Bernie would look like him twenty years from now.

"Daddy Jones!" she moved into his arms for a kiss. "So good to see you." In more ways than one. He had stepped in to save what little her mother had left. Swamped in debt after the Judge's death, Merle had been bewildered by a world she'd never had to deal with. Hiram Jones had come to the rescue, bought the big old white-elephant of a house and helped her sell off some of the family finery, the massive gold and silver bric-a-brac, the stacks of elegant china and crystal, the most expensive jewelry. Even though the antiques had brought only a fraction of what they were worth, it was in cash. It had brought order out of chaos; Merle had enough to satisfy her needs in years to come.

"Dad." Bernie always hugged his father,

not embarrassed by sentimentality. "You've got to come out to our house more often. Matty needs to know his grandfather."

The boy was watching them wide-eyed. He knew this was his mother's father, but up until now it hadn't meant much. Today he was fascinated by family lineage. "We signed the papers," he told his grand-dad. "I'm really . . ."

"You're part of our family. Matty, you always have been. Your mother was my little girl." Hiram glanced at Lindy warmly. "And now I have another daughter. Everything has turned out all right."

"Your buying my childhood home is the crowning gesture," she told him. "I am so grateful!"

"Well, the fact is, my good wife has admired this house for a long time. She always did want to live like a great lady. There isn't much left of Kansas City society these days, but when it starts to come back, she will be part of it. There's nothing like a market crash to level the playing field. Those high-toned folks will need us self-made men. Even real estate developers," he chuckled. "Reckon she'll find plenty of people to take a seat at that big old mahogany table in there." He had kept all the larger pieces of furniture that were in scale for the gracious rooms. "Wish we could keep your cook."

"Yeah," Bernie said. "Clemma is like part of the scenery here. I guess she's happy to be retiring."

"She must be over sixty," Lindy added. "My father had already given her the golden hand-shake before he died."

"What's a golden hand?" Matty demanded.

"It's a figure of speech," she explained. "A person gives an employee a retirement gift. You get it for serving in one position for many years, well and faithfully. It can be a personal item or a piece of property. In Clemma's case Dad gave her cash, to go back to her home town in southern Mississippi and open a little lunch shop."

"At her age?" Bernie was surprised.

"She's younger at heart. Looking forward to the future, she's probably better off than most of us." Lindy sighed. "I'd better go in and see how near ready Mother is."

"I told her to take her time," Hiram said. "Whenever she's finished packing I'll drive her to the Depot." Merle was going to live with a sister in Virginia.

Mounting the curved staircase, Lindy glanced back at the parquet floor of the foyer, still studded with several stands on which small sculptures sat, a reminder of the great days of formal dinners, receptions. *I wonder where the punch bowl is?* Her uncle, a diplomat, had once been given a huge punch bowl with a rim of gold leaf and an inscription from the country where he had served. There had been thirty or forty matching cups. She hoped Bernie's mother would find it in the attic. It was the sort of thing to display proudly.

But how on earth is Mrs. Jones going to get used to all those draperies that have to be cleaned, the floors to be waxed, the mahogany and walnut and cherry-wood furniture to be polished? Maybe they could afford a maid. Bernie's father had become one of Kansas City's most successful real estate developers. *What does the market crash mean to him? He always said that owning land was the one thing you could count on.*

Upstairs she paused at her own suite, but it was depressing. The little princess bed was gone, the chaise lounge looked shabby in the bare light of uncurtained windows. Going on down the hall she went into the master bedroom, glad to see a fire burning on the hearth. Merle stood amid open suitcases, looking frustrated.

Handsome as always, carefully groomed, but her eyes had lost the lustrous joy that had always been hers, the zest for living.

"You know," she said, as if they'd just been having a conversation, "I really dislike Mr. Hoover. I know it isn't patriotic to say anything against one's President, but the man is simply out of touch. He keeps saying everything's fine and dandy out here in the country. I swear I believe I am going to vote next election, just so I can help run him out of office. Terrible man!"

"A lot of people agree with you," Lindy went and hugged her, with a world of love.

It seemed to retrieve Merle from some inner place where she had gone to brood. She smiled brightly. "How are you, dear? You look splendid. That's a very nice dress. How did the proceedings go?"

"The adoption is a *fait accompli*. Matthew is officially ours."

"Good. That deserves a small token, I think." Merle went to her dressing table and took out a box. "I've been waiting to give this to the boy — to remember Judge Forrest." She opened it to show Lindy. The heavy gold pocket watch was so familiar it brought tears to her eyes. "Don't let him forget his grandfather, dear."

"Never!" It came out on an odd pitch, Lindy swallowed hard. "Mother, this all can't last forever. We'll have you back here again, in your own town, some day after things get better. I just know it!"

"I'm sure you're right, darling. Now go along with your little family. I'll be happy thinking of you, and your Bernie. He has turned out to be a strong, dependable man. Don't worry about me. I'll be fine once I'm out of here. I must admit I don't like anti-climaxes. The sooner I get on my way the better." She kissed her daughter fervently and gave her a small nudge toward the door.

Everything was a blur as Lindy went down the long staircase for the last time. Hurrying past the two men still talking on the porch she went straight to the little roadster, where Matty was waiting in the back seat.

Giving him the little box, she said, "This is your inheritance from your Grandfather Forrest. It's been passed from father to son, but he had no son, so it comes to you as his grandson."

In speechless awe Matty took the handsome object out and held it up to the light. Finally, he said, "That's better than a hand shake. That's real gold."

"Yes it is. It's a very valuable piece. You probably shouldn't show it around too freely these days. When people are short of money they get desperate. Especially don't take it over to Hooverville." The shanty town had acquired a name of late.

The boy looked at her with those vivid eyes, layered now with dawning maturity. "I don't go across the tracks much any more. The last time — I don't know, Momma, it was kind of bad. One of the kids in the tents asked me if I had anything to eat. So I thought I'd go home and make him a sandwich, he looked really hungry. But then there were twenty kids all around me, and they were really hungry too. And we didn't have that much bread to make everybody a sandwich, and anyway, what good is one sandwich? So I told them we were poor too. Anyhow I haven't been back since."

Bernie joined them then, sliding into the driver's seat. "Dad said tell you to come back and visit any time. He means it, Lindy. He loves you too. Wow, what you got there, Matt?"

"My inher . . . inherit. . . ."

"Inheritance. A bequest from my father, one of those family-tradition things," Lindy explained.

"It's a beauty." Bernie sounded cheerful, but his eyes were shadowed, as always, by latent worry. He knew more about the climate in the country than she did, Lindy knew. He had told her privately that the President's assurances of prosperity being right around the corner were wrong. "Put

276

that in a safe place, son."

"There's a little space under the stairs down in the basement," Matty said enthusiastically. "Willy calls it his 'hidey-hole.' It's where he keeps his gold money."

Lindy was shocked. "I didn't know that. And you shouldn't be spilling Willy's secrets, son."

"He wouldn't mind. He trusts us. Anyway, he says it's safer than putting it in a bank. Poppa, when a bank fails, what happens to all the money in it?"

Bernie got the car in gear. "When a bank fails," he said, "it means they don't *have* any money." And the grimness in his face deepened.

■ ■ ■ ■

1932

■ ■ ■ ■

TWENTY

Around the press room they sat like actors waiting for a play to begin. Bernie, at his easel, was doodling cartoons of the others — Hobby at the coffee urn, head shining like a polished doorknob, Willy sitting a straight chair backward over by the clean-up sink, arms and legs askew, looking somehow like his own drumsticks, Lin and Matty at the composing table, poring over a game of dominoes as if their lives depended on it. Pete got up from his desk and began to pace the floor. Pausing at the window he stared out at the town, burnt dry under the early heat of summer. June had been a killer. And July looked worse, even on this second day of the month.

"Maybe this isn't the best time to ask," Hobby said abruptly into the silence, "but I wonder, Pete, if you could spare me for a few weeks? I haven't been too successful drumming up new business for us. The regular advertisers will hang in as long as they can. They don't need me leaning on them."

Koslow stood blinking, hauling his thoughts back from somewhere else. "Sure, Hobby. What's up?"

"Well, some of the fellows over there —" a nod toward the ragged tent camp across the tracks — "want to join the Bonus Army. All over the country veterans are forming companies, going to march on Washington and demand the bonuses they promised us after the War."

"Those aren't supposed to be paid out until 1945," Bernie said. "Congress just killed a bill to release them early."

"And that's what got us thinking, we should kind of stroll over to White House and put the nudge on old Herbert to ease up and give us the money now. Reckon he could do it if he wanted to. If we sort of camp on his doorstep, it might bring the truth home to him: we need help."

"Wish you luck," Pete said dryly.

"We're calling it the 'Bonus Expeditionary Force.' " Hobby grinned. "It's going to be run just like the Army with rules and officers and flags. I'll send you some pictures, maybe you can write us up in the paper."

"Glad to," Pete nodded, but his mind had

already strayed back to its inner focus.

"I win!" Matthew announced loudly. "I beat Momma at dominoes."

"He's getting good," Lindy confessed.

The boy looked at the big clock over the door. "People are going to be mad when the paper's late. They'll think it's my fault it didn't come on time."

"No, they won't." Bernie laid down his stick of charcoal and got up. "They know the nominating convention is deadlocked, they'll have heard it on the radio. They will understand why we had to hold the front page. The whole thing should have been over by now. Politics is getting to be a blood sport."

"Yeah," Hobby agreed. "When do they start the fourth balloting?"

"Not until eight tonight Chicago time." Pete looked at his watch. "But I've got a friend in the Hearst camp, he'll know when the McAdoo delegation decides to make its move. He's going to call me, give us a chance to scoop some of the other papers."

"McAdoo?" Matty thought it was a funny name. "McAdoodle Doo! What does Mc-Adoo do?"

"He's in charge of the California vote," Pete told him seriously. "Hearst has been holding them in reserve, waiting to see who's winning. Roosevelt has a majority of the delegates to the convention, but under the rules he needs two-thirds to be nominated. Al Smith is backing Baker, that's why they're deadlocked. And Hearst hates Baker. So it just makes sense he'll throw his weight for Roosevelt. I don't know what's taking him so long."

"Texas," Bernie said. "It's going to depend on Garner. I'll bet right now Hearst is on the wire, twisting Garner's arm. If they don't break the deadlock this time, the fringe vote may peel away from Roosevelt, and the rush will be on, somebody else will step in. There's always a dark horse waiting."

"What difference does it make?" Matty roamed the room restlessly.

"The man who wins the Democratic nomination at this convention will undoubtedly be our next President," Hobby informed him. "And with the country dying before our eyes, it matters. Baker is a throwback. Roosevelt — well, nobody knows about Roosevelt. But his campaign song is 'Happy Days are Here Again.' I'd elect him on that alone. He's a rich man, so you have to figure he knows something about making money."

"He inherited it . . ." Bernie was saying

when the door burst open, a man stood there, bib-overalls and a straw hat, a look of horror on his face.

"Pete, where's your father?" It sounded almost like an accusation.

"Dad?" Koslow frowned. "I don't know. I suppose he's at home. Why?"

"No, he ain't. Ain't nobody there. He probably run out on us. There won't be nobody to open the Bank come Tuesday morning."

"Now stop that, Jeremiah!" Pete said sharply. "What are you in such a sweat about?"

"Well, Amos Quinn won't be there, that's certain!"

Lindy was as puzzled as the others. Quinn was the teller who took care of the window at the People's Bank and Trust. A middle-aging man, he'd been a main stay of the institution since it was founded. Since the tight times, there was no assistant manager. The only other employee was a bookkeeper behind the scenes. Mr. Koslow sat in an office and handled loans. But Amos was the face that people looked to when they came to deposit or withdraw or just hobnob about interest rates.

"What's the matter with —"

"Amos? Well, what's the matter is he don't

have a head no more." Jeremiah Utley seemed to take a grim pleasure in delivering the news. "What's the matter is he done took a double-barrel shotgun and blew his own face off. That's what's the matter."

"Where did you hear that?" Bernie gripped his shoulder and shook it.

"Hear it? I seen it. I just come from his daddy's farm. Amos went out to the barn and blasted hisself to kingdom-come."

Lindy was aware of Matty lurking, wide-eyed in the background. "Mr. Utley," she said firmly, "try to calm down a little. You're among friends. Please control yourself." The words seemed to make a slight impact on the man.

He glanced around at them all. "Well, it was a bad thing, and it's gonna get worse come Tuesday morning when we all go to the bank and there ain't nobody to open the doors."

"That's nonsense," Pete told him firmly. "The bank will be open, my father will be there. If necessary I will be there. It will be business as usual. Here, have a cup of coffee, get your breath a little."

"No, thankee. I got to tell folks . . ."

Slamming back out into the afternoon heat, he seemed to leave a vacuum behind.

"Good Lord," Pete muttered. "He's going

286

to get the wind up all over town. We'll have a panic on our hands."

"Thank heaven for the Fourth of July," Lindy said. "This long holiday weekend will give the news time to sink in and folks to settle down. Poor Amos."

They were all aware that the man had been in a state of deep sorrow since the death of his wife, a couple of months ago. But everyone goes through periods of grief, they don't shoot themselves.

"Probably had something to do with the fact that his father is about to lose his farm," Pete told them. "Couldn't pay the taxes. It'll be going on the auction block, come Tuesday."

"Things are tough all over," Hobby remarked with a hunch of shoulder. "You just have to . . ."

He was interrupted by the telephone, its clang made them all jump. Pete hurried over to answer it. A few low questions and he hung up, already heading for the press.

"It's done. It's official. Let's go. Garner will throw his votes to Roosevelt. Probably be the Vice Presidential nominee. McAdoo will make a speech tonight when he votes California on the balloting. The bottom line is: Franklin Roosevelt is the Democratic candidate for President." He was locking up the front page, which was already set with its banner headline:

DEMS PICK ROOSEVELT

"Have you got the cartoon page ready, G. B.? I can help you with the caption. My friend had a look at the acceptance speech," Pete added. "The key words are 'new deal.' I don't have the exact quote."

Bernie laughed out loud. "I must by psychic. I already drew the picture — Roosevelt at the head of a poker table. I captioned it: IT'S TIME WE HAD A NEW DEALER. I'll just cut off the last two letters."

"Fellows get ready to fold and bundle," Pete directed Willy and Hobby. "And you can go get your bike, Matt. We'll give you the first copies that come off the press. You take the east side of town. Lin can take the car and deliver the west. We need to give people something to talk about instead of — this other."

As they went out the back door together Lindy put an arm around Matthew's shoulders. Pale and confused, the boy looked to be struggling with some question.

"I kinda liked Amos," he said as they walked across to the house.

"So did I. Poor man, you never can tell what someone's suffering inside. He probably reached a point where he couldn't stand the grief coming at him from all directions. A stronger person would cry, maybe, and then brace up and go on living."

"Like me and Tyler," Matty said half to himself. "I cried after they took him away. I was sorry he didn't like me."

"I think maybe he loved you a lot, but the part inside that made him a good man was already damaged and just went to pieces under the stress of those cannons. It wasn't anything to do with you. But it was awful, I'm sure, and I'm glad you got past it."

"Yeah." Moving a little more lightly, Matt ran to the barn and came back out with his bicycle hung with empty canvas bags. "See you later," he called back as he wheeled it over to the press building.

An uneasiness hung over the town that weekend, heavy as the heat that had settled in like a blanket of wool. Not a breath of breeze all day Saturday, but in the early hours of Sunday morning a blast hit the house. Dust storm. *That's all we needed,* Lin cringed inwardly, it was the hardest part of living on the plains, that wind. She got up just as a red sun cleared the eastern hills and dressed for church.

Bernie hauled on his Sunday pants. "I may be damned," he told her, "but I am not wearing a coat today."

Nobody was. Even Absalom stood before them in shirt sleeves and spoke a little desperately against the gusts that shook the frame building. " 'And there came a great wind from the wilderness and smote the four corners of the house . . . and Job fell down upon the ground and worshipped. He said, the Lord giveth and the Lord hath taken away, blessed be the name of the Lord. In all this Job sinned not, nor charged God foolishly.' "

The preacher was sweating and pale, obviously struggling to make his message more inclusive. The wind was only a metaphor for disaster that seemed to loom over them, the sense that something nameless was about to happen.

It was a nervous congregation that gathered in the Sunday school room below the church for the usual after-sermon cup of coffee, though today it was cold drinks. Lindy went to help Maizie with the big pitchers of lemonade and iced tea. The other women ferried trays of glasses and cookies over to the far end of the room where the men had gathered together in front of the big blackboard, which bore a chalk inscription:

NO FOURTH OF JULY CELEBRATION

"Well, if this isn't the last straw!" Cora fretted. "It's like canceling the United States of America."

"Nonsense," Lindy told her sharply, "it would be impossible to shoot off fireworks in that wind. And with polio getting so bad, it's just as well for the children to stay away from the swimming pool. The United States will survive just fine!" *Will you listen to that tone I just used!* But somebody had to speak some sense in the absence of their usual mentor.

"Has anybody heard any news about Gertrude?" Agatha asked with a frown. "They say she was taken by a seizure. Couldn't breathe. I hope *she* doesn't have polio."

By now they knew the wife of the banker had been rushed to the hospital in Topeka, Friday afternoon, which accounted for Mr. Koslow's absence that day. Polio? The word sent a riffle of horror through the group. It had been a bad summer for the disease. Like a predator lurking in dark shadows it could strike without warning, its cause unknown, its results usually lethal.

"Well, we all pray for her, and you can't blame Mr. Koslow for staying at her side. But it still leaves us without anybody at the bank," Agatha contended grimly. "My husband said we should take our money out right now."

Again Lindy spoke out with a confidence she didn't feel. "There's nothing wrong with the bank. If everybody gets into a panic they could cause a failure, just by their own actions. I'm sure Mr. Koslow will be back by Tuesday morning."

But as she watched the men, she could see that it was far from a sure thing. Bernie was arguing with them now, shaking his head, Absalom Stark apparently giving him support, while the others bristled and stiffened and took on postures that seemed oddly defiant. The debate was held in lowered tones, but an occasional word rose above the mutter.

". . . all over the country, man!"

"If the American Trust can go under . . ."

". . . new Emergency Relief Board . . ." that was Absalom.

And Bernie was saying, "Give the thing a chance . . ."

"You give it a chance. Me, I'm gonna . . ." The voices suddenly grew more hushed, but the angry tones were hardly abated.

Abruptly Bernie left the crowd and came over to Lindy.

"We're going home," he said. "Sorry to cut the fellowship time short, but we're needed elsewhere." His smile to the ladies was preoccupied. As they went out the wind struck them like a blow.

"What's up?" Lindy asked, as he helped her into the truck. In harsh weather they used the newspaper's sturdy vehicle.

He swung up behind the wheel. "We've got trouble," he said. "There's going to be a run on the bank Tuesday morning."

TWENTY-ONE

At four a.m. the veils of darkness were beginning to shift, a faint wash of light showing in the eastern sky as they silently made their way across the barnyard and around to the back door of the People's Bank and Trust. Once inside, Bernie said in a hushed voice, "Reminds me of the dawn of battle on the Argonne. Everything dead quiet before the guns let loose."

Matty grinned feverishly in the yellow light of the vestibule. "Tell about it again, Poppa. How many guns?"

"Thirty-five miles of artillery lined up hub-to-hub, all opened fire at once."

Lindy had some private doubts about the effect of Bernie's war stories on the boy's imagination which was easily enflamed. "Thank goodness we aren't going to have any violence this morning." And even as she spoke, Hobby Carter let himself in the back door to join them; dressed in Army uniform, he had a pistol hanging at his side.

"Morning, everybody."

"What's the idea, Hobby? You'd think this was a war." Bernie didn't look pleased.

"Just figured it might sober folks up if I stood around and looked like I was guarding the place. Those guys across the tracks know all about what's happening here. They know there will be a lot of loose cash flowing when we start paying off the customers. Pretty tempting, don't you think? I figured I would remind folks of the dangers of carrying a bunch of greenbacks around the streets. Maybe they'll even think twice about withdrawing their savings."

"You know, that's a good idea," Lindy said. "Especially if we're going to pay them in small bills."

It had been Pete's idea, to amass a stock of ones, fives and tens and count them out slowly to give people time to reconsider. He was out now, going around to see his father's friends at the Kansas City Mercantile, the Topeka Sentinel, the St. Joseph First National, all of whom were willing to interrupt their holiday and go into their vaults for small currency.

"Any further news on Gertrude Koslow?" Hobby asked.

"Not that I've heard. Mr. Koslow is still

over in Topeka at the hospital." Bernie led the way to the tellers' cages in the front of the bank. "When does the auction start out at the Quinn place?"

"Nine o'clock." Pete had come in from the rear quietly to join them, hauling large canvas sacks in either hand. Dumping them in the antiroom, he unlocked them to display their contents. "All small bills, mostly ones."

"How's your mother?" Lindy asked.

"They've got her on an iron lung. Yeah, it's polio. All you can do is pray. I told Dad to stay there, we can handle this. He gave me leave to try anything I could think of, so here's what I want you to do . . ." He drew Bernie aside. Hobby was over by the front door, peering out between the closed blinds.

"Getting light out there. And they're already starting to gather."

"More coming from the other side of town." It was Willy ducking in the back door with a stack of bakery boxes. "I brought us some doughnuts. Don't this bank have a coffee machine?"

"Yes. Wonderful." Lindy went to look for it. "We'll make them feel welcome. We'll take the edge off their nerves with some refreshments. Good thought, my friend."

She helped him carry the heavy urn to the

front of the bank and station it on a table near the door. "Cups . . ."

"They got lots of paper cups over at the Grange Hall," Matty said. "They didn't get to use them for the picnic yesterday since the Fourth of July got cancelled."

"Let's see, who could we call to open the place up . . ."

"I can get in," the boy said, with a grin, "I know how. I'll bring back all the cups I can put in my bicycle bags." He was gone before she could say *no*.

"Matty," she called after him. "Leave them a receipt."

"Okay," Pete joined them. "Coffee and doughnuts is a good idea, all right, treat this like a party. Everybody going to act cool, as if we have a rush on the bank every day. Hobby, you can offer to walk them to their cars so they won't get robbed in the parking lot. Because a couple of hundred one-dollar bills is going to make quite an arm load, and shucks, we don't have any bags to put them in, sorry." In a grim way he was enjoying himself, but there was a shadow of fear in his readable blue eyes.

"Pete," Lindy murmured, "truth: how much money do you have on hand."

"Not enough to pay out all those ac-

297

counts," he muttered, his lips hardly moving.

"Where's Bernie?"

"I sent him on a special undercover assignment."

"You can't tell even me?"

"Lin, it may not work. Now what?"

A knock at the back door, Willy let Absalom in. The preacher was in full black with collar reversed, his pudgy face already glistening with sweat. Behind him the sun was shooting long rays across the tops of the Bluffs.

"I thought if there was trouble I might help stem the flood with a little oratory." He spoke to Koslow, but included them all. "If you think I'd be in the way . . ."

"Not at all!" Pete assured him. "We've planned to welcome our clients in with good will galore. You can take care of that part." But he frowned slightly — the funereal attire didn't send the right message.

"I've got an idea," Lindy said, and ran back to the storeroom at the rear. She had noticed a box full of holiday trappings, never put out on the Fourth. Grabbing up a red-white-and-blue garland of tinsel, she had to suppress an impulse to laugh hysterically. But it was with proper diffidence that she draped it around the pastor's shoulders like a prayer shawl. "If you don't think it's sacrilegious . . ." she began.

"Not at all," Absalom assured her stoutly. "Quite suitable to our cause. I shall greet the clamoring crowds with prayers to the Lord and the Democratic Party to deliver us from evil."

"As a figure of authority," Pete added, "you can keep them from crowding the foyer. At a certain point, we'll have to make them line up in the street and be admitted one at a time as others leave. Right now, what with my mother getting polio, I am nervous about contagion."

"Good point." Absalom accepted a paper cup from Willy. "Thank you, young man. I wonder why it never gets too hot for coffee."

"Did Matthew get back with the cups?" Lindy glanced around.

"There was a dispenser full of 'em in the rest room," Willy told her. "They'll hold us for a while."

"Folks are piling up out-front," Hobby called, from his post at the window. "And it's still three hours until ten o'clock."

"I don't intend to make them wait," Pete announced. "Unlock the doors, Hobby."

The next few hours was one of the rare

times in Lindy's life that she couldn't recall clearly in the years afterward. It came back to her in snapshots, scraps of conversation. A vivid image of Pete in shirtsleeves, looking like a warrior with those heavy shoulders, tousled hair, but always the big smile.

"Hi, Hank, how's it going? You ever get that roof mended? They say it's like to rain, next October. Let's see, your account amounts to two hundred twenty-one dollars and forty five cents, nice little nest egg. And you want to close it out? Okay, here you go. One . . . two . . . three . . . sorry I'm not as fast as poor old Amos, and to make it worse I banged my thumb in the car door this morning, but I'll get there . . . four . . . five . . ."

Willy: "Lin, we need more doughnuts."

"I'll run over . . ."

"No, I'll go, but I need some money, I don't have any more small change handy."

"In my kitchen drawer, I always keep a few dollars . . ."

Matty: "I got the cups. What'll I do now?"

Hobby: "Hank, looks like you got your hands full. Let me help you out to your car. Oh, you walked? Well, sorry I can't see you all the way home. Got to stick by my post here. Some new fellows came into Hooverville yesterday, I don't like the looks of 'em."

"Lindy?" A soft voice, little Randy Perkins, the grocery store clerk. "Tell me, is there really enough money back there in the vault to pay all these people?"

She shrugged her shoulders. "All I know is, it's the most cash I ever saw at one time in my life."

And later a shrill voice, rising over the others — Bucky Wilmott, the owner of JOE'S DINER (nobody could remember who Joe was). Bucky was Irish and wiry as a brass brush. "Listen, you say you got enough, even if we all take our money out. So if that's true, the bank will still be here tomorrow, won't it, Pete?"

Suddenly the clatter of voices went quiet, waiting for the answer.

The big man went on counting. ". . . forty-seven, forty-eight and thirteen cents. And thanks for your business, George. Now what was the question? What's going to happen to the bank? Well, my dad started this institution because the town needed it. If the town decides it doesn't need it any more, I guess he'll close up. But not until every account has been settled. Next . . ."

"But what'll we do with our money then?"

George Diggs, trying to stuff wads of one-dollar bills in his overall pockets, said, "I know what I'm gonna do. I'm putting mine into tin cans and bury them . . . never mind where."

"Can't write a check on a tin can."

"Good Lord, I'd have to go clear to Topeka to deposit my day's receipts."

Absalom Stark by the door: "I'm sorry Yantsy, but I can't let any more folks in here, it's not safe. Anyway, it's probably hotter inside than out." His black suit was showing large patches of sweat. "Good time to ponder hell fires," he added facetiously.

At one point Lindy had crossed the street to go home, made enough lemonade to fill two gallon jars and carried it back to the bank. The room was still choked with milling people, the odor of humanity beginning to thicken in spite of the large fans in opposite corners of the lobby. She took the pitcher to Willy who was dispensing the last of the coffee.

"It's not very cold. Tell them I couldn't bring an ice box with me." She sounded silly, even to herself. It was getting to the point of laugh-or-cry.

And then Bernie was back. He came in from the rear, a new sunburn blistering his nose, hair tousled, but a look of victory on his face. Pete stopped counting and the customers fell quiet, sensing an announcement.

Bernie waved nonchalantly. "We did it."

"Good work!" Turning to the crowd Pete said, "I asked Bernie to go out to the auction at the Quinn farm and bid on it. These tax-delinquency foreclosures are being tracked by big corporations who are picking up our land for pennies. Back taxes on the Quinn place were only a hundred and some dollars. It's worth five times that much. So my father gave the word to go and buy it. What did you have to pay, G.B.?"

"Three hundred and twenty-six bucks. When I told Mr. Quinn he could stay on as a sharecropper he sat down and cried."

"If the bank could afford to buy it," somebody asked, "why didn't they give Quinn a loan?"

"Couldn't." Pete shook his head. "There's a limit to how much a bank can lend in proportion to its assets. Dad wouldn't go over that. He did this out of his own pocket, as a tribute to all the years Amos put in here at the bank. That's what a man does, who values his friends."

In the stillness, Bucky Wilmott said, "Aw shoot. I'm going home."

Excerpt from Lindy's letter:

The truth is, I think they had all changed their minds by then, they just needed an

303

excuse. So the town is back to normal, people seem to be knuckling down to the hard reality of the Depression. And I got to thinking how much it depends on how the women react, to keep everyone calm. I remember, Mother, that in times of crisis you always insisted we sit down together at table and have a quiet meal.

So I wrote an essay for the paper, about how wives save pennies, how they stash them in cookie jars and dole them out when most needed to lighten the family's spirits. I wanted to make the women aware of what a big part they play in the outlook of the town. I said sometimes the best way to cheer people up was to bake a fancy dessert, and I finished with your recipe for spice chiffon cake. It must have hit the spot, everybody has been complimenting me.

And when I went over to the paper this morning I found I had a desk of my own, with a name plate on it: cooking editor. Before I could get too puffed up Pete put it in perspective. He said, "This paper could use more input from the ladies. Lin, see if you can get your gal-friends to submit stuff. We could have a special corner for tips on housework and gardening and dress patterns . . ." Well, you get the idea. Namely, that my contribution means no more to him than the idle prattle of a backyard gossip. And here I was thinking of myself as a writer. Ah well.

■ ■ ■ ■

1933

■ ■ ■ ■

TWENTY-TWO

They drove in Bernie's truck the few blocks to the Courthouse, with Willy and Matthew crouched on bales of old newspapers in the back. Nobody was comfortable, but Bernie had said, "We'd better ride. We don't want to look like a parade marching through town." And Willy snickered. Matthew was unnaturally silent.

Lindy still had misgivings. In this last year the mood of the country had changed, she had to admit. There was a flavor of hope in the air, of desperate optimism. "We have nothing to fear but fear itself," the President had said. A gifted orator, his speeches were powerful. But how much of it was bluff? It's all very well to banish the big fears, that the United States would fold up under its own weight. But what about the little personal spurts of dread? Like this one, today, this meeting that had them all afraid.

"No one will know you are giving depositions," Austin DeMille had assured them. But how could he be certain? What ears are cocked in a place like the Courthouse?

Matthew was almost pop-eyed with excitement as they got out of the car beneath the pile of the old fieldstone building. "You reckon anybody's in jail in there?"

He had been on a sharp edge since the news last Saturday — the shooting in Kansas City. They were calling it the "Union Station Massacre." Three gangsters with tommy-guns had attacked a detail of men escorting a convict to Leavenworth. In the parking lot outside the Depot a fire fight had taken place leaving five men dead, including an F.B.I. agent. The next day Bernie had received a call from Austin DeMille relaying a request from the Federal Bureau for the taking of a deposition in regard to the old arson at The Settlement House and the death of his sister. The Feds were ready to step up their case against Pendergast.

"I'll be glad to get this over with," Bernie said. "After we give our depositions we'll all be on record. It will be too late to silence us. It should be the end to our worries. And in a little burg like Pawnee Bluffs, if they come skulking around looking for revenge they'd be noticed pretty fast and run out of town."

I hope. Lindy wondered if he was right or whether this was just a reassurance for the boy. And for Willy, who had the most reason to be nervous. *He's the only one who can identify the goons that fired the House. Poor guy, he looks incredibly hot in that suit.*

Blue serge, it was a winter garment. A red tie somehow conveyed an air of defiance, but his brown face was shining with sweat like polished walnut. He mopped at it with a handkerchief as they went in.

In a back room a long library table had been set up for the deposition. A floor fan was oscillating briskly in the corner. Chairs were set around and a stenographer was seated at the far end with a notebook and tablet. A tiny aging man with only a few scant hairs combed across a dome of baldness, the veins on his hands stood out like a kind of decoration. But the old fingers moved with alacrity as he began to write in a strange hieroglyphic across the page, setting up the place, the people present and the date of the meeting, June 21, 1933.

"As a rule we don't admit minors to a deposition." The Bureau had sent a middle-aged man of athletic build and carriage, moved like a policeman but talked like a lawyer. "Only the testifying parties can be present."

311

"Matthew was an eyewitness," Bernie said dryly. "Even if he was six weeks old, he was the one most affected by the death of his mother. We felt he should be here."

Looking slightly stumped, the F.B.I. frowned. Then on an impulse, he said, "My name's Earl Harding. Let's all relax." It was the right move; after that everyone sat easier.

Deposing Bernie and Lindy first, as collateral witnesses, Earl began to concentrate on Willy's testimony. "Mr. Bickford, how did you happen to be present when the fire occurred?"

Gravely Willy said, "I was living in the wood shed behind the hotel at the time. Everybody had gone off in the bus, so I figured I should keep an eye on the place."

"And what exactly did you see?"

"Out by the front porch I seen — saw — four fellows in sheets, planted a cross they made out of two-by-fours, then set it afire. I remembered how the Klan did that all over the South, to scare off Nigras. There was some coloreds living at the House then. Voorhees, old Tom's boy, he'd told Hereford he couldn't have 'em living in the same building with whites."

"Did you hear this exchange?" Earl interrupted.

"No. Not in person. I heard Hereford talking about it to the men afterward. He told 'em he wasn't going to let the Boss run his Settlement House."

"By 'the Boss' you refer to Thomas Pendergast?"

"Yes sir."

"Go on."

"Well, you'd think old Tom would be put-out. He don't take 'no' kindly. So it seemed kind of funny when he set up this picnic for the guys. He sent around the bus and took 'em out to Swope Park, gave 'em soda pop and sandwiches and all. Only soon as they was — were gone, here come these goons in the white sheets with that cross. Had cans of gasoline, poured it on the porch and threw some on the walls and set a match to it. That old hotel went up like a pile of kindling."

"Did you know Mrs. Romney was inside?"

"No sir. I heard the baby crying, though, and I run into the kitchen. It was already full of smoke, I couldn't see nothing. But I knew where the crib was under the sink, so I grabbed Matty up and ran out. Never did know where his mom was at. She didn't make a sound, reckon she was too hard asleep. They said afterward she breathed in a lot of that smoke and never woke up."

"Yes, the record shows smoke inhalation

as the cause of death. Now you mentioned at the time that you knew who the men were — the ones in the sheets."

"Sure. I seen — saw their faces. I lived in the Bottoms all my life, I know who folks are. These was some of Tom's boys. They weren't no Ku Klux Klan. He just white-sheeted 'em to throw the blame on the Klan."

"Yes, well you can't exactly testify to that as a fact. But if you can identify the perpetrators it will help us draw our own conclusions. I have here some photos. Will you take a look and see if any of these men were present at the fire?"

A dozen or so pictures, Willy took them one at a time and laid them out on the table. "That's Mick Golphin," he said, tossing one aside. "Muggsy Mick. Helps drive the ghosts around on election day, he was there."

"Excuse me . . . ghosts?"

"The needy folks that Tom pays to go around to the polls. Vote four, five times. Call 'em ghosts, because they give 'em names they get out of the graveyard. To sign on their ballot, y'know." He tossed forth another picture. "And this is Louie the Lizard, I don't know his last name, but he was always hanging around Voorhees, and so was this one, Vic Jeeter, got that scar in a knife fight they said. Those three was at the House that day, wearing the white hoods, but you could see their faces plenty good. Fourth one I don't see here. Al Vinick. He was some kind of muscle that Tom kept around as a body guard. Probably dead by now."

The hunched man at the foot of the table was writing full speed, his bony hands skittering across the page. When he looked up, Earl nodded.

"We're off the record now. This was excellent information, son," he told Willy. "We'll be able to add it to a lot of other testimony and . . ."

"Hey!" Matthew had drifted over to the window. "Here comes Pete, *and he's got Hobby with him!* I bet he could tell you stuff, he lived at the Settlement House."

Bernie went to join him. "I'll be darned. It's good to see Hobby again. And it's true, he was there at the time, but he was on the picnic with the rest of us."

"All the same, one more affidavit can't hurt," Earl said. "Young man, if you will, go get them and tell them where we're meeting."

When he walked in Hobby looked jaunty in a seersucker suit and blue bow tie, straw skimmer. Evidently he hadn't suffered in the months he'd been away with the "Bonus Army."

When he and the other veterans had left for Washington last year, he'd been in a tattered uniform that was too tight in the waist and frayed around the cuffs. According to the newspapers, the protest had been a crushing defeat, with the President refusing to budge an inch on advancing the servicemen the bonuses they had been promised after the War. The thing had ended in a riot.

For months there had been no word from him, so now it was a moment of celebration as Bernie shook hands and Lindy hugged and Matthew pummeled while the F.B.I. waited patiently.

Cheerfully, Hobby was saying, "My first stop was *The Whistle,* of course. When Pete told me what's going on here, I thought I might help. I happened to be in the office at the Settlement House the day Voorhees came in and threatened Hereford, about his accepting Negroes, and so forth. I can testify to that."

"Good! Please," Earl nodded. "Sit down."

The pictures were still out on the table, Hobby bent over them. "Hey, I know that one. Muggsy, his name was. A guard out at the work farm where I got sent for a month of hard labor for driving two miles over the speed limit. They called it Old Tom's boarding house — Pendergast made money off the meals he supplied to the inmates. You'd have to be kind to call it 'food.' "

"That's very interesting," Earl said, nodding to the stenographer who got out his pad again. "Let's go back to the beginning. Your full name please?"

"Zachariah Carter, nickname 'Hobby' because I liked to hobnob with everybody when I was a kid."

"Address?"

"Don't have one right now."

"Yes, he does," Pete said. "Make it *The Pawnee Whistle.* For the present he can use one of the empty rooms upstairs. We'll fix him up with a bed and so forth . . .."

An hour later, depositions concluded, affidavits signed, the group broke up and Earl and his stenographer piled into a sedate blue Packard sedan, leaving the others to get on with their reunion.

"Who's hungry? Let's do it up proper and have lunch at The Tonowanda, my treat." Hobby said it so proudly there could be no refusing. The restaurant was the only place in town that sported white table cloths. Its clientele usually consisted of lawyers and

Circuit Court Judges and their cronies.

"There's no hamburgers on the menu," Matty whispered plaintively to Lindy.

"Order the Salisbury steak on a bun," she murmured.

"So what have you been up to, old buddy?" Sitting next to Hobby, Bernie looked happier than he had in months. Ever since last fall when Pendergast's people had carried the elections across the State of Missouri, even ramming through the Machine's man as Governor, Bernie had been gloomy. His cartoon that week had been of a weedy, run-down building labeled Missouri Capitol with a gross figure lolling on its steps, carrying a bull whip. Caption: UNCLE TOM'S CABIN. The phrase had been picked up by other newspapers around the State. It was said that The Boss didn't much like it. "Fill us in," he went on, "what's the rest of the world like out there?"

"Been on a pretty wild ride ever since I left this place," Hobby marveled. "Trip to Washington was okay, we had backing from some veterans' groups, rode the train properly instead of the baggage cars. Set up a camp near the Potomac, some mud flats called 'Anacostia.' Word was: keep it neat, keep it clean, keep it respectful. We maintained military discipline, had our own

318

M.P.'s., got a lot of positive publicity, even from the New York papers. Veterans began to join us from the eastern states."

"How many in all?" Pete asked.

"They say it was close to 20,000 men, which is why, I guess, old Herbert got nervous. He turned down our request real fast, but we didn't go away. We just hung around, trying to get the members of Congress interested — which they weren't. And yet there we were, all us heroes. With elections coming up, I think the President kind of panicked. He sent the United States Army against us. Can you imagine, our own countrymen being ordered to attack us with cavalry and tanks? Led by a General with stars all over his shoulders — man named Douglas MacArthur — he ordered his troops to run us out. They set fire to the camp and that was the end of that."

"It was on the wire services," Pete said, "but the accounts were garbled. I couldn't make out who was to blame, and they didn't say anything about tanks."

"Well, seeing us run for our lives probably scared off the editors. If a President can turn on his own veterans, he can sure enough wipe out a few newspapers."

"Maybe we should run the story now."

"Na-a-ah." Hobby dug into his roast beef.

"Day late and a dollar short."

"Anyway, you seem to have survived in style," Bernie said. "Good-looking suit."

"Yeah, I had to buy that for my job. I've been working for the new administration, limo driver to the big shots. And let me tell you, carting those politicians around beats reading the paper any day. You get to hear the news before it happens. And right now it's happening fast. FDR is a sprinter, he came out of the gates at a gallop."

"Sure did put a stop to the banking panic," Pete nodded, gnawing a drumstick with unapologetic relish. "Our bank has been certified sound and our deposits insured up to $2,500 under the new FDIC."

"And the minute they announced the CCC program," Bernie added, "about half of Hooverville signed up and rode off on the trains to go plant trees out west for a dollar a day and keep. Which left us with mostly scum of the earth. You don't want to go back to a tent over there, Hobby."

"No, I know that. We ought to clean that place out. A man willing to work doesn't have to scrounge now. We've got the NRA. And I just heard the other day about a new program they're going to call the WPA, to build post offices and public buildings, even grant money to artists to paint murals."

"Shoot, G.B., that sounds like it's right down your alley," Pete kidded.

Lindy tasted her filet of sole. It was overcooked and the peas were out of a can, but that didn't matter. As she listened to the men, the growing enthusiasm in their voices, she was filled with an optimism she hadn't felt in years. Watching Willy, she wondered if he was getting the same boost. But the deposition had left him moody.

In a pause he said, "Anybody tell me why the President's down on gold?"

Pete took a long pull from his glass of iced tea. "I can. It had to be done, Willy. Roosevelt's been creating new programs that cost a lot of money. Under the old standard we couldn't pay for them unless each dollar was backed by an equivalent amount of gold. He had to change that, so he could print more paper money to buy our way back to prosperity. It's a tricky economic move, means the government will be operating at a deficit, but if it puts people back to work then a little debt seems worth it."

"Did you cash yours in?" Lindy asked and the boy shook his head.

"I can always sell it over in Chinatown in Kansas City, they purely love gold. They send it back to their old folks in China."

Matthew was scooping up the last of his

ice cream, already fidgeting to be on the go. It was a restlessness he hadn't outgrown yet, though he tended to be more cautious than in time gone by. "Can I be excused please?" Off and gone. He'd be heading for the barbershop to tell tall tales of Washington, D. C. to the old-timers who sat beneath the striped pole.

Pete sighed and pushed back from the table. "I ought to be getting back to the paper too. Hobby, I think I'll do an interview with you, just the stuff we've been discussing here — it would be interesting to our readers."

As they drove into the yard behind the press building Lindy came alert. She wasn't sure why until Bernie said, "Who left the back door open?"

"I locked it before we left for the Courthouse." Pete was out of the car, hurrying with Bernie on his heels. In the rear hall of the building Willy headed straight for the door to the basement. Its padlock was still intact. Lindy followed the men into the big press room, to be jolted to a halt. Sheets of drafting paper covered with cartoons were scattered all over the floor, drowned in India ink. It had been lavished all over the furniture, the walls.

"Your drawings . . ." she breathed.

"Don't worry. The originals — the best of them — are in the vault." One of the benefits of an ex-bank building.

Meanwhile Pete headed for his big rolltop desk. It had been vandalized, the lock broken on the petty cash drawer.

"They poured water in here," he said, puzzled, reaching for the empty cash box only to recoil in shock, his hand held out stiffly before him. "Acid . . . don't come near . . ." he almost strangled on the words.

Hobby ran to him and half-dragged him toward the sink. Big florid face drained of color, Pete was shaking with pain as Lindy turned on the tap and they held his hand under it. Stiff as a board, transfixed by soundless agony, he hung there over the drain precariously.

"Willy, run over to the kitchen and get my baking soda. Shelf by the stove, a yellow box. And bring the bucket from the back porch." Across the room she heard Bernie talking to Doc Menlo, as she helped Hobby get the massive bulk of the man over to the sofa.

"Doc's coming. Says don't let him go into shock. There's got to be some blankets upstairs." Bernie was already out the door.

Stretched out flat, Pete was chalk-white, lids ajar, blue eyes clouded. Between clenched teeth he said, "You guys keep things going . . ." Then, "Lindy . . . you better learn the keyboard . . . Monster."

As she sat before the linotype that night Lindy realized what Pete was getting at. The keyboard bore no resemblance to a typewriter, studded with ninety-one keys, capitol letters in white on the right side, lower case in black on the left, with a center section in blue that held the punctuation and numbers, plus space bands that had to be inserted. The keys were arranged in the order of their frequency, the first vertical line consisting of ETAOIN.

With one hesitant finger Lindy began to compose:

June 19, Pawnee Bluffs, Kansas. Today our quiet little town was brutalized by forces from outside the realm of law. The press room of this newspaper was vandalized and our editor, Pete Koslow had to be taken to the emergency room at the hospital in Topeka with severe acid burns on his hand due to the diabolical actions of persons unknown, but suspected to be miscreants from across our eastern border.

She paused as she heard the truck drive in. When Bernie came through the door he looked angry and weary and yet energized.

"How's Pete?" she asked.

He went straight to his easel. "They've got him sedated. The damned stuff burned nearly to the bone, they're not even sure how much use he'll have of his right hand in the future. So I told him: If you want I will never do another cartoon against the Pendergast machine. Say the word." He got out a piece of charcoal, then looked at her over his shoulder. "You know what he said? He said, 'I've got an idea for your next one. Draw a kind of squatty fortress half falling down and the Boss looking scared to death, sitting behind a crumbling wall, holding a tommy-gun. And the caption is, I THINK I HEARD THE PAWNEE WHISTLE'."

■ ■ ■ ■ ■

1934

■ ■ ■ ■ ■

TWENTY-THREE

This was Lindy's favorite time, in the darkness of their bedroom when Bernie held her close. Tonight, like a miracle, there was a stir of cooler air, a promise of Fall. She always welcomed that inner whisper when the seasons turned. And how they all needed that.

The desire for a new shift in the world was almost painful. Everyone felt it. Last year had been the worst anybody could remember, for heat, for dust, for lack of money, lack of energy, loss of confidence. After the first surge of the new President's programs, the tide of the Depression had swept back in on the hot winds. One dust storm that started up in the Dakotas had darkened the skies clear to the eastern states, giving them a taste of what the plains had learned to expect. Like nothing else it had created a genuine horror in the city folk, who had never before seen a wall of sand. Like the haboob of the Sahara, one paper had said. There followed a lot of talk of conservation, improved farming methods, crop rotation. A lot of talk.

"They say," she spoke into the darkness, she knew Bernie was awake, "they say the land should be left fallow for a year, so that natural grasses come back and hold the soil down. They say the earth needs to renew itself. But what's a farmer to do for cash if he doesn't plant crops?"

"Huh?" His mind had been a long way off elsewhere. "Oh, well, the people who preach haven't been in the church themselves. They'd think deeper if there was no wheat to make flour with or corn for the feedlots, no beef on their table. When it comes to that they'll get down to real programs."

But what kind of program can stop the wind? Or bring a little rain? The night air was dry as if baked in an oven. Even with that hint of coolness there was no longed-for smell of showers. *Never mind, they will come this winter. There will be snow. At least we have always had snow.*

"Anyway, I'm glad it's September," she said. It was even bearable to hold him close to her tonight, and Bernie responded suddenly, fiercely almost. For a while there was no more talk.

When she came awake, Lindy saw a paling of light beyond the window and got up. First day of school for Matthew, she wanted to fix him a special lunch. The two of them had become closer since the devastating experiment of the circus. He was a different person, warmer and more able to communicate. The affection she felt now was far removed from the years before when the feeling was mixed with duty and pity and dismay. Now there were times when she looked at the boy with a sense of deep fellowship.

As she brushed out her hair, only a little gray in the red-squirrel curls, Bernie came up behind and gave her a swift peck on the cheek. "That was good last night."

And once more the marvel came over her, that she was his wife and that they were still in love. As he began to shave, she said, "I don't know why, but I feel as if we're about to launch on a new time in our lives. Winter coming, I think things are going to get better. I feel as if we're out of the woods."

"Well, it's been over a year since the disaster." The shock of that day had taken a while to wear off.

And for Pete it was still an ever-present shadow on his life. His hand had healed but the tendons had been so damaged he could

331

hardly use his fingers. Hobby had fixed up an apartment for himself on the floor above the pressroom; he helped Pete with his daily chores, buttoning buttons, tying shoe laces, but it was weighing heavily on the big man, to be so helpless. The smile hardly ever flashed these days, and his face had set into premature age-lines.

Bernie was going on, "I have to hand it to Pete. He insists now that we go right on needling the Boss, and nothing new has happened, so maybe Pendergast has learned he can't stop us. Now, with elections coming on in November, I've been thinking of starting a new series of cartoons."

Lindy didn't answer that. It sent a small frisson of doubt over her precarious optimism. "How many ways can you think of to tweak the man's tail?" she asked it lightly, but he was quick to pick up a hint of disapproval.

"I know. You think I'm obsessed and you think it's time I slacked off my war. And I feel bad about Pete. He's been a good sport about me putting us all at risk, but I still feel guilty about what happened to him. How are things going these days?"

She knew what he meant. It had been a tough adjustment for Koslow to dictate the paper, all its news columns, its editorials. At first they had tried to compose it together, with him standing behind her at the lino-type machine while Lindy punched the keys, but she was far too slow to keep up with his stream of thought. So they had turned to dictation — Lindy had learned shorthand in finishing school. She could take his words down and transcribe them at her own pace.

"It's working," she said. "But he told me, it's difficult to think out loud, when he's so used to writing everything down. And I am still woefully slow with the typing. I can barely do four lines a minute. The good linotypist can do seven or eight."

"Don't apologize," Bernie told her fondly. "Without you I don't think we'd have a paper."

Lindy smiled. "Thank you, kind sir. But the truth is, you probably could get a more experienced steno than I am."

"Not one that makes great pancakes too." They had taken their conversation down to the kitchen now, Bernie still dressed in his bathrobe. As she put the bacon on she saw Willy heading for the barn and went to the back door.

"How about some breakfast?"

He flashed his boyish smile and reversed course. "Don't mind if I do." Always careful not to take too much for granted, he never dropped in at meal time uninvited.

Matthew could be heard descending the stairs vigorously. Bernie poured some orange juice all around. "Where are you off to so early, William?"

"Got a call last night, fellow up in St. Joe. He wants to start a jazz band, wanted some advice. Wants to get the 12th Street sound."

"Well, he picked the right person." Bernie turned to Matty. "Morning, son. Ready for school?"

"Yeah. Got to be at the bus stop at eight o'clock," Matty told them. "Listen, what's it going to be like? High school, I mean?"

"Oh, the people in Olathe are pretty much like the ones here, I'd say. Some good, some bad. Just keep your head down until you see the lie of the land."

Lindy poured batter onto the griddle. "Somebody put the syrup on the table, please?"

"I know that, I don't care about the other kids." Matty frowned. "I mean the subjects, like biology and history."

Willy grinned. "Don't look at me, I never done school. But I come close, other night, got me a lesson in drumming."

"Somebody good enough to teach you new tricks? I don't believe it!" Bernie poured the coffee.

"Man, yes. Fellow named Gene Krupa. He sat in with the band last Saturday night. Makes those sticks fly. Told us about a new kind of music, haven't heard it much yet, they call it 'swing.' Fellow name of Benny Goodman is playing it all over the country. Going to put jazz out of business, they say."

"Well, it's for certain that drums will never be obsolete."

"Lin, I purely do admire them words of yours. Not to mention the good food."

Bernie was shoveling down the pancakes. "Good breakfast, my love. I may need it, these fancy luncheons never have very good chow, for some reason."

"What luncheon is this?" Willy asked.

"Pete and I are invited to the Fifth Avenue Hotel in Topeka. Have you know, we're being presented with a plaque for our achievements with *The Whistle*. We will be the guests of honor and Pete will make a speech."

Lindy had known of it for several days. She wondered if it was that which had given her the sense of euphoria. More likely the pleasures of the midnight bed. As she gave Matty his lunch and watched him run off down the street at a trot, it came over her again — a pure and simple happiness. Willy, heading on out to his journey, contributed to the feeling. He looked jaunty in his new Fall suit and spiffy blue golf cap.

Bernie stood beside her at the window, his arm around her, last night's memories still warming him too. "There goes our little family. Well, I guess I'd better get dressed in my luncheon duds. This trip will give Pete and me a chance to talk about future policy for *The Whistle*. Maybe I really should let the Boss alone. The Federal Bureau will take Tom down eventually."

"But you can't let go of your vendetta," she teased.

"Yeah. Truth is I'm worried about this coming election in November. The Machine has a man running for a seat in the United States Senate. That would give Pendergast a chance to get his fingers on national policy. Who knows how much power his guy could eventually wield — fellow named Harry Truman? I know him, slightly, he was at Camp Donophan just ahead of me. Went over to France in the first contingent of troops. Came home a Captain, his men think he hung the moon. So he'll probably win the election on his own steam. Of course your friend, Austin DeMille, and his Republicans are trying hard to sell their own candidate. I might have a chance to influence people on this one. I keep thinking I ought to try. I'd hate to see old Tom pushing the buttons in Washington, D.C."

A half hour later, as she watched her men drive off in the newspaper truck, Lindy put editorial problems behind her and turned to thoughts of her own column. Standing on the back porch in the early sunlight she examined the theme that had occurred to her yesterday, the darning of socks. She had got into the habit of sleeping on her ideas to test them, but even now in the brilliance of the morning it still seemed appropriate.

A woman's way, to weave a new patch across the hole in the heel of a sock. If it's done right the wearer never knows it's been mended. Takes patience, tiny stitches . . . she began to write the column in her head. It was the one moment of her week in which she felt a sense of achievement, beyond the daily housewifely chores. Excitement quickened her, the act of her own creation — it lifted her inside to a height of satisfaction she would never have dreamed. So many worn places in the life of a family, needing a woman's touch . . .

Her inspiration was brought up short by the sight of Willy's station wagon turning in at the yard behind the house, moving slowly. He nursed the odd-looking wooden bodied vehicle across toward the barn. Lindy ran to open the doors, inner alarms going off all over the place.

"What's the matter, why are you back so soon?"

Once inside he cut the engine and got out. His clothes were grungy with dirt and his hands and face smudged with oil. "Got car trouble. Worst kind, steering wheel. I thought it felt odd as I drove out, so I stopped . . ." he was pulling on some coveralls. "Looked underneath and felt around, something wrong with the linkage. So I come back real careful, it's no good when you can't steer."

"Well, thank the Lord you made it without getting into an accident." She stood by as he scrounged his way under the wagon, nothing showing but the well-shined shoes.

"Ho-boy." His voice came distantly, and he began to squirm back out again. "Lin, somebody's trying to kill me."

"No!"

"Yeah. They cut almost through the rod that connects the wheels to the steering column. Hacksaw, I'd say at a guess. You can see the tool marks. That thing's hanging by a thread. One good bump and she's broke, you're in the ditch, at forty-five miles an hour."

"Oh, Willy. This is bad. We've got to call those government men. They're still after Pendergast, and he knows now that you can testify against him. That has to be it."

He nodded. "What I figure, too."

"Well, we'd better wait for Bernie and Pete. They'll know how to proceed. Meantime, let's get you to your appointment. I'll help you move your drums into the truck." Bernie had bought a second van to handle the out-of-town deliveries. Not much to look at, but it was sturdy.

"Hold on a minute," Willy stopped her, his brown face knotted in an alien frown. The boy never scowled, she realized, it wasn't in his nature. Slinging himself down and under the vehicle, he wriggled forward, then back out again.

"It's been jimmied, too. Same thing, hacksaw blade, cut right through the steering rod to about an eighth of an inch."

They stared at each other, coming separately to the same frightening conclusion. Lindy ran for the house, Willy at her heels. *It's a good road all the way to Topeka. Maybe they'll make it just fine. They've got to.* She picked up the phone, a familiar voice said, "Number plea-uz."

"Rose, it's Lindy Jones. Can you put me through to the First Avenue Hotel in Topeka? I don't have the number."

"Hold on." The lifeline of the community, Rose Feltsham had been the town's only telephone operator since the first poles went up. "I've got it, Lindy, I'm putting it through right now."

And almost at once a voice came distantly. "First Avenue Hotel, can I help you?"

"Yes. I'm trying to reach a couple of men who will be attending the luncheon up there today —"

"Excuse me, madam, but we do not have any events scheduled for our dining room this week."

"Something . . . the Midwestern Publishers . . ." she fumbled.

"I'm sorry, I have never heard of such an organization."

As if a hammer had fallen, an explosion detonated in her head. "Oh . . . my . . . Lord . . ." Trying to gather her wits, she said, "If anyone comes to your desk asking for directions, will you please tell them to call home at once. It's a matter of life and death."

By the time she had put the phone down Willy was on the move, running back to the barn. In a daze, Lindy followed him. "It was a trick," she said, "to get them out on the road."

He had already crawled under the roadster to check it. In a minute he was back out. "They didn't hurt your car. It's an old model, the steering is harder to get at, got to take the oil pan out to reach it. I'll go after 'em, Lin, I'll catch 'em up."

"No." Instinctively she knew she couldn't sit by waiting. "I'll go. Willy, would you stay here and wait, in case they call. If I don't get back right away, will you take care of Matty. Please."

"Any way you want it," he said, with his unfailing intuition.

It's always been like that between us, he knows exactly what I need, what I'm thinking . . . Lindy found herself driving recklessly fast north along the Topeka highway. As the miles slipped by beneath her wheels a desperate optimism rose. *They made it this far, it's going to be okay. This is a pretty good road, no bumps in it. Maybe Pete got the same feeling that there was something wrong with the way the truck was driving, maybe they turned off to find a garage in one of the little farm towns. God in heaven, please let them be safe. Please!*

And then she topped a rise, saw the city of Topeka ahead with its taller buildings. A mile short of town a small crowd of people along the highway made her heart sink like a stone in dark water. They were looking down at wreckage in the ditch below the shoulder of the road — she couldn't see it, but she knew what it was. Pulling up to the scene, she was out of the car and running.

About to plunge down the embankment, she was caught and held by a strong hand. Whirling in an agony of fear, she saw a badge, the word SHERIFF. "Let me go, that's my husband's truck, he was driving to Topeka . . ."

"Yes, ma'am. But there's no point going down there, the accident happened a half-hour ago. The ambulance took them away. The one still alive they were going to transport to St. Francis Hospital. The other would be at the coroner's by now."

"Names . . ." she was gasping for air.

"I'm sorry, ma'am, I only got here myself a few minutes ago. I was tied up with a big accident over west on Highway 60. Cattle truck overturned, animals wandering around on the road, it was a mess. Anyway, I don't know the names of the folks involved here. My officer took their wallets for safe-keeping. He was in a rush to get the fellow to the hospital." He showed her two wallets, one of them Bernie's. But then of course it was, the truck in the ditch bore the logo of *The Whistle.* "You shouldn't ought to be driving, ma'am . . ."

But he was speaking now to empty air. Lindy plunged back into the roadster and got it going, her mind a broken record repeating *Bernie, Bernie, Bernie . . .*

TWENTY-FOUR

Lindy sat there by the bed in a state almost of stupor. She was aware of comings and goings, but mainly she was fixed on the motionless figure with all the scratches on his face. From the windshield, she had been told. The terribly white bandage around his head made his pallid skin look lifeless, the freckles standing out unnaturally dark. The sheets were awkward on the casts that immobilized his legs. But he was alive. She had to keep reminding herself, even though it wasn't the husband she knew. Poor damaged man, in a coma, no telling what the lasting effects would be on the brain, the doctors had told her. She had listened to them without hearing, the prognostications. She couldn't realize, she couldn't believe, she couldn't think.

She wanted Matty, that much she knew. *Willy will take care of him.* But she wanted him at her side. The doctor said something about hospital rules, no children allowed in the critical ward. She tried to accept it — the boy must have a lot of homework his first day of school. Dark outside now.

Aware of another familiar face, kindly, flushed, beads of sweat. Absalom Stark. "Is there any one passage in the Bible that Bernie likes?"

Her answer was automatic. "Third Ecclesiastes."

He didn't even have to open the Book. He just began to recite: "To everything there is a season and a time for every purpose unto heaven. A time to be born, a time to die . . ."

After a while he was gone.

A strong hand lay on her shoulder, she looked up to find Hiram Jones beside her. Tough, shrewd, angry now as he looked at his son. "My wife is coming back from Colorado, she'll be in on the morning train."

Then, another time it was Hobby. "Listen, Lin, I don't want to upset you with a lot of questions, but if you want to put out a paper, I think Willy and I could handle it. One issue, to let people know. Don't answer now, we have until Thursday to decide."

Surprising herself, Lindy spoke up without hesitation. "Yes. We'll print it as usual." *Only suppose . . . what if he doesn't . . . what will the headline be?* "Bernie would want us to carry on," she said. "We can discuss it tomorrow." She wanted to let the sheltering numbness move in again and remove her from the awful pending future.

Then as the evening wore on and the halls outside grew very quiet she heard a footstep. The door of the room opened and a boyish face edged around it, those strange blue eyes. Then Matty was inside very softly, closing the door behind him. Dressed in his windbreaker, looking a little scuffed, he came to her side and crouched down.

"I had to climb the fire escape. Willy gave me a boost. They wouldn't let me in," he whispered fiercely. "They called me a 'child!' "

"I'll set them straight on that," she said grimly. "Bring the chair over, sit with me." She clung to his fingers hard for a minute.

Settling down at her side he produced a paper bag from inside the coat. "I brought you a sandwich."

Oh Lord, I can't — "Thanks, sweetheart." She forced herself to take a bite.

"I told 'em no mayonnaise."

"It tastes good." And once she got started, it did fill a need. After that they sat there wordless, watching the still figure on the bed.

"Is Poppa going to die?" Matty asked once

in hushed tones, eyes stark with awe.

"God only knows." But for some reason Lindy felt he had a better chance now with his family beside him. So when the nurse looked in, she braced herself for an argument. But the woman just considered the two of them, nodded and left.

Hours later, Lindy was aware when Matty began to flag. "You should go home now," she said. "You need to do your homework. Your dad would want you to go on to school. We don't know how long he'll be unconscious. I'm going to stay all night."

Some time in the late evening two orderlies moved a bed into the room. The nurse was back offering a pill.

Lindy shook her head. "No sedative." But she did stretch out on the cot, which was near enough that she could reach Bernie's hand. It lay limp at his side, that marvelously gifted hand which could create likenesses in a few swift movements. It looked as if it had never been in an accident. *Thank God at least for that.*

But what good, if his mind was ruined, if his quick wit had suffered irreparable harm? *I'd rather he be dead, because he'd rather he'd be dead.* She shivered convulsively and the nurse laid another blanket over her. Alone at last she reached out from under the covers and found Bernie's fingers and gripped them. No response, but she felt he must know, at some level of his subconscious, that she was with him.

She was still holding his hand when she came awake to find the room swept by sunlight. Bernie still lay unconscious, but the doctor bending over him was alert and smiling. Not the perfunctory professional smile, or the painful grimace of sympathy. He looked like a man who had done a difficult job well.

"Your husband has taken a turn for the better. Amazing what complete rest will do — the body wants to recover. He's in a normal sleep now, and I intend to keep him under for another twenty-four hours." A middle-aged man, face lined with every long night's waking, the doctor came around the bed and helped her get up. "You look exhausted, Mrs. Jones. I prescribe that you go home and get some rest. Don't want to have a second patient in the ward. I'll call you at once if there's any change."

"Call me at the office of *The Whistle*, please," she said. "I have a newspaper to get out."

TWENTY-FIVE

The last edition of The Pawnee Whistle. It's got to be good, it must look professional, do justice to the events, sign off in a dignified way.

With a return of purpose Lindy got a sense of orientation, she felt able to go through the motions — wash the face, comb the hair, find the car keys. Find the car! She wasn't even sure where she had left it. It was in a No Parking zone near the Emergency Room door with a ticket tucked under the windshield wiper.

She drove cautiously, paying attention to traffic, aware that her reflexes were slow. When she passed the accident site she only glanced at the wreckage. The truck lay on its side, the picture of the Indian hardly damaged. But the undercarriage was twisted out of all recognition, wheels folded, radiator burst, the hood pleated like an accordion. Quickly she turned away, but the picture was burned on her memory forever.

She remembered the day Bernie had painted the logo on the side of the new truck — long years ago, but she could still see him perched on a stool, laying in the outlines of an Indian head, wearing an eye-shade with pens and pencils stuck in it for feathers. Blindly she followed the white line on the highway until the turn-off to the town and home.

It had never felt so much like home as it did today, under the September sun, quiet and a little shabby. She turned into the barn and parked the roadster next to Willy's station wagon. He must have fixed it, to have driven up to Topeka yesterday. Or was it day before yesterday? Lindy spilled out of the car and rushed for the press building. If it was already Thursday there wasn't a moment to waste.

In the big room they were waiting. Perched on stools around the composing table they looked worried, Hobby and Willy and Matthew.

"Here she is!"

"What day is this?" she demanded.

They almost smiled. Hobby said, "It's only Wednesday, we were about to try to get the press going. Of course, without you there wasn't going to be much of a paper.

How is Bernie?"

"He's passed the crisis point, the doctor is optimistic. And he would want this last issue of The Whistle to be a good one, so I decided to come home. Matthew, why aren't you in school?"

Hobby said, "I spoke to the principal. Matty is excused."

"We already did the front page, we ran off a proof." Willy showed it to her, a large portrait of Pete and the black banner head: PUBLISHER MURDERED.

Lindy started to choke up. She had hardly come to realize it yet, that Pete was gone. Now the sense of loss threatened to swamp her, but she fought it off. There was no time for tears. "That's good. How did you manage it, Willy?"

"Pete showed me a long time ago how to make up a headline out of that big type. One piece at a time. Don't need no machine for that."

It was a good picture. Taken a few years earlier, it made him look boyish and happy, the way he'd want to be remembered.

"There's a write-up in the morgue," Hobby added. "Well, don't look at me, that's what he called that file where he kept biographies of us all. And a lot of celebrities too, already written up so we could pull

351

them at a minute's notice and stick them in the paper." He led her over to the cabinet.

"I never knew that." Lindy wondered how much else she didn't know about the big man who had been a central figure in her life for the last decade. She started to glance down the page and realized there was no time for that, either. Taking it over to the linotype, she said, "I'll get it set."

"The ads are all in place, I just kept them where they were last week," Hobby was showing her the layout. "But we need the story of the wreck for the second page, and we need an editorial."

"Ought to be a biography on Bernie too," Willy suggested. "I mean it don't have to be a obit-chew-ary. But folks ought to know about how he fought in the War. And how he come to be a cartoonist and all."

"You mean his education at M.U." Lindy nodded. "Okay."

"I mean how God told him to go to that school, spoke the words right in his ear."

They fell silent, pondering that. Matty's eyes were bright with curiosity, at the idea of celestial communication.

Lindy said, "I know Bernie felt he was guided by a higher power, but . . ."

"You didn't know the Lord saved his life?" Willy glanced around at them. "Told me, long time ago, how on the way home from France he was gonna kill hisself. Lord talked him out of it. I'm not kidding you, he said was just lucky he learned how to listen. Told me if people would listen hard enough they'd get the answers they need, right from the Lord's own voice. And on the train home, He sent him the message, how he was supposed to be a artist. Only what I wonder now is, with the paper gone what's he gonna do when he gets well, Lin? Paint signs all his life?"

Lindy tried to clear her head. A whole new brew of questions was stirring in her, she couldn't think. "Let me just finish this column, about the wreck." That, at least, was clear in her mind.

Slowly she began to peck out the words on the Monster's strange keyboard, and thank heaven for it. She couldn't even have tried to set the type by hand, the way Pete used to, his big fingers flying . . . What did he once tell her, how to begin a news story? Who, what, when, where and why.

"On Monday morning the editor of this paper, Pete Koslow, and his co-publisher, Bernie Jones, headed for Topeka to attend a luncheon where they were supposed to be honored, an affair that was totally bogus. Bait in a trap, it was cleverly set to prompt them to take to the highway where it was intended they would die in a rigged accident."

"Here comes Mr. Jones," Willy said, from over at the window. "Hope it's not — hope it's good news."

Lindy rushed to greet Hiram at the door and was reassured by the smile. He hugged her. "Just came from the hospital up in Topeka. He's doing well, still knocked out by all those needles they've got in him, but the doctor says he has stabilized and is improving. Even a chance he may walk again."

The words startled Lindy, she hadn't even thought to ask about that.

"Of course it's going to take months of nursing. Wanted to tell you, if you decide to bring him home to Kansas City, you can live at our house. Your old house, of course."

"I don't — I guess we'll just have to play it by ear. But I appreciate —"

"Doesn't have to be decided right now. What does, though, is the future of this paper. Yesterday I did some calling around, trying to put together a group that might buy *The Whistle*. Hard to tempt people to take risks right now. Roosevelt's got the country moving, but he's doing it on credit. Don't know how much of that they'll give him, Congress, I mean. Anyway people are leery about a small-town newspaper as an investment. Costs can eat up the profits fast."

"We were doing all right before the crash," Hobby told him. "Once the economy picks up . . ."

"Exactly. That's what I told them," Hiram said. "I may get some backers yet, but then we'd have to find an editor and so forth. So what I wanted to tell you, Lindy — you are empowered to make decisions on this, aren't you?"

"Yes. Austin DeMille drew up papers so that in case of Pete's death the paper would belong to Bernie, and I have my husband's power of attorney. Count on a lawyer to think of all contingencies," she added dryly.

"Well, you may be getting offers, even tempting ones, to sell the paper fast. It's a potentially valuable property. I'd advise you to hold off as long as you can, let me try to find the right buyer."

"Why valuable?" Hobby asked. "If we are just scraping by?"

"It's like this," Hiram told him. "I own that piece of land east of town, could turn into a suburb of Kansas City. Well-off middle-class people, pay their taxes and so forth. But to attract them the town needs a hospital, it needs a high school, a radio station. It needs to start thinking bigger, which is where the paper comes in. Actually, it's the backbone of a community. Once the economy picks up it will be worth plenty. Well, I've got to go along. I just wanted you to think about the future, call me before you sign any papers."

After he had gone a heaviness seemed to settle on the big room. Lindy went back to the linotype. Hobby to his window, as if watching for the enemy. Out of the silence, Matty blurted.

"Will we have to move out of our house?"

Another whole element of the question that Lindy hadn't thought of yet. *Not back to Kansas City!* Why the protest rang so loudly in her head she couldn't say. She just knew it would mean the end of Bernie's life.

"Don't worry," Willy was telling the boy, "Other places can be good too."

"But I like it here."

Nobody contested that. Trying to rally her thoughts, Lindy attacked the news story again. But almost at once Hobby reported a newcomer heading for the building.

"Not from around here. Looks like a lawyer."

"Nobody ever looks like a lawyer, even lawyers." Lindy was feeling a little light-headed. She heard Willy say, "Matt, go over to the house and fix your ma a sandwich. She's feeling skimpy."

The man did look like a lawyer, gray silk business suit, four-in-hand striped tie, very white handkerchief in the breast pocket of the well-tailored jacket. Levett Pilcher, he offered his card.

"Owner of this establishment? Good, I understand it may be for sale. I've been traveling the midwest looking for sound investments. I believe this little town is full of promise."

Coming so soon upon her father-in-law's warning, the words brought Lindy to attention. As the man went on with his sales pitch, she was listening between the lines. "Yes," she said. "I might be interested. But only if conditions were right. For instance I would want written guarantees that the paper would continue to publish and all the personnel involved in it would be kept on for a period of five years."

Mr. Pilcher laughed politely. "You can't be serious. No one would sign such a contract. The whole benefit of buying a piece of property is the right to use it as one pleases. After all, five thousand dollars should be severance pay enough. The physical plant is hardly worth that. Naturally there would have to be changes made."

"Uh-huh," she nodded. "I'm sure. Well, I suggest that you go back to Mr. Pendergast and tell him: no deal."

"Beg pardon? I don't know any Mr. Pendergast, but I can promise you —"

"Your business card says you have offices in Kansas City and you claim you don't know Tom Pendergast?" The rise of rage in her throat almost choked Lindy. She saw it mirrored in Hobby's face, in Willy's tight jaw. It must have communicated itself to Pilcher, because he left without further argument.

Matty was back now with a big bowl of steaming beef stew. *I hope he turned the stove off.* Lindy ate it fast with amazing appetite. She finished copying Pete's obituary onto the machine. The adjoining article about Bernie she made up off the top of her head, and if it sounded like the cry of a loving wife, so be it. She left out the part where God spoke to him.

Hours later, sitting back from the keyboard with the page ready to lock up, she had time to wonder: why had he never told her, but confided such an intimate moment to Willy? Shy of offending her and her

Anglican heritage? In the Episcopal Church it was hardly expected that the Lord would speak words in your personal ear.

Hobby came to her, by then it was almost three. "We're looking good to publish by noon tomorrow, which is what we need to meet our deadlines. No one will expect the paper to have a full array of news. But we do need an editorial."

"You mean to let people know what the future of the paper will be," she said, and he nodded.

Some mad notion was fermenting in her like cider in October. Before she could frame it in words, another visitor came through the front door almost diffidently. It had been over a year since the depositions but she recognized him at once.

"Mr. Harding. How's the F.B.I. doing these days? Catching lots of evil-doers, ridding our world of scum?" The bitterness rose uninvited. This man had promised them he'd put Tom Pendergast away.

"Not soon enough," he said readily. "Mrs. Jones, I am so sorry for this new outrage. I am assuming it's the work of our mutual nemesis? The minute I heard I put men on the trail, trying to trace what must have happened. They tell me the steering mechanism on your husband's truck was tampered with."

"Willy can explain it better than I can. The other truck is in the barn. You can see the sabotage for yourself. But before you go, here's a business card. A man just gave it to me, pretending to be an independent entrepreneur, wanted to buy *The Whistle*. And when I confronted him, claimed he never heard of Tom Pendergast. Maybe he will be a lead."

"Every little bit helps," the G-man told her grimly. "And believe me, it won't be long now. We are closing in on that old hoodlum. You can assure your husband that the Boss's days are numbered." He followed Willy to the door, then glanced back. "I hope this doesn't mean you're going to close down the paper?"

Hobby said quickly, "That hasn't been decided yet." And when he was gone he turned to Lindy. "Has it?"

She shook her head. "If you don't mind, I'd like to be alone to think out what I'm going to say."

"I'll just go on out to the barn and give them my expertise on the rigging of accidents." He bent down and gave her a kiss on the cheek. "Think hard, old buddy."

Matty started toward the door, unwillingly.

"Not you, son. Please sit here with me." Wearily Lindy leaned back in the steno chair and closed her eyes. She had gone beyond weariness to a kind of fierce contention. *Well, obviously I can't put the paper out all by myself. The men are wonderful, they want to help, but the news has to be written. It has to be analyzed and evaluated and editorialized. Each story has to be a complete piece of work — like my column only twenty times over every week. Even when Bernie comes home he couldn't help with that. His talent is in his drawing pen.*

Bernie . . . was it true he had tried to kill himself? He had never hinted at such a thing. But that was a time of War. In such a terrible crisis, you could imagine things — like a personal word from on high. *I have to figure this out by myself. No matter how hard I listen no benevolent deity is going to help me.*

Are you sure of that?

The words shook her. They were of a deeper caliber than any thought she'd ever had. She couldn't equate them with her musings. As if a voice had spoken in her ear.

Tentatively, feeling shy and skeptical still,

she said, "If I take this on, it would mean total commitment. When would I have time for all the rest of my family's needs?" She had uttered the question aloud. There wasn't an answer, of course, not from the Almighty.

But over by the drawing board Matty said, "I could help. I could learn to cook." He wasn't kidding. He meant every word, his face grave and determined. She could see what he would look like years from now.

It did something strange, the simple declaration. It gave her a sense of balance again. *Everybody, all of them, they don't want this paper to go under. I've got a unique band of supporters.* And suddenly she was sure what the answer was. She could manage it, the paper and her family. She could take care of Bernie once he was home on familiar ground, so long as she didn't cut that right out from under their feet. To sell out, for five-thousand dollars? *For heaven-sake I've got twice that in cash in a safe deposit box, my dowry money.* It would keep the paper going until the economy rallied and the ads started selling again. To give up when you haven't spent your last penny and ounce of effort would be plain cowardly. Worse than that. Everything Bernie hated would triumph.

A man could get over an attack on his life, but never recover from losing his life's work.

The voice again: this time she was sure. Even though it sounded like her own thoughts, a message had come from somewhere beyond. It raised the hairs on her neck, filled her with awe. She no longer questioned it — in fact, in a strange way, she felt as if she'd just met an old friend of Bernie's.

EDITORIAL

To all of our faithful readers who have stood by during our tragedy this paper wants to give thanks, to ask for your continued prayers, and to announce that The Pawnee Whistle will continue to publish the news, for your benefit, for your information, and for the good of the community. We are committed to the truth and pledge to follow it wherever it leads. As the Good Book says, we will gather stones together, we might even throw a few. But mostly we will use them to build a paper that would make Pete Koslow proud.

Signed: Bernard Jones, Publisher
Lindy Jones, Editor-in-Chief

William Bickford, City Editor
Hobby Carter, Business Dept.
Matthew Jones, Circulation Dept.

Later, when Bernie was well enough to read, Lindy showed it to him. And for the first time in long days, he smiled.

AUTHOR'S NOTE

The reader may be interested to know that a federal investigation into the 1936 elections revealed that the Pendergast machine had bought approximately 60,000 "ghost" votes, in some districts the registration numbers actually exceeding the total population. In the process of collecting data, Treasury investigators turned up proof that Pendergast had failed to reveal huge sums of income on his tax returns. And on Friday, April 7, 1939, at the personal instigation of J. Edgar Hoover, the Boss was indicted for tax evasion. He pleaded guilty and was sentenced to three years at Leavenworth, later reduced to 15 months because of his failing health. The Machine was effectively ended and T.J. died in 1945, a discredited broken man.

ABOUT THE AUTHOR

Annabel Johnson is the author of over two-dozen novels, the product of a long career during which she has written in every genre, though her favorite is historical fiction. For her novel *THE BURNING GLASS* she received the Golden Spur from the Western Writers of America. Her most recent book, *ONE MAN'S WAR,* published under her pseudonym A.E. Johnson, was based on her father's memoirs of World War I. Her present novel is a sequel to that, a story of the Gilded Age of flappers and jazz, followed by the Depression, all told from a woman's point of view.

Born in Kansas City, Missouri, in 1921, she still has vivid memories of her first encounter with a crystal set, of the various old automobiles (now classics) which the family owned, and of the marvelous jazz music her father and mother, and a half dozen friends used to create in the family living room. Her first writing job was a column for a local weekly newspaper, much like the one in her book. From these recollections and much further research she has tried to recreate a short but memorable era in our recent history which was the moment at which women began to come into their own.

After long years of traveling the west with her husband, Edgar, a sometime co-author of her books, now deceased, she has come to live in the desert she has always loved, a lively adult community in Mesa, Arizona, where she continues to write and enjoy the golden years of life.